The Devil is an English Gentleman

By JOHN COURNOS

VOLUME ONE

FARRAR & RINEHART
INCORPORATED

On Murray Hill   New York

For

HELEN

*whose affection and faith have helped
this book to come into being*

CONTENTS

BOOK ONE: ROMANCE

CHAPTER   PAGE

  I. The March of Progress 3

  II. The Romantic Soul 15

  III. Blood Will Tell 25

  IV. Decidedly, Blood Will Tell 39

  V. The Unforgivable Sin 55

  VI. A Fateful Evening 66

  VII. Don Juan of Weimar 80

  VIII. God's Humor 91

  IX. Woman Who Wanted the Moon 109

  X. A Lyrical Interlude 125

  XI. In Which An Old Dream Is Continued. . 142

  XII. An Astounding Proposal 155

  XIII. Trial Marriage 171

  XIV. Trial Honeymoon 191

  XV. Legal Tie 206

  XVI. Ravenford Manor 217

BOOK TWO: REALITY

  XVII. Homecoming 239

  XVIII. Life's Like That 256

  XIX. Irony 272

  XX. The Waning Dream 285

CHAPTER ONE

The March of Progress

THERE is a short stretch of Sussex coastland which does not present quite the same appearance that it did a generation ago. There may be other spots along the coast whose face has undergone the accelerated transformations of our time; but our interest may be said to lie in the particular spot and in the particular human beings who have inhabited it.

Not many years ago this place had been wasteland and green pasture, bordered on the sea side by one almost unbroken hedge of tamarisks; immediately behind this hedge, nearly hidden from view, was the gravel beach; and audible to the ear was the rhythmic rasp of the smooth stones as the lapping tides washed them up and down, up and down. On stormy days, when the white capped, writhen sea, undeterred by the intersecting groynes built by human hands to soften its assaults, dashed with fury against the shore and withdrew with an impotent foaming and cataracts of spray, the rasp loudened, rising to a roar; and between these intermittent roars there were silences, tense, ominous, and profound, like the silences of some primordial void, above which only the swiftly circling gulls sent forth their shrill, clarion sounding cries.

The sea, the elements, the lapping tides, the roar of storm, changeless and immune against the mutilating hand of man, are here and will endure as long as the world endures. But the land goes on changing, and the human beings go on changing with it. No longer the green pastures, the sheep-inhabited landscape otherwise desolate; no longer the fringe of the tamarisks delicately spun like a fine lace. There is revealed, instead, a panorama of modern gabled houses all built on a depressingly uniform post-war pattern of stucco and red tiles, habitations comfortable within and less flimsy than they appear on the outside. They are separated by straight streets and smallish low-fenced gardens, the larger of which can boast of tennis and croquet courts. The tiny newly planted trees provide but little shade, while here and there the low hedges, bushes and miniature trees are trimmed to unnatural, fantastic shapes which one associates with the verdure of a toy world. In the centre of this meticulously planned hodge-podge of pretension and artifice, grandiloquently calling itself Garden City, there is a tiny square, rounded off at the corners by a series of iron railings, behind which, in variegated confusion, carefully set out flowers bloom. In its middle, protected by a circular enclosure, there is a circular bed of tulips, set out in serried circles, each a different color, one encompassing the other. Along the outer railings of the square there is a number of benches, in the summer too much exposed to the sun to attract sitters; and as yet no lovers' joined initials nor coupled hearts have been scratched on their virgin planks. The only lettering indeed to be seen is the lettering formally printed on the ubiquitous signs warning hawkers to keep out of this bourgeois paradise. And only the shrilly crying gulls are allowed to set defiance to the regulation strictly forbidding all unnecessary noises. The streets, for the most part, are equally deserted of hawkers and of inhabitants occupying the complacent homes. Only now and then, a limousine drawing into or pulling out of a garage gives expressive vent to the modern temper of the place; while out of a rambler-framed window strange cracklings and chortlings, mingling at intervals with popular instrumental tunes and curious not quite human voices, give ample token of the presence of some mechanical zealot "listening in."

From this communal centre a linear flower-bordered path leads to a broad esplanade built over a sea wall; a parapet marks the line where the tamarisks once had been. A half-dozen or more detached houses, separated by gardens and lawns, obviously the largest and most opulent habitations of Garden City, are recessed here; their spacious windows open out to sea. The esplanade does not run the length of Garden City; the parapet stops at either end of this row of houses. The sea wall also terminates too soon at either end. As one looks down over the parapet to the right, one sees the gravel beach, the uninterrupted series of sheltering groynes, the line of surviving tamarisks, the less choice houses stretching in serried rows, and their lawns and gardens. To the left of the parapet quite a different sort of landscape is to be seen. Here the last remnant of the old pasture land appears to view; the old native still remembers it as a part of the larger pasture before Garden City had been built. Yet he will note one vital difference from its former state; and that is, the grave inroads made by the sea. The tamarisks no longer show an unbroken front. There are intermittent gaps where the untrammelled sea has bitten into the clayey soil and has made semi-circular indentations resembling gigantic bites by some vast monster. The impoverished owner of this land could not afford to repair the groynes half demolished by the hungry onslaughts of the sea; and every succeeding year has shown a coast line increasingly ravaged by the elements. Fearful lest ultimately the sea work its way round the sea-wall and threaten Garden City on the left flank, the distraught owners, known as the Wilson Development Company Limited, have again and again made better and better offers for their purchase, only to meet with a scornful, curt refusal from Richard Thorley, the last of the Thorleys. Richard's father, Henry Thorley, had at a time of acute financial distress, disposed of half his holdings to Mr. James Wilson, father of the present proprietor, and, regretful of his bargain, on his death enjoined upon his son at all costs to resist any further encroachment on part of the new order. And Richard, hard pressed as he was, obeyed his father, and, resisting all temptation, refused to sell a single foot of the land, though he appeared to be willing to let Nepture have a good many feet for nothing. Satisfied in his conscience, Richard was not troubled by visits from his father's ghost, from which it is to be inferred that the parent was fully gratified with the staunch behaviour of his son. Ghosts of the dead visit living relatives and friends only when they want something from them. And Henry Thorley wanted nothing from Richard.

The feud, if feud it was, between the lords fighting for the land had at one time extended to the neighbouring village of Ravenford, whose inhabitants deeply resented the usurpation of their time-honoured name; for Garden City, for all practical purposes, assumed the title of Ravenford-on-Sea.

Old Ravenford, situated half a mile inland, and boasting an old inn and a dozen or more authentic black and white houses, did not at first take kindly to the London-journeying folk, with their limousines and new-fangled notions; the establishment by the Wilson Development Company Limited of a row of shops on the immediate outskirts of the new settlement did not add to the friendliness of the villagers.

With time even the worst of feuds grow threadbare, and when the young nowadays grow up they no longer walk in the way of their fathers. Instead, to use the parlance of the time, their lives are so "speeded up" that they can scarcely be said to walk at all. In old Ravenford some of the barns have been turned into garages, and it may be only a matter of time when the word "barn" will become an anachronism; that is, as far as this particular village is concerned. The old folk are also beginning to reconcile themselves to the changes, and not a few are pleased because, Ravenford-on-Sea having become something of a summer resort, the overflow of profitable visitors is filling the spare rooms of the old cottages and the hitherto sparse purses of the villagers. The only hotel is unable to accommodate all who want to come, and during the tennis tournaments week the prices take a big upward leap, and every available room is snatched at a premium. Prosperity, for the first time, has struck the village of Ravenford; in consequence of which the then still young Richard Thorley was coming more and more to be regarded as old-fashioned and "queer." There were indeed one or two grumblers who went so far as to insinuate that he was an enemy of society. And, in a fashion, he was; he had the effrontery to think and to act as if human society had great need of a different kind of improvement than the Wilsons of the

Garden City could give it. That, to be sure, was to prove his undoing.

But this is anticipating. This strange history goes back to the time before Ravenford-on-Sea so miraculously—or so diabolically, as some would have it—sprang into being; to the time when Ravenford Manor, occupied for generations by the Thorleys, was the main human focus between the tamarisk-lined coast and the downs rising northward a mile or more distant. It had been at one time the Mount Olympus and the Mount Sinai to the villagers and small landholders and labourers of the surrounding radius; tradition affirmed that the Thorleys ruled the land firmly but justly. In politics they were Tories, disdaining liberal ideas but insisting on "fair play"—as they saw it. The genealogy of the Thorleys has been fully and competently dwelt upon in county histories; there is no need to recapitulate it here except to say that the Thorley blood contains a mixture of the Vikings and the Normans, and possibly of the Saxons —though on this latter point there is some disagreement among authorities—in any case, a robust enough concoction of races which in the solution has operated nobly and, on the whole, as far as we know, for the public good. Our history properly begins more recently when, to the dismay of the natives, a drop, and truly a fatal drop, of Russian blood was added to the solution. Incredibly strange and appallingly destructive were its effects on the Thorley family history.

It began three generations ago, when one William Thorley, who had begat Henry who had begat Richard, shedding his traditional Thorley insularity, had ventured forth on a journey across the North Sea and, penetrating into

"barbarous Muscovy," as all the living Thorleys regarded
the Tsar's domains—though the journey was undertaken
some years after the Crimean War—had, after a year's
mysterious absence, returned; bringing back with him, as
the new mistress of Ravenford Manor, a Russian bride,
lovely as she was alien, with strangely fair hair and dark
almost raven-black eyes, with long curling lashes, and pale
white skin scarcely perceptibly flushed a faint rose. And
her speech was as soft and mellifluous as any heard from
the loveliest Italian mouth. She spoke English, which she
had learned from tutors and governesses, with a slight
accent which cultured visitors to the Thorley home found
charming; and in other ways they found in her many
exotic enchantments. The master of Ravenford himself
never could resist following with admiring eyes the graceful movements of her lithe, firm-bosomed, slender-waisted
figure. And he never failed to plunge into ecstasy when
she let her long flaxen hair down; not only did it fall below
her waist, but it spread increasingly downward, enveloping
her in its flowing abundance. A young Royal Academician
of the day who painted her—fire unfortunately has destroyed this likeness of her—had aptly, in a moment of
enthusiasm, referred to it as "a Niagara of hair."

But if she shone for others, Olga Thorley herself was
not long happy in the insular atmosphere of her new home.
William had been so thoughtless as to bring her there in
the autumn. Could anything have been less auspicious
than to arrive in the damp and fog of early November and
face the prospect of a long English winter? Had William
Thorley possessed the common sense with which the
British race is credited, he would have straightway can-
celled his stay in Ravenford Manor and fled with his bride

to Italy. But he reasoned quite differently. He said to himself, "Love is all. Love should conquer. She will love me in the rain and in the fog, as well as in the sun!" It all seemed very simple to him.

But she was increasingly miserable, as the long dark days dragged on and on within the walls of that many-roomed mansion. And she soon began to pine for her native land, for the chaste white snows madly swept by the wild troikas, for the crisp dry air violated by the crackling of the whip and the many-belled tintinabulation; and again for the deep sonorous ringing of the larger bells on feast days from the multiple sun-glinting spires and minarets; and for the fervently tender ceremonies remembered from girlhood, such as the exchange, amidst the hypnotic fumes of incense, of the Eastern kiss, and the solemn interchange of those solemn words, "The Lord is risen!" "The Lord is risen indeed!"

Everything was strange to her in this sunless isle with its loury skies, in those long months of greyness when not a ray of light or joy penetrated the bleak habitation. The human beings who walked about in the visible world, whether within the large house or in the landscape to be seen out of the window of her upper chamber seemed like half animate shadows propelling themselves with effort through the dense atmosphere, as it were, blurs of protoplasm floating in unformed chaos.

The men who came to the house, friends of her husband's, dignified and reserved like himself, lacked the fire which men of her race bred in the Caucasus had taught her to look for in men. Gentlemen they were called, and gentlemen they were. They had ease and good manners, and they kept their secret emotions pretty well in check,

until Olga began to wonder if this fabulous self-control
were not an illusion created to conceal the fact that there
was nothing to control.   Granted they were Spartans,
whose hard virtue had been ingrained in the race through
the many generations—what of that?   She could respect
it, she could admire it; she could hardly be expected to
love it.   And she was one of those intensely romantic persons to whom loving was a need, and ecstasy the very
essence of living.   Instead, her life was becoming a perpetual contemplation of a tantalizingly calm mask which,
far from inspiring her to calm, awakened in her a terrible
desire to slash it open with a rapier, with that irresistible
vim with which one sometimes stirs banked-up fires.   What
was under that mask?   The sulky fires of Caliban?   The
ethereal fancies of Ariel?   Chained passions?   Fettered
desires?   She was eager to know.

Her husband seemed a different man from the man who
had wooed her on her father's estate in the wilds of the
Caucasus.   English to the core, with the long head and
face so characteristic of the English aristocratic type, he was
tall, handsome, well set-up, with fair hair and long moustaches and hirsute side appendages descending well below
the temples and a long firm shaven chin.   It was not that
he was really different.   He *was* different in her circle at
home.   There, among men of her race, he was distinguished for his stately bearing, his aloofness, calm, reserve.
He had stood out like a superior being from another world.
He shone in that background of unbridled Tartar exuberance, of active Slavic chaos; he was a Greek god, a serene
statue, unmoved by the restless world around him.   And
he had awakened her admiration and love.   There was
the assurance of his race perceived by her senses, there was

something nobly equestrian in the way his head and shoulders were flung back. And she herself was as a high-strung spirited horse yearning for a rider as noble and controlled as he appeared to be.

During his visit to her father's estate they had often gone out on horseback jaunts together; and she had observed how motionless he sat, and how erect; and what marvellous control he had over his horse and over his own body. He sat there, one with his horse; and in a moment of illumination the meaning with which the Greeks had endowed the creature called the centaur had suddenly come to her: man, who was half god half beast; his intelligence resident in the topmost part of him longing to soar into the heights, his beast-like body holding him to earth, to earthly nature. And she had conceived an idea of this Englishman as of a half-god, as of a centaur held to earth by his earthly fetters. Her own countrymen, in comparison, were fauns, wild and goat-like, and obscene. Their appearance in civilized European attire did not dissipate this impression. They surely were not centaurs; at best, untamed horses madly romping about and shaking their manes in a frenzy of wild delight.

In short, Olga Thorley was an imaginative, romantic woman. It was, perhaps, natural that her sentimentalizings about this quiet, statue-like Englishman, should in his own land suffer the rude shock of disillusion commensurate with her previous exalted idea of him. Now that she was in the land of dignified god-men, she found them on the whole a tame lot. They were brave and considerate and disciplined, and gallant toward their women; but where she had expected free Athenians, she found dutiful stoics. They had gotten her respect where she wanted to give them her love. Respect was a poor sort of jade. In the quiet of her upper room, looking out to sea, she sometimes laughed hysterically at the thought that instead of the noble centaur she had expected to find she had found in life but a poor jade. She herself, she felt, was becoming a poor jade in the process.

Apropos of this, a brief letter of hers remains among the archives of the Royal Academician who had painted her portrait, a letter significant for a few words her spirit and the nature of its conflict with a life so antipathetic to it. In it she wrote:

"The human emotions are wild horses, and the human mind is the driver directing them. But now the horses are cowed, and the driver sits quietly in his seat, no longer the man who has need to exert himself to control the weary jade."

These extraordinary words might, in the usual course of events, have passed for an abstract expression of philosophy, strange to be sure coming from a woman, especially from so charming and exquisite a member of her sex—there can be little doubt that she enchanted all the males who saw her—were it not that the words which followed quite dissipated the notion of philosophic calm moving her to intelligent observation. Indeed, there was something heartrending and desperate in the simple words:

"I can't stand it! I can't stand it! I shall go mad, I tell you."

Comparing this note with a more formal communication written earlier, a mere invitation to dinner, both preserved by the Royal Academician—why these two and not others it was hard to tell—it was to be seen that whereas the invitation was written in a minute, meticulous hand, the hand of a gentlewoman, the calligraphy of the other epistle gave every indication of nervous tension, of stress; the very letters which formed the words appeared agitated and gave the sense of galloping after one another in a mad stampede, like wild horses running from pursuing would-be captors.

No, it was clear she did not write this letter in a mood of philosophic calm, but rather—one gathered in comparing the two epistles—in a state of mind bordering on frenzy. And there could not be any doubt as to the desperate meaning of the words, "I can't stand it! I can't stand it! I shall go mad, I tell you! . . ." There was the ultimate pathos of the final words, "Or I shall die . . ."

Well, the poor woman, longing for her native land with its uncouth madness, did not go mad. But it was not long after she had written the curious self-revealing letter that she lay down and died. She died, pining, of a broken heart. Medical science, nowadays, denies that there is such a thing as a broken heart; but she, poor woman, lived in a day before medical science was so assured of its omniscience, and she died of a broken heart in a day when hearts were still capable of being broken.

Some weeks before she died, Olga Thorley left living issue of herself. It was a boy, and he was named Henry, and he was the son of his mother.

CHAPTER TWO

The Romantic Soul

HENRY THORLEY was indeed the son of his mother. All the romantic longings of that strange exquisite woman from the Caucasus were bequeathed to the tiny lump of pulsating flesh. A handsome child, everybody said, whose eyes startled by their peculiar brilliancy, as of liquid fire. The eager zeal of latent life was visible in those large dark orbs in the small fair face, so like his mother's even in early infancy. The father watched his son's growth with wonder and apprehension. "His mother all over!" he thought and pondered gravely on the boy's future.

William Thorley was an unhappy man, but reticent about his unhappiness. He had loved Olga with all his soul, even after the first months of blissful life when all of a sudden their romance seemed to subside, like tidal waters which ebbed and ebbed and showed no signs of return. In the silence of his room he had often prayed to heaven for the miracle of renewal, as he loved her then not less than at the beginning. When with her, he had snatched at every token, however slight and infrequent, of requited affection. He could not understand her, like many another man who had once loved and been loved in return and did not know why his love increased in ratio as the love of his chosen mate diminished. At last he had been forced to do what many another man before him had been forced to do: to give up the hopeless effort, to retire within himself, welling with a sorrow he could share with no one. There was bitterness too. It came from an inner consciousness of having failed the object of his devotion. Failed? But, God, he had done everything a mortal could do to please a woman! No man could have been more devoted, more tender, more thoughtful of his love's every want. Yet he had been a ghastly failure. How ghastly, he knew from her attitude towards him. It was an attitude of indifference, and sometimes, he could not help but feel, one of repugnance. Why should it so utterly have changed from her earlier adoration? He was not aware of any change in himself from the man who, but a short year before, on horseback, wooed the Slav maiden riding at his side in the wilds of the Caucasus. He could scarcely remember when had occurred the first rift in their happy togetherness, a rift which day by day widened until death itself, with invisible hands, had closed the gap. It must have been on the day three months after their arrival at Ravenford Manor that in a twilight hour he first glimpsed the shadow in her eyes, an indefinable, impenetrable shadow, like a curtain shutting her away from him; and later on entering her room he found her sitting still with a motionless brooding stare out to the dark sea, her whole being remote from him. She neither turned her head when he entered, nor did she speak; and without addressing her, he left the room, with a shadow on his heart which never afterwards quite left him.

This happened several times. At last, fearful for her mind, and distraught by his own unhappiness, he ventured to ask her if there was any way in which he could make her lot happier; the only answer had been:

"Don't ask me! Please don't ask me! I shall go mad! I shall go mad!"

Such an answer only perturbed him the more, and in the intervals between these increasing states of what he called "home sickness" he redoubled his efforts to please her. But in his heart he knew how useless it was. He brought his native commonsense to bear, and he thought it came down to this: she was a romantic soul, a soul craving a continuity of excitement, a continuity of sentiment, such as attended the first six months of their togetheredness. She demanded of life a never-flagging romance, a perpetual honeymoon. That was all very well, and he tried to please her as best he could. But life as he saw it and as he had been trained to see it was a serious business: in the end one had to "settle down," as the phrase went. He loved her, of course; how could one help loving her? But one couldn't go on "mooning and spooning" forever, as if life were just that and no more. He was a conscious member of the British Empire, perhaps the greatest Empire the world has seen. As one of its privileged members, he had duties to perform. It was expected of him. Following in the footsteps of his father, he contemplated standing for Parliament. His constituency seldom failed to return the Conservative candidate. But just at the time when he expected his wife to become a proper helpmeet, she unwittingly threatened to disrupt him and his dreams.

In the midst of this period of stress, which members of his family began to notice, not without casting censorious glances at the suspected culprit, he tried to keep his head. But for all the training he had had in the school of self-control and his forebears before him, he found it difficult. Too late he discovered that any lapse he made from the cool godlikeness with which he had at first so profoundly impressed this alien maiden had been too fatal to overcome now by any new effort at dignity, its only effect being to awaken her contempt. Thus was he caught between two fires. If she saw him devoid of romance, she had at least expected him to maintain the calm demeanour which had first won her adoration; but as he sometimes revealed his inner torment and distress she found him now devoid of both romance and Stoic hardihood. In short, the rider was not what he had appeared to be and had been ignominiously flung from his saddle.

Now and then it dimly dawned on William Thorley that their marriage was a mistake, that an insular Englishman and a romantic maiden from the Caucasus were no pair. This but echoed the judgment of the countryside. "A decent Britisher oughtn't to 'ave wed a bloomin' furriner!" But it was surely not in any Englishman's scheme of life to admit that such a marriage having been found a mistake could in any manner whatsoever be disrupted. "Those whom God hath joined together, let no man put asunder." And Thorley, a conservative, had no doubt whatsoever of God having joined him and Olga together. He could admit of no mistake there, and for reassurance on this point he returned in his mind to the happiness of those first six months. Beyond that, he liked to think that the subsequent unhappiness was the work of the devil. He once indeed ventured to express this opinion to Olga, and was deeply hurt to see her break into hysterical laughter to the tune of the wounding words:

"But, my dear Will, you are quite right. But don't you know that the devil is an English gentleman?"

The words were cryptic to him. What did she mean?

It, somehow, sounded like an insult. Did she intend it for him in particular, or did she mean to implicate the whole British race? Either idea was untenable, and for the first time in his dealings with her he could not restrain his wrath. He said angrily:

"I should have thought it was the Tartar!"

At these words, she suddenly ceased laughing. Her face flushed, then grew pale; her eyes blazed anger. She seemed not to be able to speak. Then:

"You vile creature! Get out of my sight!"

He did not wait to hear further, and at once left her room, a prey to the most terrible misgivings. He wished he hadn't said anything. The break between them appeared complete.

But she met him at the dinner table smiling, and acted as if nothing had happened. Later, when they were alone, she expressed regret. He felt relieved. The honour of the English gentleman was vindicated.

But not for long.

The subject of the English gentleman was to come up again, and yet again, and William was to shed some of his lustre in the ordeal. Schooled at Eton and at Oxford, he found it difficult, in relation to this alien woman, to play the part he had been trained to play. And this was something of a shock to him. "Have I lost my dignity?" he repeatedly, afterwards, asked himself. Was a gentleman so vulnerable, after all? "Scratch a Russian, and find a Tartar!" Napoleon had said. And it actually occurred to William to ask: "What would one find, if one scratched an English gentleman?" The question appalled him, for this exquisite woman he loved had a way of laying him bare and scratching until what was left of the English gentleman was not a pretty sight for him to contemplate. Yet each time he accepted her challenge he meant to shine, to show Olga that the Englishman was made of the right stuff. And so he was, persisted the poor man to himself, but so fine and finished a product was scarcely to be appreciated at its full worth by so elemental a people as the Russians. As a gentleman, he must be fair to all; this seemed the fairest way to vindicate his own race without indicting another. He once ventured, rashly enough, to speak his thought aloud to her:

"You Russians have the wildness, the romance, the picturesqueness. We English have character."

"You English have chains!" she blazed.

And, as an afterthought, she added:

"And are proud of them!"

So that was how she looked at it! Well, in all fairness to her, it was a point of view. It was wrong, of course——

"But, my dear," he persisted, "character is strength. It is restraint of self. Without restraint, civilization would—"

"You English are all restraint!" she angrily interrupted. "What would be left to you without it?"

He was about to reply, but reconsidered. It was best to practice what he preached. It was so easy to be angry. And gracefully he retired to the shelter of silence. It was, in the circumstances, the only thing an English gentleman could do. If he could not retrieve what he had lost, he might at least retain what shreds of dignity were left to him. And what he had lost was so precious and, at heart he knew, irretrievable. There was little comfort in the knowledge that if the fault was not his neither was it Olga's. It was a terrible and a bitter thing to see both sides, and William, with the blood of the Thorleys in his veins,—the very name of Thorley stood for justice and fair dealing, and for pride in these—could not help but put things in a balance and weigh and see. Hardening his heart against his love, he yet profoundly pitied this alien woman who was his wife, and pitied himself not the less.

Of course, there were reconciliations, many of them. Human beings cannot live in the same house and see each other every day without some outward show of civility. In the eyes of the world they were a contented if not a happy couple. Even Olga would not have it otherwise. The frequent guests who came to the house and saw her act as hostess could scarcely have suspected the unhappiness of this charming, well-bred woman, who lavished hospitality in an amiable, gracious way; while they saw the host take evident pride in the handsome woman and follow her with eyes which clearly said that she was all in all to him. During these hours he indeed allowed himself to entertain the illusion that he and she were happy and that all was well. Incredible it seemed that it could be otherwise. It was only when the leave-takings took place his heart would be seized with the secret dread that his dream was coming to an end; a foreboding well-grounded, for it was nearly always after these exhibitions of amiability that she performed a *volte-face* and made him feel sorry he had ever been born. Hence, it was not surprising that he invariably made the effort to hold his visitors until a very late hour.

There was one visitor in particular whom William held in great esteem, for the man possessed the precious gift of being able to soothe Olga into happy moods; and all was well when he came from London for two and three-day stays. This was Wyndham Priestley, a handsome

Royal Academician of about thirty-five, who possessed ample descriptive and lyrical talents which might have served him well as a poet but which actually made him one of the galaxy of Victorian painters who, in the fashion of the time, only succeeded in painting mediocre "subject pictures" acclaimed by the generation as "works of genius" and subsequently distributed in reproduction by soap firms and Christmas pictorials. They bore such titles as "Diana at the Bath," "Penelope at the Loom," "Horatio Holding the Bridge," "The Fond Father," "Nelson Calling on All Englishmen to Do Their Duty," etc., etc. Well, you know the sort of thing. Priestley was somewhat superior to the others in this dubious art, in that he took pride in his line and strove to achieve a sensuousness of colour; but that is neither here and there. After all, the essential thing about Priestley was that he was thoroughly charming as a man, and that he thoroughly charmed Olga Thorley.

With his sensitive long oval face, fair hair, ruddy complexion, and the bluest of blue eyes nearly always mischievous and laughing, he disarmed all who came in contact with him; moreover, he managed to maintain his position as a gentleman without the coolness and reserve which marked the others, without the restraint and dignity which so often provided a parody of themselves. He was good-natured and gay, bubbling over with good spirits—an ardent soul, Olga called him—and he could hold the audience of a drawing room by the warmth and rhythm of his melodious speech. He and Olga made good friends from the beginning, and she was rarely moody in his presence. There was no doubt he had the power of keeping her from being bored. Like all ardent, romantic souls, she intensely suffered from the incurable malady of boredom, that most virulent form of "home sickness," which at twilight makes one long to be on the move seeing strange peoples and places, to go in quest of that hypothetical isle or oasis where one might contentedly and even happily rest one's head for the remainder of one's days.

There was something of the pixie about Priestley. He could keep up a stream of running talk and sprightly comments, and he had the gift of story telling almost Irish in graphic charm and fantasy, while his voice in itself exercised upon Olga a hypnotic potency, subduing her recalcitrant spirit to an opiate mood. He had no ideas, no particular philosophy; his mind was a playground in which all sorts of fancies cut wild capers irresponsibly, in cornucopian confusion; and Olga, fascinated, listened. And, in spite of the appearance he presented of a jovial sprite, he became in a manner the confessor of William Thorley's unhappy wife. They were drawn together in the hours in which she sat for him, while he painted a portrait which was to be the sensation of the exhibition she did not live to see. What might have happened between them had she lived on it is hard to say. Her husband's deliberate gallantry in putting no restraint on their intercourse served well its purpose. There was nothing secretive about Olga, and Priestley was a gentleman.

Then came the time when they could not see each other. For Olga grew big with child. William awaited the event with joy, for already it somewhat softened the prospective mother; and he fervently hoped that with the infant's birth, a new life would begin for both of them. He was doomed to disappointment. Scarcely a few weeks passed after Henry's birth before Olga began to pine and fret; again her twilight hours became unbearable. Then one day she contracted a fever, and it was presumed that she died of it. That was the verdict of the doctor, but William possessed his own secret knowledge of the matter. He had seen her lose all desire to live, he had seen her yearn for death. She had no will to resist the Reaper.

William was inconsolable. He had conceived the idea that he was responsible for her death; he had even called himself her murderer. Oppressed with this idea, he fell into lassitude, and took little interest in things other than those which immediately concerned his household and estate. He became a gentleman farmer. Urged by his friends to put into effect his original idea of standing for Parliament he mildly shrugged and replied that there were better men than he to make laws for others. His astonished friends said sympathetically among themselves that it must have been a marvellous love affair to have so affected poor Will. This was true enough in its way. He remembered Olga as she was in the full bloom of their romance; and he refused to believe that that which followed was anything more than a figment of some unpleasant dream. Now that she was dead he felt closer to her than when she was alive. He too was a romantic soul—in his own fashion.

Only one other thing now obsessed him, and that was his son. With wonder and trepidation he watched the young boy's growth, and in those large brown eyes of his in the small fair face he saw the living soul of the departed. With a curious prescience, he foresaw that the boy would be no ordinary Englishman, no traditional Thorley. There was something in those eyes which presaged a life different from the life of his male forebears, but where it would lead, and if its goal was for good or evil, was beyond his ken.

CHAPTER THREE

Blood Will Tell

O NE lovely forenoon, in the corridors and dormitories of ———— School intense excitement prevailed. The whole school, numbering some three hundred boys, had been ordered at a certain hour to appear in the immense Assembly Hall. It was not an hour in which the hall was generally used for any definite purpose. The summons was mysterious, everyone wondered what was up. At break, the boys talked vociferously among themselves, propounding theories, all wide of the mark. One thing was certain: something portentous was to happen; the very atmosphere of the place was charged with that portentous certainty. The more robust boys were jubilant with expectation, the more sensitive nervous with apprehension.

The truth leaking out at last from a quarter most directly concerned with it spread fast through the small community. For among the boys of one of the lower forms it was known from the beginning that one of their number had been summoned by the headmaster to answer the charge of a most heinous felony. Peter Smallpeice, a first-year boy, was the culprit, accused of appropriating to his own use a belt belonging to one of his room-mates, Andrew Carling, who reported the matter to the prefect, who reported it to the head.

Peter was a small, lean, sallow-complexioned boy, with a long lean face, high cheek-bones and hollow eyes which habitually wore a frightened look. He had long unruly brown hair which, in spite of efforts, insisted on sticking out in wisps, accentuating his peaked expression. He came from one of the poorer families represented in that school. His father was a country solicitor who, at some material sacrifice, wished to give his son advantages he had not had himself. Peter was not good at sports, in itself a reprehensible circumstance, and he was not popular, though before the belt episode nothing tangible could be held against him. He was quiet and he kept mostly to himself, but in his duties as "fag" he encountered some trying experiences. The boy for whom he fagged was a bit of a bully who resented the pathetic looking boy and exercised against him that abstract malice inherent in human beings in varying degrees, more in some than in others. He made Peter Smallpeice's life miserable, and Peter, mindful of the sacrifices his parents made for his sake, bore his many trials with infinite fortitude; waiting patiently for the time when he would be a "fag" no more and some other boy would be doing the fagging for him.

Peter had that morning inadvertently picked up a belt belonging to another boy and put it on; it had lain where his own should have been. Andrew Carling, whose property it was, discovering it on Peter and resenting the search to which he had been subjected, reported the matter to the prefect who in his turn reported it to the head, who summoned Peter. The boy pleaded that what he had done he had done without intent to steal. But the headmaster was obdurate and decreed that Peter should receive a reprimand and twenty strokes of the cane before the assembled classes. The poor boy wept, entreated, and falling on his knees implored to be let off, but all to no avail. The sentence was passed and must be executed. Three o'clock was the time set.

The terrible hour had come. Smallpeice's Golgotha was ready there at one end of the immense room in the shape of a platform customarily used for lectures and gala occasions. For the time being, save for a table and some chairs, it was empty. A portrait of Queen Victoria, flanked by portraits of Gladstone and Disraeli, looked down on the auditorium.

The three hundred odd boys filed to their places with a great clamour of voices and a noisy shuffling of feet, in preparation for the spectacle. There were some faltering hearts among them. And there were others glad because of the diversion about to be offered them. It takes many kinds of people to make a world, and a school is no exception to the rule.

At last all were seated, including the boy to be offered as the sacrifice, the sport for many. Peter Smallpeice, occupying one of the rear seats, sat there stunned, dumb with horror, scarcely able to breathe. Now and then he trembled violently, as one in the throes of ague. Not far from him, a row or two to the rear, sat another boy eyeing him out of startled large brown eyes, and it was to be seen that he was profoundly distraught by the plight of Smallpeice and the humiliation to which the poor boy was on the eve of being subjected.

The whispering ceased, silence possessed the whole assembly, as the headmaster, accompanied by the mathematics master, emerged from an open side door and ascended the platform.

The headmaster, Mr. Cecil Pertwee, a tall gaunt clean-shaven man of about sixty, with an almost hairless head and a straight almost lipless mouth, which took a sharp downward curve at the corners, stood for some moments behind the table contemplating his audience in silence. The mathematics master, Mr. Ronald Rudwick, a shortish, plumpish figure, with round face and discoloured red-brown walrus moustaches, and gimlet-like round blue eyes, sat down in a chair to the left of the table, and looked out of his spectacles with a fixed stare directed at the culprit whom his searching gaze soon found. He knew his duty, and he would be there to do it when the time came. At his side, on the table, lay a long switch which had already done yeoman service in his capable hands. A little more than three years had passed since Mr. Pertwee himself manipulated the switch. His once good right arm was half lame with rheumatism, and he relegated the duty of chastisement to Mr. Rudwick, who as mathematics master could be depended upon to count his strokes without risk of miscalculation.

Mr. Pertwee, standing erect there in spite of his sixty years, with marked deliberation drew out a little snuff box from a pocket, and after sniffing from the finger tips a few grains of the powder up his nostrils he pulled out a hand-kerchief and sneezed vigorously, always with him a portentous token. He was ready for his peroration.

"Boys," he began, slowly, with a grave air, "I regret to say that a painful, an onerous duty falls upon me today. I am addressing myself as a gentleman to gentlemen, I hope; or at any rate, to sons of gentlemen. A gentleman, I trust I may say, with no exaggeration, is the noblest work of God. Without gentlemen civilization would be a failure. I assert, with no fear of contradiction, that the mighty British Empire rests on the shoulders of gentlemen. This is an axiom . . ."

He paused, and glanced around him, as if to see if his words produced the desired effect.

"What is a gentleman? I ask you," he resumed. "A gentleman, I may say, is not merely one who exercises courtesy and restraint, not merely one in command of manners not within compass of the common herd. He is also,"—at this point he slightly raised his voice—"one who perceives what his duty is towards others and himself and does it, however painful it may be, fearlessly and without regard as to whom it may or may not hurt. Indeed, it may hurt himself more than him for whom he may happen to serve as a direct or indirect instrument for the infliction of a just punishment . . ."

Again he deliberately paused, while he helped himself to another pinch of snuff. Then, after giving vent to the inevitable sneeze hardly less vigorous than the first, he went on:

"A deplorable thing has happened today. I say deplorable because no other word in the English language so adequately describes the unseemly conduct of one who, presumably a gentleman among other gentlemen, has deviated from that path of Christian rectitude which gentlemen in all circumstances are expected to follow. I say the word deplorable deliberately and without any reserve whatsoever. It is all the more deplorable—and this I may asseverate with some pride—because the thing that has happened has never, to my knowledge,—certainly not within my whole range of experience and hearsay—happened within the precincts of this school; the long annals of this institution are quite free from all taint of dishonour . . .

"All the more shame, I say,"—Mr. Pertwee raised his voice in a volume of indignation—"to the young man who has this day departed from the knightly virtue of the English gentleman to ways befitting those belonging to a lower order! And all the more reason, I insist that the felon should be made an example of; that the whole world may see what is to be expected of an English gentleman!

"As the head of an educational institution whose duty it is to train gentlemen in the way they should go—it would be false modesty on my part if I did not stress the responsibility and gravity of my proud task—a heavy burden devolves upon me, and I should be false to my duty if I did not take immediate and definite steps to eradicate the virus of dishonour from the living organism of this small community whose chief pride has its source in the maintenance of its honour.

"Within recent years there has been sprung upon us a new idea, the Darwinian theory of evolution, with regard to which, as some of you may know, there has been considerable debate, pro and con. It is not for me to say how much or how little truth there is in the theory. Personally, I cannot bring myself to believe that we, human beings, can be descended from the monkeys. I don't feel the least atavistic inclination to hop from tree to tree and crack some hard nuts!" Mr. Pertwee gave a weak little chuckle, in appreciation of his own nimble wit, and looked around with satisfaction at the responsive smiles. "We have, to be sure, our own hard nuts to crack here! . . . However I may disagree with that statesman politically, I prefer, generally speaking, in this matter of evolution, to stand with Disraeli, 'on the side of the angels.' Yet this evolution theory may, with some truth, in a limited sense, be applied to the undoubted development of human beings, exemplified in the production of the highest type of man, the English gentleman. And to that extent I am willing to aid Nature in its sublime process."

Having delivered himself of this noble exordium, the noble Mr. Pertwee thought his effort deserved a double pinch of snuff, after applying which to his noble nostrils, he resumed:

"I said that what happened this morning within the precincts of this school was deplorable. This is what happened. One boy, without leave, has appropriated to his own use the property of another. Respect of another's property is one of the first tenets of a gentleman. To be sure, the property so appropriated, was only a belt, a little thing, a trifle, you will say. But the very art of being a gentleman hangs on respecting trifles. It is the principle that matters. Is there, in principle, any actual difference between robbing another of a belt and robbing a bank? I, for one, say No! No! A thousand times No!" The headmaster emphasized his statement by pounding the table with a clenched fist. "The property of another, however trifling, should at all times be respected. I cannot emphasize this point too much. What would happen to society if we all took to pilfering? Anarchy would prevail, and chaos. With all our strength we must combat such tendencies. We must make every effort to extirpate them at the root. And we cannot help a boy better than by demonstrating to him the evil of his ways before it is too late. It is equally important to demonstrate this to the whole assembly, so that if there is any similar latent tendency in any of the other boys it may be nipped in the bud, so to speak. The honour of every individual here, the honour of the school, the very honour of the country and its glorious Empire demand it!"

With keen satisfaction with his own eloquence, Mr. Pertwee surveyed the assembly and seeing some frightened faces there he concluded that his peroration was not wholly lost on the young men. Mopping his forehead with a handkerchief, he called in a tone of command:

"Smallpeice, come forward!"

In answer to the call, a whimpering boy rose from his seat and haltingly made his way up the aisle, followed by all eyes. He stumbled and almost fell as he walked up the four or five steps which led to the platform, and was helped by the flung-out willing hand of Mr. Rudwick, as if that worthy were apprehensive of the escape of his prospective prey.

Once on the platform, the boy stood in a lost sort of way. Then, suddenly galvanized into life, he implored for mercy, crying:

"I didn't do it to steal! I swear it! I swear it!"

Was there a heart there moved to pity? It was hard to say. Save for the boy's whimpering an intense silence reigned. The headmaster, with disapproval, eyed the boy unable to take punishment "like a man," and motioned to Mr. Rudwick to take charge of the ceremonies.

"Rudwick, you may begin!"

That gentleman, thus appealed to, pushed his chair forward and, taking the stunned boy by the hand, commanded him to bend his body in such a way as to permit him to rest his hands on the seat of the chair, while his buttocks and legs alone were visible to the auditorium. This much accomplished, Mr. Rudwick seized the switch from the table and lifted it to strike the first blow, when a sudden commotion in the rear of the hall caused him to suspend operations. The whole assembly hall was astir with excitement. Without warning, the boy with the large brown eyes who had watched Smallpeice so sympathetically from a seat not far from him sprang from his place and, to the wonder of all, running impetuously up the aisle, quickly mounted the platform and, in a passionate outburst, addressed himself to the headmaster:

"Please, please don't beat him! He's not guilty. I know he's not guilty! But guilty or not, please don't beat him! Beat me, if you must beat some one! I'm willing to take his place! I beg of you, let me take his strokes! Please!"

Consternation appeared on the face of the headmaster, as he gazed, tongue-tied, at the handsome flushed boy with the appealing large brown eyes looking so steadily into his. The headmaster, averting his gaze, looked helplessly at his assistant, who blinked, and, thinking to help out matters, suggested with a malignant chuckle:

"Do you think I'd better thrash them both?"

And it was to be seen at once that nothing would have suited Mr. Rudwick better. One was one, but one plus one was two. Good arithmetic, if not exactly higher mathematics.

But Mr. Pertwee either did not hear or deliberately ignored the Solomonic proposal. For reasons of his own, it did not suit his purpose to administer chastisement to Peter Smallpeice's champion. It vexed him to think that of all the boys this boy, so habitually well-behaved and contemplative, should have ventured on so dramatic an entrance. And Mr. Pertwee knew and respected his father, a gentleman of gentlemen. It was a ticklish position for any self-respecting man to be put in.

The moments ticked by, long eternities. Something must be done, and that quickly. For once in his life, Mr. Pertwee found it hard making up his mind. He decided to temporize.

"Henry Thorley!" he said, at last—for the boy was none other than William Thorley's son—"Go at once to my study, and wait for me there."

The handsome boy, rendered still handsomer by the pink flush which suffused his habitually pale face, stood hesitating. He ran a distraught hand through his soft brown hair and, with the other indicating Peter who stood close by as much stunned as the rest, said with evident perturbation:

"Very well, sir. But may I ask, will Smallpeice be let off? I can't stand the thought of his being beaten. I can't, sir. And I'm willing to take his place!"

"Go, I tell you!" shouted the old man, peremptorily, with not a little exasperation. "Go! Wait for me in the study!"

Crestfallen, Henry Thorley descended from the platform and, with bowed head, walked down the aisle and out of the room, leaving behind him an army of astonished stares. Such audacity had not been known in all the glorious annals of —— School, and not a few there but envied his courage—or was it rashness?—in challenging old Pertwee of all men. The majority were thrilled by the extraordinary spectacle and wondered as to the outcome. None envied Henry in that; the headmaster was not a man to be trifled with. But did they really know old Pertwee? The truth was, old Pertwee did not know himself—not at this moment, at any rate. He was nonplussed; a struggle was going on in his confused soul which, if it were only known, would have astonished most those who knew him best.

It was expected that another peroration would follow on the subject of insubordination, but this time the boys were spared such refined torture. Instead, in a voice faltering with emotion, the nature of which was hard to fathom, the headmaster commanded:

"Rudwick, go ahead!"

This time Smallpeice did not protest. Taking courage, perhaps, from his champion's example, he contritely resumed his previous unnatural position, while Mr. Rudwick, resentful of the delay, with unwonted vigour began to lay it on with the switch across the boy's buttocks tightly encased in the stretched trousers. The boy writhed and winced, but gritting his teeth did not cry out. Shame and humiliation were his, but they were tempered by the newly gained secret knowledge which inspired him with a courage he had not thought he possessed. Nevertheless, at the ninth stroke he was ready to swoon. Rudwick had struck harder than if there had been no interference; in his bitter fancy he was striking at Henry as well as at Peter. He could not understand his chief allowing the other boy to go.

But at this point of the proceedings there was another surprise in store for the irate mathematics master as well as for the assembly, already so amply thrilled that afternoon; for just as Rudwick's hand was uplifted for the tenth stroke old Pertwee's voice came thundering:

"Enough! Stop!"

It was a curious voice, unusual for the headmaster. The old firmness was gone from it. It seemed like a broken cry forced on him by something deep within himself. What was it? Had Henry Thorley's desperate intervention struck something in the secret recesses of him never touched before? Did the man really possess an unsuspected spring of compassion unwittingly tapped by the strange action of the gracious boy? It was hard to tell. But it was certain that his cry to Rudwick had something in it curiously pathetic, curiously perverse, something not to be expected from a man who had never before been known to show pity. What was it? What happened? There was mystification in all faces, and not a little open resentment in Mr. Rudwick's; the mathematics master was a realist and loathed all mystery which he could not explain. There was a job to do, and he was there to do it. He had been commanded to deliver twenty strokes, and he was there to deliver twenty strokes. Could anything more be expected of any man? And here was a man in Pertwee's position suddenly turned blithering idiot, going back on his own word, the word of a gentleman. Could anything be more discouraging?

Mr. Pertwee, oblivious of the sensation he had created and of the feelings of resentment he had aroused in Mr. Rudwick and of the mystery he had suddenly, as it were in an instant, become, did not wait to witness the effect of his two short words, and, turning his back on Mr. Rudwick and the Assembly, rapidly descended from the platform and stalked out of the doorway on the left through which he had previously so ceremoniously entered.

Mr. Rudwick, taking matters in hand, in a few words declared the extraordinary session at an end. The boys, rising simultaneously from their seats, once more, with clamour and a loud shuffling of feet, began to file out of the room, talking animatedly concerning the unprecedented events of that exciting afternoon; while poor Smallpeice, stiffened by the position which he had held and the severe punishment he had received, limped painfully along, shame and humiliation filling his heart and, now that the ordeal was over, tears pouring from his eyes copiously and without restraint.

What passed in the subsequent interview between the headmaster and young Thorley never became known; both maintained a strict reticence. It was clear however that something had to be done, that Henry could not violate the discipline of a school without suffering for it. And it came to pass that on the following day the father, William Thorley, now a middle-aged grey-haired man, urgently summoned from Ravenford by Mr. Pertwee arrived at the school, where he immediately went into conference with the headmaster in his study. After an hour's deliberation, the elder Thorley issued forth from the school, accompanied by his son. The pair, arm in arm, were seen to enter a closed carriage which drove them to the station a mile and a half distant. Henry's bags went with them. It was clear to those who witnessed the departure that young Thorley was no longer a pupil at the school, but whether he was expelled or left of his own will or by the wish of his father it never became known. The father did not show any anger, nor did he appear upset about the occurrence in which his son had played so dramatic a part. Once in the carriage, he turned to Henry and said quite softly:

"You appear to have upset old man Pertwee in a way I did not believe was possible. He's really a decent sort, you know, though he doesn't often show it! What did you say to him?"

"Nothing much. We differed in our definition of the word 'Gentleman,'" came the surprising reply.

"I should have thought it was more serious. What was your definition?" the Thorley senior asked, with some curiosity.

"I said that I was under the impression that a gentleman was a *gentle* man," said the boy shyly.

"Ha! Ha! Ha!" William Thorley burst into a boisterous laugh. The observation of his son struck him as naïve in the extreme; yet, to be sure, there was a note of fundamental truth in it too. And there was a simplicity about it which pleased him.

"Why do you laugh?" Henry asked, turning a puzzled face to his father. "Isn't it rather obvious?"

Thorley Senior, recovering his composure, gently patted his son's back. "That's just it, of course!" he hastened to say. "It's so confoundedly obvious! That's why old Pertwee never saw it. How I should have loved to have seen his face when you make the sage observation!" And, glancing with pride at Henry, he again broke irresistibly into laughter; which subsiding, he fell into a pensive mood, and his eyes grew sad. He was thinking:

"Yes. Every bit the son of his mother!"

CHAPTER FOUR

Decidedly, Blood Will Tell

TWELVE years later—he was twenty-seven then—
Henry Thorley returned from the Continent, where,
after the unfortunate caning episode at Mr. Pertwee's school, he had been sent to be educated, at first by
private tutors, later at the universities. He had been at
Weimar, at Heidelberg and at the Sorbonne; and in the
long holidays he travelled hither and thither, to Greece and
to Spain, to Egypt and the Holy Land, and, for sentimental
reasons, to Russia, always driven by some inexorable demon
who would not let him rest. Knowledge quenched the
thirst of his mind, but not of his heart, and, troubled in
spirit, he felt himself consumed with a disruptive inner
flame which, notwithstanding the outlet provided by numerous journeys, plunged him into moods of introspection
and dream. His philosophical studies pursued in Germany
only encouraged a latent tendency to speculation, and
inspired him with yearnings towards the perfect, the absolute, the unattainable. He was not content to see them
remain yearnings, but longed to see them embodied in
reality, in the substance of everyday life. And, his father
having but lately died, he had been called home to manage
his estates. What a discouraging outlook for so high-
minded a young man! But he did not flinch from his
new earthly responsibilities and duties. On the contrary,
he welcomed them as a heaven-granted opportunity for the

practical realization of his dreams. He hastened back to England to take hold of things.

His father, whom from time to time he met on the Continent and at home, he respected and liked, though their relation never attained the intimacy of a deeper affection; because, in spite of the blood bond, there was no common ground of approach. The Thorley Senior, while kindly and denying his son nothing, was reserved and self-controlled, while Henry was exuberant and impetuous, with a tendency to extremes, excessive joy or excessive melancholy, and with that streak of wild fancy which ever drove him to seek more than he could find.

On the other hand, his mother, whom he had never seen, exercised a fateful influence over his whole existence, and precisely because he had not seen her she stirred his imagination with that potency which always has its source in mystery. He loved her as one loves perfection, and this love was fostered by the gallantry of Thorley Senior who painted the strange woman who had been his wife in most glowing colours and, in excessive zeal, asserted that he had been unworthy of her; which his son, while charitable to his father, was only too ready to believe. Eager for everything which had to do with his mother, Henry hungrily listened to all who knew her, and during his visits to England assiduously cultivated the company of Mr. Priestley, who only too willingly fostered the ideal picture which had grown up in the young man's mind. His mother was the most perfect of all perfect things; that was what he desired to believe, and he believed it with all the inducing strength of his youthful desire.

Henry was now a handsome young man, with a oval pale face, almost regular in feature, with thin silken hair very much like his mother's—he had seen a precious lock of it in his father's keeping—and large brooding brown eyes which emitted flame-like gleams dangerous for their power to ignite feminine hearts. Many woman instinctively feared him as one who might demand much, which was indeed true; for no man can demand so much of a woman as he who adores a mother whom he has never seen. Yes, decidedly, one can love easier something which one has not seen.

His German education emphasized this aspect of his naturally romantic character. The so-called "ideal woman" —in those days no contemptible phrase—was one of his obsessions. This hypothetical being was his innermost need, and she was not to be found, though spurious specimens abounded. In his too energetic quest of her, he made experiments and often fell in love, nearly always at first sight. For the most part, these "affairs" were brief, all too brief. There was no woman who answered his purpose, no woman whose charms outlasted his passion. And permanence was what he sought most of all in a woman in whose company he must needs spend the rest of his life. He associated permanence with the ideal. And his mother alone was permanent in his mind. There was something degrading in the reiterated discovery of the kaleidoscopic nature of woman; reality mocked him with its permanent impermanence. Somewhere in this world there must be, he thought, the one woman specifically created to merge her psyche with his, and his failure to find her tortured and consumed him. In the lack of his heart's desire he likened himself to a man without a home, to an eternal wanderer taking temporary shelter in devious places always in the hope of finding a constant habitation. He was the supreme

romantic temperament still possible in the early eighties
before the industrial florescence and the Great War had set
the final blight on such human illusions.

Henry returned to England with two ideas in mind,
though he regarded them as one and inseparable. There
was the woman to be found congenial to him. And there
was the work to be found equally in harmony with his
best self. Happiness was the end of life—that seemed to
him the first and the last axiom of existence—and happiness
could be had only by a harmonious marriage of all the
faculties. And he decided that once having found his
woman, together they would work to make a Merrie England of the little spot of earth of which he was the steward;
there must be a woman somewhere, a woman of his kind,
who would be willing to share in this task of service.
Social reforms were in the air, and romantically he was
infected with this idea of service, an idea coloured by the
aesthetics of Ruskin, the Rosettis and William Morris. He
thought himself practical, but not in the ordinary sense of
the word; for he observed with increasing alarm the
growth of the machine and the industrial world and he
looked askance at all social movements which operated
under the name of "practical organization." He thought
they "spoiled half the fun." Christ may have been the first
Socialist as some have asserted, but Christ did not work on
a system based on statistics, and "organized charity" was
no part of His scheme. Love, love must be the motive
behind all social service—love as Christ and the poets
understood it—and there was nothing so practical as love.

And so the woman he must find must be Mary, unafraid
of wasting precious ointment in the name of love; but she
must be something of Martha too, for the house must be

kept in order, and there was work to be done in the world.

It happened two years after his arrival in England. It was after dinner. Henry Thorley, still a young bachelor, was sitting with some friends in a house facing Regent's Park, sipping coffee with a liqueur. His hosts were the Wilsons—James and Marjorie—a prosperous newly-wed couple. James's father and Henry's had been friends, and for a while James and Henry had gone together to the same public school, at which Henry's tenure had been cut short by the caning episode. James had gone on to Oxford and was by way of becoming a politician, and he was painting to Henry the glories of following a similar course.

"You, Henry, are lost at Ravenford. With your great gifts you ought to be doing something. As you are something of a social reformer, why don't you go into politics and put your ideas and ideals into practice?"

"Perhaps you're right," said Henry dubiously, with a remote look in his eyes.

"Of course, I'm right!" asserted James with the assurance of one who was stating an incontestable fact. "You have the presence, the intellect, and the gift of gab. You can swing a constituency, you know, if you only will!"

"One good politician more or less—what does it matter?"

"But it does matter!" Marjorie added her persuasion to that of her husband. "The Empire has need of every man!" The latter phrase she had caught from her husband, who was not tired of reiterating it. She was a good-looking plump little woman, with a lovely complexion, and bright blue eyes which had cheer in them, and rather often fondly regarded the husband.

Henry smiled whimsically at the zeal of his friends. "I wouldn't be in the boots of Gladstone himself—no, not at any price!" he asserted with some energy. "The British Empire can take of itself. What matters to me is just life. I want it in the full meaning of the word. Life! What I can't stand is boredom, stagnation! And I don't ask it for myself alone, but for all! As things are, I see nothing but intolerable boredom. Everywhere!"

"But, my dear man," exclaimed James, with some show of exasperation, "you ignore the adventure of modern science, of new discoveries! Take the theory of evolution. What a new world it has opened up to us—men of today!"

"It doesn't console me for what we have lost!"

"Yes, just fancy, Henry!" Marjorie said, with a grimace at her husband. "Jimmy insists that I've come of a monkey. I don't like the idea at all!"

"Nor do I," said Henry, with a friendly smile. "If we are to believe wholeheartedly in the idea, then we shall be mere monkeys to the generations of the future. In any case, the original monkeys are still with us, and——"

"What, do you mean to say you don't believe in evolution?" asked James, in astonishment, as if Henry had uttered a sacrilege. Evolution seemed such an obvious fact to him.

"I didn't say so," said Henry calmly. "But I do say that the idea is not at all flattering to us. We've managed, to be sure, to dispense with tails, which proves to some people our superiority to the beast. But what else must we drop to be superior to ourselves? It's all so purely arbitrary. A generation may arise without noses, and that generation will surely assert that a noseless generation is superior to one which could boast of a proboscis. But that will get us nowhere! Nor make us a jot happier! I personally shall continue to think that Marjorie looks lovelier with a nose than without one."

"You with your paradoxes!" returned James. "To accept your analogy, you think Marjorie would look better with a tail?" He laughed triumphantly.

"I'm sure she'd have a nice one—a lovely bushy one!" rejoined Henry, with a gay laugh, in which his companions joined.

"A dubious compliment. It doesn't sound quite nice!" said Marjorie, blushing.

The conversation, she thought, was becoming embarrassing. But could anyone take umbrage at anything Henry said? He was a gentleman, "a perfect dear," not given to ribaldry for ribaldry's sake. She liked him. And she was used to these talks on evolution. Evolution was in the air. It formed the subject of much earnest talk. It also furnished a topic for small talk and badinage. It was father to the word Progress, which had become the Shibboleth of the day. Indeed, that was almost the next word that came from her husband's lips.

"Then you deny the idea of progress?"

"Progress? There's no such thing. We're too prone to assume that there is a rising continuity of things. As a matter of fact, we have good reason to believe that things completed and perfected have a decided tendency to devolute. A flower at the height of its bloom withers and fades, a ripe cheese falls apart, the mellow summer turns to autumn and winter blasts, a beautiful woman grows in loveliness but she too goes the way of all flesh. You too lightly assume that we are more intelligent and beauty-loving than the Greeks, more ethical than the ancient Jews, more law-minded and disciplined than the Romans, more rich in the sacrament of mystery than the Egyptians. We are indeed poorer in many things . . ."

"No, no!" cried James. "There's more humanity today, more human kindness. And science is doing much to ease life, to make life more comfortable, to give human beings better health, more leisure . . ."

"Granted all that. But science has also the decided tendency to make life more dull. Tell me, what's the good of a long life if it's a constant agony of boredom? What's the use of more leisure if there's nothing interesting to occupy it? Speaking for myself, I'd rather have a shorter life but full of intense living, far better have a Cleopatra for an hour than some complacent Martha for a life-time! Yes, yes—but our life makes Cleopatras impossible, impossible!"

Henry worked himself up into a passion. It was to be seen that there was something peculiarly intimate to him in the idea he was propounding, that he felt it with his whole heart and soul.

"Still harping on Cleopatra!" cried Marjorie, laughing. "A nice piece of baggage, I must say! You wouldn't know what to do with her if you had her!" But she looked at Henry, and was in doubt. Flushed as he was with drink and his own talk, he certainly looked handsome, and virile too. "Well," she added thoughtfully, "I wish you luck. I hope you find your Cleopatra!"

James slapped Henry on the shoulder. "I wish you happiness, old chap! Only take my word for it, find yourself the right girl and get married! Only don't go in for a Cleopatra! She'd lead you a gay dance, my dear fellow!

Marry a nice girl who'll only think of your comfort, health and happiness!"

Henry laughed. "She'd drive me to drink! No, it's Cleopatra or nothing! I shan't marry!"

"I'm afraid you won't," Marjorie laughed. "Not if you hold out for Cleopatra!"

"Never fear," James contradicted her. "You must beware, Marjie, of anyone who says he won't marry. There was old Jerome Hopkinson. You remember what happened to him!"

"Rather!"

"He was a handsome young man, was Jerome," resumed James. "Well-to-do. Firsts at Balliol, and all that. Headed for a distinguished diplomatic career. For ages he'd been saying, 'I won't marry! I won't marry!' A wife was a coffin to a man, was his way of putting it. And there were all the matrons and the fond mammas with daughters to dispose of, conspiring and dangling and angling. And he always laughed at them and their transparent efforts to entangle him. 'Not for me,' he'd say. 'I couldn't stand having the same woman hanging round me all the time!' He didn't mind flirting and philandering. Many a girl's heart fluttered with hope for a while. But in the end they gave him up. 'An impossible man!' they always said. 'No one would have him!' Of course, it was a case of sour grapes. Then he was sent on a several weeks' mission to India. And just imagine the feelings of the fond mammas and their pretty daughters when one day he reappeared among them with a full-fledged wife. He had picked her up—she was a mere chit of a girl then—on the boat on his way back, without, mind you, so much as an introduction from anyone. For a while his return was the talk of his circle. What mean things they didn't say about the Hopkinsons—the women, I mean! Then the rumour got around that they weren't happy together, and there was more excitement, more talk. 'Serves him right!' they said. 'He should have looked before he leapt!' But all the time, they were thinking: 'If he'd only leapt for us! If he'd only married one of us!' I was sorry for Hopkinson. A really decent chap he was. All the same, he brought it all on his own head. You see, he had married a Cleopatra of sorts. You know the kind of woman I mean. Men get infatuated at the mere sight of Elaine—that's the lady's name! I often wondered what made her marry Jerome. She's not really the marrying sort, you know. Still, a Cleopatra, if you like!"

"The poor man died," said Marjorie, warningly.

"Died?" asked Henry, absently, a remote look in his eyes.

"Yes, he died," said James, italicising his voice, as if he meant to rub it in.

"I never met this Hopkinson," said Henry, slowly, "but I imagine *I'd* have liked him. A man after my own heart, from what you tell me!" Exasperated by his host's matter-of-fact attitude, he had an urging impulse to put in a word for the unknown-to-him Hopkinson; he was indeed defending his own attitude, which had been challenged by the complacent James.

"All the same," said his host sententiously, "take warning and don't follow in the footsteps of our friend Hopkinson! It's bound to be disastrous. Romance is all very well in its place, but safety lies in common sense!"

"How long was he happy? Was he happy at all?" Henry asked, ignoring the speaker's platitudes.

"He was happy enough, I dare say. That is, the first six months or so. Deliciously happy, they say. But the poor chap paid for it afterwards, and heavily!"

"H'm . . ." Henry grunted. "Six months, you say? Six months is a long time. I should say it was worth it! Most men live a long life without knowing a moment of real happiness. And his appears to have been ecstatic. Six whole months! Goethe says somewhere that he hadn't three. And he lived to be over eighty!" Sipping his benedictine, Henry lapsed into a reverie. Presently, he started, like one suddenly awakened from a dream. "By the way," he asked, "where is this Elaine now?"

James and Marjorie laughed simultaneously.

"Now you've started him off, Jimmy!" said Marjorie.

"Where's this Elaine?" Henry repeated.

"Where? I haven't the least idea, old chap. Most likely she's making some other man's life miserable!"

"Or happy . . ." Henry interpolated.

"If you insist. Though I stick to the notion that she can keep a man happy only the first six months!"

"Then you don't know where she is?" persisted Henry, ignoring the other's comments.

"No . . ."

"What a strange, persistent man you are!" laughed Marjorie, and looked at him narrowly. She was thinking he was absurd, yet found this absurdity curiously pleasing. Here, at all events, was a man who had a capacity for loving, and secretly she could not help wishing that James could show something of the same ardent temperament. But she mustn't expect too much of James, who had his work cut for him. He had a career to make—the Empire had need of such men, so his friends assured her—and he hadn't the time to waste on a woman. As it was, she had made a good match and was reasonably happy. Only this man made her feel strangely uncomfortable, made her in some curious way aware that she was not getting out of life as much as there was to be got out of it.

"You were always an odd sort of fellow, Henry," said James, refilling his guest's liqueur glass. "Do you remember the day you stood up for that poor devil Smallpeice? How agog we all were that anyone could have dared to do it! I ran into him the other day. That's what made me think of it. That and old Pertwee's remarks on evolution. They were silly, of course! But you appear to have made a lasting impression on Smallpeice."

"I have? How do you mean?"

"Well, he and I had a chat over coffee, and I asked him how he was getting on." James paused, glancing whimsically from Marjorie to Henry. "What do you suppose the poor fellow said?"

"I haven't the least notion!"

"Well, he said he didn't think it was important to get on!"

"That sounds sensible!" Henry laughed. "What's Smallpeice doing?"

"He's a solicitor of sorts," James replied, not without condescension. "He has a very odd clientele. Very odd, indeed!" He laughed.

"How, pray?"

"Well, his chief idea in life seems to be to protect the poor against the rich, and his speciality appears to be to undertake cases in which there isn't the least hope of reward!" Again he laughed, as he added, "Why, the poor fellow was actually down at the heels!"

"And you think I've had something to do with all this?"

"Decidedly. He's confessed as much. He said that that famous day had revolutionized his life, and that your example had forced him to the conclusion that there was nothing nobler than to be of service to others! His father, I understand, who had sacrificed a great deal to put him through school, died heart-broken. So you see what you have to answer for!"

"Answer? To whom?" Henry flung the question defiantly. In some strange way he felt elated about the news of Smallpeice's mission. At the same time, the goodnaturedly contemptuous tone in which James had detailed the matter depressed and vexed him. "To whom?" he repeated, almost peremptorily, with just a touch of unaccustomed brusqueness.

"To God, of course! But you appear put out, old chap!"

"Not at all, Jimmy," he said, moderating his tone to gentleness. Then, after a pause: "You say God. But surely, Jimmy, you don't believe in Him?"

"I don't believe in God?" cried James, in astonishment. "Of course, I do! We're both good church members, aren't we, Marjie? But what makes you say that?"

Henry laughed. Half seriously, half in jest, he said: "I imagine your faith in evolution is stronger than your faith in God."

"Frankly, I don't see that the two are incompatible!"

"Perhaps not. Still, you must either believe that God created the world or that evolution had everything to do with it. If we assume that things grow and develop of themselves, out of protoplasm to an infinite variety of conscious and unconscious life, then we must agree that all intelligence, including the human intelligence, is in no way dependent upon the caprice of a deity——"

"It doesn't follow at all," James interrupted with some heat. "A watch, we know, is an intelligent device. But we also know that a watchmaker has made it. In short, God has created the process of evolution in the same way that the watchmaker has made his watch. And the watch processes and the evolutionary process go on working with equal efficiency after their creators have finished with them, though, to be sure," he added with a sly smile, "they both may need an occasional winding up, so to speak! The analogy only proves," he concluded, in triumph, "the intelligence of the deity."

"A poor analogy," retorted Henry. "The watch, we'll agree, is a mechanism devised by an intelligent man, but it remains a mechanism without any creative intelligence of its own. Besides, it does not of its own accord evolve into a superior watch. Indeed, in time it will wear out and not perform at all! In short, if we are to accept the analogy, then, in order to have a better world God will have to scrap this world in the same way one scraps a wornout watch."

"Let me put it like this," James made haste to say. "The process of evolution is like a watch-piece with the added distinction of having a creative intelligence of its own!"

"Good!" exclaimed Henry, undaunted. "Granted that is so, then man and all creation have emancipated themselves of God; since it must be assumed that God Himself cannot stay the processes which he has set in motion. Isn't that the rational conclusion to your premisses?"

James appeared nonplussed.

"You can't have it both ways," went on Henry relentlessly. "You must concede either that God, or some mysterious force we call God, guide this world, or that God has abdicated his task in favour of natural processes which you call evolution!"

"I believe in Progress!" protested James doggedly, giving no answer to the dilemma propounded by his guest.

"Another name for godlessness," asserted Henry calmly, pressing his host hard.

"What do *you* believe in?"

"I? I believe in God—and the devil!" Henry laughed.

"In a personal God? A personal devil?" James found it better tactics to ask questions than to answer them.

"I don't know. But I do know that there is an eternal conflict between the two, between the forces of good and evil, and light and darkness. The conflict may go on eternally. It's hard to tell. At this moment the devil appears to have the upper hand. Undoubtedly he rejoices in the existence of this human faith in evolution, for it is a weapon in his hand with which he may counter God!"

"How then would you judge a civilization if not by Progress?" James was vexed and desperate.

"I should judge it," replied Henry promptly, "by its charity toward the beggar!"

"What are you saying, man?" exclaimed James, throwing up his hands in disgust. "Are you serious? That's absurd!"

"Let us not forget," returned Henry, "that charity towards the beggar produced Homer, who gave rise to the most balanced and sane civilization the world has yet seen!"

"Children! Children!" cried Marjorie, with a laugh, meant to be conciliatory. "James, you'd better serve Henry with a whiskey and soda!" The argument was getting beyond her depth, and she sought to divert the conversation into quieter channels. She eventually succeeded.

Thus the rest of the evening passed, as most such evenings do, in small talk, in badinage, in everything which did not concern human beings over-deeply.

And at last, Henry, his mind confused with talk, and his senses warm with stimulation that comes with drink, went out into the street, murky with the fog of a London November night.

"A queer fellow," said James, turning to his wife. "I wonder what end he'll come to! No good one, I'm afraid. Anyhow, whether he denies science or not, he's a pretty good example of what heredity will do. They say his Russian mother was a strange woman!"

His wife said nothing. There was something about Henry Thorley that had touched her deeper than she would ever have cared to confess to her husband.

CHAPTER FIVE

The Unforgivable Sin

THE air was cool and damp, dense with fog, which swathed everything as with yielding layers of smoky cotton wool.

Henry Thorley walked the streets, his head in a turmoil, his heart sad with an incomprehensible gnawing. The sight of complacent people, coming in conflict with his own brooding restless spirit, often reacted on him like that. Life appeared a confused murky affair, like the streets on this foggy night, with human shadows passing him by. He himself was as a shadow walking in dream, and there was no reality about this life, no sense of living. The street lamps, dimly flickering, stretched like an eternity of reluctant beacons, leading nowhere. What was at the end of this long road of murky lights? Only another street, with more moving shadows, nothing else. At rare intervals, there was audible the clatter of horses' hooves, the rattling of a shadowy hansom over cobblestones; this too was a part of the sinister unreality. It was a city of men doomed to walk like shadows, to indulge in shadowy thoughts and shadowy feelings. Where was he going? To his hotel in the Strand, of course, but that too, in spite of its lights and the fire which would greet him in the lounge grate was no more than a shadowy oasis, peopled with the same shadowy beings only a little more defined.

Plunged in this mood of abstraction, enwombed in the

cloud of fog, he had walked the whole length of Great Portland Street, and was now approaching the more populous district bordering on Oxford Street. Veering to the right, he turned toward Oxford Circus. Armies of shadows jostled one another across the intersecting streets; life passed on in a sluggish stream, broken into numerous eddies running turbidly this way and that. Horse 'buses, with indeterminate human figures within and without, and hansoms with a solitary figure perched in the rear like some mammoth insect rolled by slowly; a barrel-organ was playing "Annie Laurie" out of tune; the air was full of inarticulate blurred cries, commingling in an immense cacophany, devised as it were by some uncouth titan bent on distressing delicate ears.

Everything merged for Henry into an inchoate, amorphous mass . . . Cant! Cant! That's all it was, this silly talk of progress. Cant! Cant! That's all it was, this absurd notion that everything was for the best, that humanity was advancing in one breathless impulse toward ultimate perfection. What was it all but cant, cant?

Henry's thoughts crowded in his mind. There too a dense fog prevailed. And his thoughts stirred sluggishly through this fog, exploding now and then in tiny outbursts of light, like the dimly flickering street lights, eternally recurring. Cant! Cant! he went on, thinking of the Wilsons. All that was cant, cant!

Beggars huddled in the doorways, taking shelter from the cold. Old men and old women. They sat for the most part motionless, in warped gargoyle-like postures, as if congealed, and their heads were bowed in comfortless sleep. Others were awake and, grimacing, stretched out their hands and begged plaintively for alms. He gave them all the coppers he had, and when these were exhausted he gave them six-pences, then shillings. He moved on, his heart full of unutterable compassion for these victims of Progress. Cant! Cant! his voice went on, tirelessly repeating.

He crossed Piccadilly Circus, brushing past beshawled mis-shapen, squatting flower women huddled in the center; and was soon in Trafalgar Square, going toward the Strand; but moved by some irrepressible demon, he skirted his hotel and, turning into Craven Street, reminiscent of his beloved Heine who lived here for a space to curse London, he directed his steps toward the Embankment.

An almost impenetrable fog, rising from the Thames, lay athwart the earth, pressed against her in intimate embrace, and exhaled a heavy damp odour, clutching at the throat. Henry could see two, perhaps three, yards ahead of him; no more. The street lamps, appearing at regular intervals, cast downward a nimbus of blurred unearthly light and sometimes faintly revealed a bench upon which reposed a group of human figures huddled together for warmth and sitting so still as to give an impression of sculpture strangely blurred like the unfinished shapes roughly hewn by Michelangelo, and striving to come to full birth. It was as if he had suddenly descended into the underworld inhabited by a race of blurred beings. They were alive, for he heard someone groaning, someone cursing, someone muttering, and these sounds had a strange stertorous quality as of blurred life gasping for breath. Voices, approaching, came out of the fog: " 'Jack,' sez I to 'im, sez I, 'ef you don't want a black eye an' a bloody nose, then keep off from what isn't yourn. Lily is my wench!' " This was followed by a boisterous laugh. "An' what did he say?" uttered another voice. " 'E sez,

sez he—" But the talkers passed by, and Henry was not
to learn what Jack had to say to the challenge. Blurred
words and blurred laughter reached him, like a muffled
reverberation from an overgrown sepulchre. "A penny,
kind gentleman!" came a broken senile voice out of the
darkness, as a warped little old woman, having the appearance of a Leonardo grotesque, suddenly emerged before him with an outstretched bony hand. He gave her a
florin, and passed on. It fascinated him, and it oppressed
him: this Dantesque unreality with its element of macabre.
And there momentarily flashed across his mind the too
comfortable house he had just left, with its dozen of large
over-furnished rooms, full of opulent cumulations; the increasingly smug face of its owner, the rising barrister and
politician; and the nourished, pretty but otherwise undis-
tinguished face of his wife, Marjorie. His conversation
with the Wilsons recurred to him. Progress, indeed! What
an absurd notion! Cant! Cant! That was good news,
though, about Peter Smallpeice. He must look him up.
It was true, then, about bread cast upon the water. It
was no fiction. Once upon a time there lived someone
called Christ. . . . And so the world was like a watch!
Tick-tack! Tick-tack! Tick-tack! A pretty bad sort of
watch. Even if it were a good one—what of that? What
was the use of tick-tacking one's life away? Tick-tack!
Tick-tack! Tick-tack! It was no life. Not for anyone.
And the best of watches, sooner or later, find their way
to the dust-heap. He wished he had said that to James.
There were other things he wished he had said to him.
He laughed aloud, wondering how his laugh sounded to
other souls walking there in darkness. Again he laughed,
as he remembered James's face as it had appeared to him

that evening. Of course, he, Henry, had been at the time slightly under the influence of liqour, a virtue in his case— so he thought—for spirits had a way of intensifying the clarity of his vision; and he had seen James as sharply as a Daumier or a Gavarni might have seen him; if the portrait appeared exaggerated in detail it was astonishingly accurate in essentials, more so indeed than when seen in soberness. Gad, how he wished he could wield a pencil and show up the fellow in his true colours: the modern acquisitive man who had acquired principles and a religion which he did not practice and wealth which he put away and then imagined he was among the fit because he managed to survive!

As for Marjorie, she was a nice well-meaning woman, even a very desirable woman—in her fashion. James had desired her, and, well—he bought her, offering the highest price for her in the open market. Of course, they called it a good match, and James himself referred to their union as a "romance." Cant! Cant! Henry shouted lustily into the fog, not caring who heard him.

Henry's depression gave way to anger. What right had these people to plume themselves on progress, while these derelicts, these degraded shapes of men and women, drifted hungry and shelterless in the smoky darkness. Cant! Cant! Henry shouted furiously into the murky air.

He tried to think of pleasanter things. Inevitably a vision of his mother rose up before him, the mother who died before he was old enough to remember, the mother now resurrected for him in all the roseate glory of ideal womanhood. The portrait painted by the Royal Academician, the scraps of letters left by her, the things said of her by his father and by persons who had known her—indeed anything that in any way concerned her—were all treasured by Henry, and all these things, abetted by his own fantasy illuming the flimsiest facts, conspired to create a divinity to be worshipped and adored.   And he did worship and adore.   He vowed that he would never wed a woman unless she was like the woman of the portrait so vivid in his mind.   Was there one like her in the flesh in this wretchedly poor, too poor world, who would gratify his intense craving, his illimitable demand?   For he felt himself to be a species of the Knight of La Mancha, tilting at windmills, but without the spur conferred by a Dulcinea or some like creature, fancied or real.   He saw how far more absurd was his own position than of the imagined knight conjured out of the hat which graced Cervantes's head. For, alas, he lived in an age which ridiculed everything except its own follies.   The particular folly of the age, thought Henry, was rationalism, whose function it was to reason everything irrational out of existence.   Yet for him only the irrational seemed to give sanction to human existence and to justify it.   For him love and the dance, and madness, the frenzied living, the exuberance of body and mind, were their own justification.   But what science could accept of these was only that to him relatively inessential part: survival and continuity of the race.   Bah!— he thought—the race be damned!   Better live intensely, fully, madly, then let the lethal waters submerge him, leaving no ripple.   The scientific explanation of love, with the nature of its implied justification, was then, really, love's degradation.   James's love for Marjorie, and Marjorie's love for James—these were the things which seemed to matter; more little Jameses of the same species and more little Marjories of the same species were the sole justifica-

tion of human existence. But was it really important?
It was important to James and to Marjorie.

He, Henry, was not important either. But the things
which were important to him were not the sort of things
important to James and Marjorie. They represented a new
order of things, and he was a rebel against that order.
He remembered: at one moment that evening they had
been extolling the new electric lights which were coming
into fashion just then among the opulent, and to confute
them he passionately went to the other extreme and de-
fended the ancient torch. In response to their half contemptuous, half amused questioning, he had replied:

"Why not? Your new electric lights—what are they?
They cast, it is true, a bright light. But it is even, unchang-
ing, monotonous, cold, sterile, providing no penumbra, no
chiarascuro, scarcely throwing a shadow!"

"That is its peculiar merit," James had said.

"Merit?" he had retorted. "If evenness, uniformity, un-
changeableness, monotony and boredom are merits, then
these lights have merits. Come to think of it, they are the
most perfect symbol of the coming mechanical man!"

Seeing James and Marjorie only laugh at this outburst,
he had gone on:

"I'll go further and say that the ancient torch was an
excellent symbol of the life of the peoples who used it.
There was the real, the living darkness, full of unknown
dangers; and there was the living torch projected into the
darkness, flaring, sputtering, now blown out by the wind
then relit again, and in the nimbus of its light are dancing
palpitating shadows, and among these the shadows of
stalwart men and gracefully draped women fully prepared
for life or death. Or it may be the lone figure of the

woman Hero waving her torch of love to light the way
to Leander across the Hellespont! There's real light and
love and life for you! Don't talk to me about your new-
fangled lights!"

He knew how absurd it all sounded to them, and with
anger he remembered how contemptuously they had
laughed.

There was neither night nor love nor life for him. There
was only this eternal fog of discontent, and in this fog
he had snatched at love, snatched at life. Once or twice
he thought he had had it; first appearances deceived him.
Aloud, he broke into

> . . . for several virtues
> Have I liked several women; never any
> With so full soul, but some defect in her
> Did quarrel with noblest grace she owed,
> And put it to the foil: but you, O you,
> So perfect and so peerless, are created
> Of every creature's best!

Yes, he had snatched, snatched. . . . It was terrible to
have this yearning in one's soul, and always to snatch,
snatch. . . . A terrible anger rose up in him, full of
challenge, of defiance! Against what? Against whom?
. . . Something deep within him stirred, threatened to
explode.

Something did explode. . . . The terrible reprehensible
thing happened. . . .

It broke from him suddenly, unpremeditatingly.
"I curse You, God. . . ."

How terrible, he thought. Oh, what had he done?

"I curse. . . ."

He paused, as if apprehensive of the repetition of the blasphemy. But some sinister force within him—he did not know whence it came—goaded him on, urged him to utter the awful words.

"I curse You, God! I curse You!"

This time the words came determinedly, without faltering. He felt an infusion of sinister strength, of defiance. Was it thus that Lucifer felt when, as the favourite angel sitting on God's right hand, he had hurled his defiance against his Master?

"Yes, a watch. . . . Tick-tack! Tick-tack! . . ." Henry muttered. "That's what the world is—a blasted watch, that keeps bad time! . . . I curse You. . . ."

Oh, what had he done? What was he doing? How had he come to utter words of so terrible a portent? He was not like that silly ostrich, James Wilson, who hid his head in evolution, in progress, in that kind of vile sand. He was a believer in God. A believer. No mere pew-holder. No mere practicer of lip-service. To the core of him a believer. He had prayed, and he had prayed, and God had not appeared to have listened to him. Perhaps, now, God would listen to his curses. He had begged, he had entreated, he had supplicated; and he had been ignored. Perhaps, God did not like beggars, liked men to be manly, to stand up to Him, to demand their rights instead of cringe on their knees. God had made men "in His own image," and He had given them the power to bless and to curse, and, in rare cases, the intelligence which made man akin to God. God was great and exalted because He had all the human virtues *in excelsis* and because the

harmonious joining of these in One made for divine perfection.

So thought Henry, lapsing into reverie. If God was
cruel, He would punish him; if God was just, He would
give him his due; if God was merciful, He would forgive
him; if God was generous, He would give him his heart's
desire; if God was a humourist, He would laugh at Henry's
effort to force His hand. If God, in His omnipotence, was
all these things—what then?

"God, I curse You . . ." he madly raved on.

He reiterated his utterance with growing defiance. He
did it despite the increasingly potent feeling that his defiance would cost him dearly. This was different from
defying Mr. Pertwee. Then, at least, his defiance had the
merit of being in behalf of someone else. Yet its nature
was, perhaps, the same and in accord with Henry's character. As to now, what were the odds? He couldn't go
on living as he did, like a poor sort of watch perpetually
ticking in this perpetual fog. Tick-tack! Tick-tack! Tick-
tack! forever and ever.

"Oh, God! I curse You. . . ."

It was sheer folly, of course. If there was a God, it
was foolish for him to be defying a Power which might
cast him into the lowest depths. If there was no God, it
was equally foolish, for in that case he was defying nothing, challenging the empty air. . . . But he had a deep-
rooted faith in a Power that was called God—call it, if
you will, by any other name—and to defy this Power
demanded all his courage, however foolish such a course
appeared.

He felt dreadfully alone. The night's fog encompassed
him, but was it not the same every day? He was never

more alone than among people. Nevertheless, he eagerly sought new people, always in the vain hope of something or somebody turning up, perhaps a new face which might give him pleasure for an hour or a day, since there seemed to be none which could give it for eternity. And always there was the faint hope that sometime and somewhere in the social purlieus of the fog-ridden city he would find the one fair face which would shed radiance for him, and for him alone.

Was it not for the absence of this sought-for elusive face that he had committed the unpardonable sin, had cursed his God in whom he believed so fervently and so profoundly?

Later Henry Thorley could have scarcely explained why he should have chosen so drastic and blasphemous a course for attracting the attention of the Deity; but he did attract the attention of the Deity, as we shall presently see; with results which, to put it mildly, were quite astonishing: most of all to himself.

For the time being, Henry, enwombed in the dense fog, and enveloped in the exhalations of his own despair, wended his way, uttering periodically with stubborn persistence the wild unheard-of blasphemy:

"... I curse You...."

CHAPTER SIX

A Fateful Evening

ENRY awoke late the next morning, dazed and oppressed, as from a heavy nightmare. He slowly rubbed his eyes, taking stock of his surroundings, wondering where he was. Gradually, the objects assumed a familiar appearance, and partially recalled him to his senses. He was in his room in the hotel in the Strand; of that much he was aware.

But there was something else. What was it? His mind was troubled. What had happened? Something, surely, had happened. Something weighed on his soul with a tragic ponderousness. Something gnawed at his heart, as he lay there, held still by mysterious fetters. His motionless eyes for a long time contemplated the ceiling. Then the brows stirred, contracting into a frown.

"Oh God!"

The words unwittingly broke from him, as the truth broke upon him and struck his heart as with forked lightnings.

"Oh, God, what have I done?"

He lay there, as one pinioned. Oh, why had not God struck him down in the midst of his blasphemy, instead of letting him live to suffer God's vengeance? For vengeance there must and will be. A terrible vengeance. That was inevitable. He nervously laughed aloud, as a quaint thought struck him. Of course, in our day and age God did not strike men down on the spot even for so fearful a blasphemy. Such things happened in the days of long ago; in Biblical times, perhaps during the Middle Ages. Men then preferred it thus, and God obliged them. Nowadays men were not struck down dead, but were doomed to live—to expiate their sin—slowly—in agony. And he, Henry Thorley, was doomed to live—to expiate his sin— slowly—in agony.

So he was alive. As he turned his eyes, the objects in the room impressed themselves on the retina with unwonted distinctness, with that singular clairvoyance with which on the previous evening the faces of the Wilsons were made to appear in so sinister, so macabre a light. Yes, he was alive—to repent, to suffer, to expiate. What woe, what misfortune, was waiting to fall on his poor head? Recant, or weep, or implore forgiveness; it was all the same. There was no help for him now. Such things were not to be recanted, not to be washed away with tears, not to be forgiven. His innermost fears gave rise to an overpowering certainty, which lay upon his heart like a great stone.

The articles of evening dress were lying in disorder in the large chair by the grate where ragefully last night he had flung them. He contemplated them with a rueful gaze. Had he been drunk then? By no means, he decided. He had been merely exhilarated; drink had always the effect of exaggerating his present mood. And last night, his mood, originally induced by the Wilsons, had been one of despair; yes, and of revolt.

But man is a resilient animal, and in due time, suddenly bracing himself, Henry energetically sprang out of bed, vigorously performed his ablutions, and called for a hearty breakfast. A maid came and started a fire in the grate. Soon It was blazing brightly, and soon Henry was enjoying his three-course breakfast and steaming coffee. Even romantics must eat. The bacon and eggs made an appeal not to be resisted.

Only once more, unwittingly, the cry broke forth from the depths of his heart:

"Oh, God, what have I done?"

Henry had an invitation to spend the evening with Lady Brinton, and he decided to accept it. Lady Brinton, a widow, maintained a salon in Bedford Square; her soireés had the reputation of being amusing. That was chiefly because Lady Brinton had infinite tact and, with an unerring instinct, quite intuitively, she introduced "the right sort of people" to one another, and never, as many other hostesses did, for the sake of appearances, parted two persons holding animated converse in order to introduce them to others who were not congenial to them.

Like many another man of his temperament, Henry was both attracted and repelled by gatherings of people. But in running away from himself he ran to others. An amusing evening quite often made him forget; but a tedious evening intensified his misery. There were always new visitors at Lady Brinton's, and new people, if they were at all interesting or attractive, especially if they were women, had a way of prodding his curiosity. And, according to whether they were animated and interesting or not, he was in the same degree animated and interested or quite glum. In any event, hostesses were pleased to have him, as they always are to have a good-looking man. A handsome man was handsome, whether he talked or not. And Lady Brinton, in particular, loved having handsome people about her. To be sure, Henry, pendulating between two extremes of mood, had a reputation for being odd; but the mystery which was attached to him only increased the esteem in which he was held. Mystery never hurt either man or woman, but only made him or her appear more desirable. To tell the truth, Henry rather enjoyed the adoration accorded him by the other sex, though when their adoration showed signs of exceeding bounds he did not hesitate to be frankly rude to the adorer. This served still further to enhance him in her eyes. His own interest in any woman, to the chagrin of the lady, rarely lasted long; and he gained a reputation for being "fickle." This, too, for some mysterious reason, increased his worth. A more fancy adjective applied to him was "Byronic." He was not unconscious of his attractiveness for women, and he bewailed the fact that no woman remained attractive to him for very long. He vowed he would remain single, unless of course he met that hypothetical female whom, for general identification purposes, he dubbed Cleopatra. As the chances of such a ravishing personage turning up in the purlieus of Victorian London were very slim, the consensus of opinion was that Mr. Thorley would stick to his vow and remain single. The wiseacres, however, smiled, and said that a man that talked like that stood to be caught, and that he would prove lucky indeed if his wife did not turn out to be a termagant; which may or may not have been the wish which is father to the thought. Lady Brinton herself, a widow no longer young but still attractive to men, knew better what passed under the Byronic mask; she more than suspected his craving for real affection and real romance, his hunger for camaraderie, and his intense sympathy for the hungry and the downtrodden. She told him as much once or twice when she entertained him at a tête-à-tête tea in her boudoir, and to the question as what gave her such a preposterous idea of him, she replied:

"I knew your mother, you know. And you are your mother all over!"

The answer pleased him, and, it having won his confidence, he showed his pleasure simply and candidly, almost as a child might.

On another occasion, when they were alone, she complimented him on his good looks, whereupon, to the amusement of Lady Brinton, he deliberately walked over to the full-length mirror and gave himself a most critical scrutiny.

"You're really a big child!" she said, unable to restrain a laugh.

"Men have called me a fool," he observed, earnestly.

"No, no, not a fool, but a child!" she reiterated. "A really clever woman could twist you round her little finger."

"I haven't met her."

"You will!" she flung at him.

"She'll have to be Cleopatra!" he retorted.

"I'm sure you'll call her that!" she laughed.

"If I do, she'll deserve it!" It was his turn to laugh.

They enjoyed this duel of words. She liked to make him blush—he was capable of blushing—and he liked her because, for a woman, he thought her very genuine, and he knew that her regard for him was real and maternally affectionate. And she had known his mother and spoken admiringly of her. "A splendid woman," she had said, "but out of place in a drab world. I never did meet a woman who was so influenced by surroundings. The poor dear, she couldn't stand it!"

How well he knew the feeling himself. Man though he was, with a sturdy frame and robust emotions, he was apprehensive of life and of what life might do to him.

"Yes, I know," he observed. "Life's tedious, and when I think of life as it is lived, I want to die!"

"I know why you feel like that," said Lady Brinton, in a significant tone. "But the time will come when you won't feel like that. In the meantime, why don't you work for humanity?"

"I don't care for humanity!" he answered brusquely.

"I know better," she said softly. "People have seen you throwing alms to beggars!"

"That may be," he said, blushing, as if abashed at the circumstance of something being kown that he wished to conceal. "Beggars are one thing. I have a sympathy for beggars. I have respect for them as members of a time-honoured profession which so-called respectable people are trying to discredit. But these respectable people are quite another thing!"

"As always, the romantic! I was going to say, the sentimentalist!"

Henry felt vexed. "No, no!" he said quickly. "You people don't understand. It's you who are the romantics, the sentimentalists. You fall into ecstasies of adoration over evolution, and you sentimentalize about progress. And I see that some are beginning to idolize the machine! As for me, I see things as they are, and I'll have none of them. And look how they worship property and collect objects which have no use but to clog houses. What do you call that but a perverted fetish worship! There will be a grand crash one day, and he who possesses the most will have the greatest number of things tumbling about his head!"

"You talk like those terrible Socialists!"

"No!" he cried warmly. "I don't agree with them, either. And for the same reason. They too build on so-called facts, on statistics, on material considerations, and leave the human factor out of the reckoning. But to me the human factor is everything! To be human in the best sense is to be divine!"

When aroused, Henry talked fervently, and his melodious deep voice charged with fire always impressed his feminine listeners in spite of themselves. They could not resist the hypnotic persuasiveness of the man. Lady Brinton was no exception to the rule.

"You're a dear, you know, a perfect dear!" she cried. "If you'd only become a prophet, I'd follow you—yes, even to the ends of the earth. And not I alone, but thousands of women would follow you. Yes, and men too! You don't know your own strength, Henry—your own power! If you'd only do it!" She looked at his big well-shaped sensitive hands, which impressed her as hands which might have the power to heal, and at his big feet which seemed made for the walking of roads; and she thought of John the Baptist.

Henry gave an expressive grunt. "This is not an age for prophets. Who is needed today? The bridge-builder! But when you've crossed the bridge, the other side is just as tedious as this one. . . . But who has use for the word, or for the man who traffics in words? Certainly, no one wants his complacency disturbed—not in this England. . . . As it is, all I ask is to be let alone to live my life as I see fit.

But there is no life. Life is denied one!" A shade of bitterness, of torment, crept in to his voice. "I am called a romantic because I demand things which are men's and women's natural heritage, and don't want the mess of pottage for which they've exchanged it!"

"You wish to turn the clock back!" said Lady Brinton, and was immediately sorry for having spoken.

"I'm tired of hearing that platitude!" replied Henry. "It's the last refuge of the apostles of Progress. But the truth is, I want to see humanity retain something that is infinitely precious: something of the original sources of its life, the unveneered soul, its unwarped impulses and intuitions, the pure heart and the clear intelligence. Let men love, or let them fight, but let no man call his refined lust by the name of love, nor the mercenary say he's battling for principles!"

"I see what you mean," said Lady Brinton, trying to make amends for her slip. "You think men have glorified the idea of Progress to the position of a religion?"

"Yes, they have denied their God, and set up a golden calf. Only they refuse to call it a golden calf, they call it Progress. The Jews who danced round the golden calf were honester. . . ."

Goaded on by Lady Brinton, in such a manner did Henry hold forth; and she regarded him as the most amusing and interesting of all her lions.

In her invitation to him for this particular evening she wrote, "You must come. The party will be a small one, and there will be one or two very attractive ladies."

Lady Brinton was a perspicacious student of character. She knew what would make Henry Thorley come.

It was nine o'clock when Henry hailed a hansom and asked to be driven to the stately house in Bedford Square.

Lady Brinton received him in person at the door of the reception room, from which a medley of voices made itself heard. The entrance of the tall handsome man, looking handsomer if anything in evening dress, imposed silence on the party, which, as the hostess promised, was indeed small, consisting until Henry's arrival of but two men and three women, without counting Lady Brinton herself. All but one were known to him, and that was an extraordinarily attractive woman whose name he failed to catch in the introduction; seizing upon a vacant chair next to her, he sat down. No sooner he dropped into his seat than the whole company broke into a simultaneous laugh. The stranger next to him laughed very charmingly, with the rest. He turned an astonished gaze on the company. Were they making game of him? So he judged from the ejaculation which followed on the part of one of the woman:

"Didn't I tell you so, my dear?"

The lovely stranger to whom the observation was addressed made no comment, and Lady Brinton, seeing the nonplussed look in Henry's face, came to the rescue:

"They're pulling your leg, Henry. Mag said you'd be sure to take that chair—and you did! That's all!"

"Oh, so it's a conspiracy! . . Well," he said after a pause, "No one can say the fault's mine!" And he cast a gallant overt glance at his handsome neighbour.

The glance assured him that she was even handsomer than he had gathered from his first glance. She was petite; she had a lovely oval face, with fairly regular features; a white skin and jet black hair; and as she lowered her head to avert the momentary penetration of his glance he had time to observe the inexplicably alluring white parting of her hair and the large thin curving arches of her brows; as well as the white slender shoulders and graceful neck emerging from the black low-cut taffeta gown, and the seductive little valley between the firm breasts; nor did he fail to make a note of the small white ear peeping flirtatiously from under the hair and the long black ear-ring designed perhaps to call attention to it. The whole impression was one overpowering with the essence feminine. With the eye of a connoisseur, he quickly took all this in, and as quickly withdrew his gaze, adding casually:

"I'm sure I've interrupted an interesting conversation."

"We were discussing," said the young red-haired woman called "Meg," "whether women should or should not propose in Leap Year."

"I said," asserted a large well-groomed suave man of about forty—Captain Jordan, of the Coldstream Guards— "that depends!"

"What do you mean, 'that depends'?" asked his wife, a youngish pretty woman, with brown hair and brown eyes.

"Don't interrupt a superior officer," Jordan went on superciliously. "I was going to say, that depends on whether the lady has given the gentleman any previous intimation that such a proposition would be forthcoming and he, for his part, has shown due appreciation and some indication that it would be welcome. It's deucedly uncomfortable, you know, for a man to be caught unawares! Deucedly uncomfortable—really. . . ."

"Turn about is fair play, Hubert," indignantly returned

his wife. "Think of the many women taken unawares by proposals they don't want and can't accept!"

"Fiddlesticks, my dear!" asseverated the Captain, with a blustering air. "No woman's made uncomfortable in matters of this sort, even if she does usually go in for dramatics by calling for smelling-salts and falling into a faint. It's a nice gesture which pleases the fool in trousers, and when the lady comes to, she says demurely, 'Where am I?' As if she didn't know where she was all the time! But the poor benighted fool goes to a heap of trouble to tell her where she is, and falls on his knees to supplicate the lady to entertain his offer. He can't live without her, says he! 'Oh, Algy,' says she, 'you know how much I admire you and respect you, and how much I appreciate the honour you confer on me—but can't we stay friends?' That's all sheer nonsense, of course! How can a man stay friends with a woman who's goaded him on to propose and then rattled off a speech she's prepared beforehand and said to some other poor devil before and will say to another poor devil later?"

"Really," said the other man, a Mr. Ballingbroke, who had a decided Oxford voice and manner. "There's a lot of truth in that, but one can't blame the dears. It's the fashion to do that sort of thing, and they all do it. I've known three men who proposed to the same woman——"

"Were you one of them?" interrupted in a melodious voice the lady with the dark hair, addressing herself to the narrator.

"Heavens, no! I got my walking papers in quite another quarter. Quoth she to me: 'You're an awfully nice man, Paul, and I am so terribly fond of you. You know I am. It hurts me to have to say no. You deserve a good

woman. If you ever find one who will make you happy,
as I am sure you will, I shall be so glad and shall be a
sister to you both!' "

Everyone laughed, for Paul Ballingbroke was an excellent mimic, and he mimicked a lady's voice to perfection.

"But you were just telling us about the young woman
who got proposed to by three different men!"

"Oh, yes. You see, I knew them all. They happened
to meet over whiskey and soda, and casually drifted to the
subject of the lady in question. . . . You see, rumours of
a certain nature had been reaching them. . . . They compared notes and found they tallied in every particular. This
was the lady's technique: 'Any woman, George,'—or James,
or Oliver, as the case happened to be—'would feel honoured in being offered the affections of such a man as you.
I am not blind to your merits. You'd make an ideal husband whom any normal woman would be proud of. But
I fear I can never be happy with you!' 'Why not?' 'I
must have a husband of whom I'm afraid. And I'm not
afraid of you, George, not even a tiny bit! The man who
hopes to become my husband will not grovel on his knees
as you are doing, but will seize me in his arms and insist
that I marry him before I can catch my breath! That's
the sort of man I want!' . . ."

The speaker paused to see the effect the story was producing on his listeners, and seeing from the amused smiles
that the result was all he could have anticipated, resumed:

"Well, what do you suppose happened? . . . Every man
Jack of them—they were different occasions, of course!—
jumped up and tried to seize the lady, just to show they
could take the right sort of hint. But she was prepared
for them every time, and was up and behind the sofa

before the chap could get hold of her. 'Too late, my good man!' she'd shout at him. 'I'm not here to teach sucklings what to do! Try it on another lady!' She was a regular minx, she was!"

His auditors laughed boisterously, Captain Jordan louder than the rest. "The hussie!" he cried between chortles. "The hussie! . . . But it served those nincompoops right for getting down on their knees before her. . . . I didn't propose to you in that fashion, did I, dear?" said the irrepressible Captain, turning towards his wife.

"It's a fact, you didn't!" Mrs. Jordan assented, with emphasis. "You did it as if you were making an assault on an enemy! . . . Do you know what he did?" she said, turning to the company. "I was sitting at the piano, when in he rushed one day, seized me hard by the hand until it hurt, and said: 'Come along, Joan! Everything's ready! The license is in my pocket, and there's a minister waiting! All that's wanted is a bride! Never mind about putting other togs on! Come, there's not a moment to lose!' And, hardly giving me time to catch my breath, he dragged me by the wrist out of doors, pushed me into a hansom, himself following, and before I knew it I was Mrs. Jordan!"

Again, there was an outburst of laughter, while Captain Jordan, surveying the company with satisfaction, said:

"I am a man of action. I believe in quick work. The women like it too, if I know anything about the dears!"

During the recitals, Henry sat silent but amused. He could not compete with the blustering ways of the Captain, And he was thinking hard of his attractive neighbour, of whose presence he was with every moment becoming more and more aware; as when two affined souls meet. Moreover, with a curious masculine prescience, he was not unaware that she was at the same time thinking of him. Her aroma wafted itself towards his nostrils, and he had the very pleasant sensation of intimacy not to be measured by the short time in which they had known each other.

"But we were talking of Leap Year proposals,"—it was "Meg" again who spoke—"what is your opinion on the subject, Mr. Thorley?" She turned to the latest comer. "You've hardly said a word!"

"Why Leap Year?" Henry said quietly. "Why shouldn't women have the right to propose any year?"

"They don't! Isn't that enough?" returned "Meg," mockingly indignant.

"But they do!" contradicted Henry, smiling.

"Impossible! No decent woman would think of it!"

"Then I don't know any decent woman," said Henry, without changing his smiling expression.

"You mean to say that decent women have actually proposed marriage to you?" cried "Meg," with something like astonishment, and even awe.

"I'm not giving any secrets away," said Henry, and his smile was more tantalizing than before.

"Mercy! What are we coming to? It's all due to the terrible novels people are reading, I'm sure!"

"We are living in the age of Progess, Miss Worthington," Henry's voice was ironic.

"Do tell Meg and the rest the story of that German girl," called Lady Brinton. "It's quite harmless, you know. You won't be giving anything or anyone away! Not that it was exactly the young woman who proposed! ... Do tell it!"

"I don't mind in the least," said Henry, and began his story.

CHAPTER SEVEN

Don Juan of Weimar

I T happened in Goethe's town of Weimar. I was a student there, living in a little pension, of which at the time I was the only lodger. I occupied the largest room in the house. It was on the ground floor, and its windows faced the road. I was a newcomer there, and as I was rather retiring and knew no one, I rarely mingled with the students.

"One morning, about eleven, while I was preparing some studies, I chanced to look out of the window. An elegant two-horse carriage drove up and stopped before the gate. A tall, rather huge lady got out of it, and gathering up a large number of parcels piled on the seats she handed them to the driver, and then picking up the remainder, which among other things included a large bouquet of flowers, the formidable lady, her own arms full, followed by the driver, his arms full, walked up the path between the flower beds, and presently there was a knocking on the front door.

"Little suspecting that it had anything to do with me, I gave no thought to it and resumed my studies. I could hear my good-natured German landlady coming to the door and exchanging some guttural remarks with the visitor. Scarcely had I taken my quill in my hand when there was a knock on my door. In answer to my 'Come in!' the door was flung open, and, led by the landlady, the

visitors entered my room, and without a word of explanation deposited the parcels on the sofa. The driver and the
landlady then withdrew, leaving me alone with my formidable visitor, from whom I waited for a word of explanation of the extraordinary visit. However, I politely begged
her to be seated.

"'Mr. Thorley,' she began in her own language, 'Allow
me to introduce myself. I am Frau Weingartner, wife of
Herr Heinrich Weingartner. My husband is a large land-
owner here. Please don't be offended at my unceremonious
visit to a stranger in our little town. The fact is, we've
observed that you were alone here, a solitary man without
friend or acquaintance. We're a very simple hospitable
people, and we should like to make you feel thoroughly
at home. As a little token of our friendliness, I've brought
a few trifles I thought you might stand in need of!'

"Saying which, she rose from her chair and, walking
over to the sofa, she first reached for the bouquet of flowers.
'This,' she said, 'is to make your room look more cheerful,
and, without much ado, she undid the bouquet and arranged the flowers in a vase which stood on the mantel-
piece over the fireplace. 'Please get your landlady to fill
the vase with water,' she said. Then she began to undo
the parcels. All manner of things dropped out of them:
fine linen handkerchiefs, neckties, tie-pins, bon-bons, bis-
cuits, cookies, and what not?

"So far I was too stupefied by the whole amusing occurrence to raise a word of protest. Having undone the parcels and piled their contents on my table, she went on:

"'You look like a man from a well-to-do genteel family,
isn't it so? And it's terrible to be away from home, with

no one of your own blood to look after you. Have you a mother, or sisters, or brothers?'

" 'No . . . but. . . .'

" 'There!' she said. 'I'm glad I've come!'

" 'But I don't want anything, madam!' I found my tongue to protest. 'You are very good, but I'm not in the habit of accepting things from strangers!'

" 'Tut! Tut!' she said. 'We won't talk about that. I can see you're a modest self-contained young man. All the more to your credit! But it gives me some pleasure to bring these things. I wish I knew some thing you really badly wanted. . . . No, no, no! Don't say anything against it! . . . You will hurt my feelings if you say anything in protest. . . .'

"By this time I gave her up as a hopeless job, and let her go on talking. I couldn't have stopped her in any case. As for getting in a word edgewise, that was quite out of the question. She was formidable, I tell you." He paused to laugh.

"Then what happened?" asked Henry's attractive neighbour, with charming impatience. "I can guess, though! She had a young daughter!"

"Yes, she had . . ." he replied, pleased at her perspicacity and at her interest in his narrative. "But listen to the rest of the story. . . . 'We have a big house,' she said, 'and we are hospitable. You must come and see us!'

" 'Surely,' said I, rather dubiously, having no intention whatsoever of keeping up the comedy.

" 'But you must come soon!'

" 'To be sure,' said I.

" 'But when? Can you come tonight to dinner?'

" 'No, I can't come tonight. . . .'

" 'Tomorrow, then. Say tomorrow. We'll expect you!'

" 'No,' I said, wondering how I might get rid of the importunate visitor. 'I can't tomorrow. I have studies. . . .'

" 'Day after tomorrow then,' she persisted. 'You know the saying, "All study and no play makes Jack a dull boy!" '

" 'Yes, madam, I've heard of it.' By this time I felt sufficiently exasperated to want to take the woman by the scruff of the neck and push her out of doors and send the parcels after her. However, I controlled myself, and said: 'I can't come this week'—it happened to be a Monday—'I am really behind in my studies.'

" 'Come next week, then.'

" 'Let me see,' I said, fumbling for an excuse.

" 'Name your own day, Mr. Thorley. I don't want to interfere with your studies. I have a young son, and he won't study at all. Do name your own day!'

"Well, there was no way out of it. I named a day as distant as I could without appearing too rude. The end of the following week it was, I think. As obviously I knew hardly anyone there, and my lessons couldn't occupy me all day and all night and I did have to eat sometimes, it was the best I could do. She left, apparently satisfied.

"The fated evening arrived at last. I was surprised at the immense size of the house. They were apparently people of substantial means. No sooner I got into the vestibule and gave the maid my coat, hat and stick than qualms seized me, and I had the strongest imaginable impulse to run. For from the reception hall I could hear a multitude of voices, and from the number of hats and coats my eyes suddenly fell upon, there was every appearance of a grand reception for someone instead of the quiet little dinner party which I thought it would be at the worst. But I had no time to think, for presently I was ushered into a large room—indeed, a small hall would be a better name for it—full of people, and my name was announced in stentorian tones by the butler—perhaps I should call him the town crier—and immediately thirty or forty necks were craned to see me. My formidable hostess, all smiles, came forward, followed by the portly Herr Weingartner, and I was introduced all around. Conceive a picture of me, a shy foreign student of nineteen, bowing right and left to this strange large company, and heartily wishing them all at the bottom of the sea.

"The preliminary ceremony done with, a worse ordeal was before me. Barely five minutes elapsed before Frau Weingartner gave the signal, at which an invisible orchestra struck up a tune, at which the company, directed by the redoubtable lady, formed into a file of twos. To my lot was assigned a girl of about seventeen, but I was too confused to pay any attention to her or even to look at her. And in this fashion we filed into the dining-room.

"The long table was set for about forty persons. It was in its way a gorgeous affair, course following course until I began to wonder when it would all end. I won't bore you by going into detail. Certainly, the good Frau was an opulent sort of person, whether she brought parcels to a stranger or dispensed hospitality at home. Decidedly, a managing sort of woman, quite in her element. You should have seen her alloting places to the guests. It was as though she were putting children in their places on the first day of school. Gad, how she enjoyed it! Not that she wasn't good-natured, and good-hearted too! She had enough heart to go round that big table, and she made it go round! Simply wouldn't take a refusal—not from anyone. You had to take what she gave. But that's neither here nor there. . . . Imagine my amazement and horror when I found myself seated near the head of the table, to the right of the good Frau herself. For it suddenly dawned on me that I, a perfect stranger to the town and the assembly gathered there, was the guest of honour!"

"Well, I'll be dashed!" suddenly broke out the Captain, unable to restrain his feelings any longer. "I call it a bit thick myself. She was something of a Tartar, wasn't she? The idea of playing a joke like that on an honest Englishman! You should have got up from the table, you should! That would have gone Frau Whatever-you-call-her one better. Upon my word, Thorley, you should ——"

"You're interrupting the story, Captain Jordan," said the diminutive Mrs. Jordan to her mighty husband.

"So I am. I beg your pardon, old chap! Do go on!" said the big man with mild contriteness. "The women folk are dying to hear you!"

"Yes, I'm the guest of honour, I thought to myself," resumed Henry. "But why? Who was I? What have I done? How in heaven's name have I deserved the honour? I racked my mind for a possible solution, but could find no answer. I was nobody in that town, I was nothing to these people, and not a soul there knew anything about me. Was I by some chance invited by a lunatic to a lunatic asylum? For a moment I took the idea seriously and was frightened. No, that could not be. They were mostly young jolly people, and the older folk were really too bourgeois to be mad. I must try another tack. Then I thought that perhaps they've taken me for a Prince travelling incognito and have decided to do me honour. What would happen, thought I, if they suddenly discovered their mistake! Such things have happened before. . . . Then the dreadful thought struck me: suppose they should call for a speech! Perspiration covered me from head to foot at the mere idea.

"My reflections, however, were cut short, by the serving of the soup and by my hostess nudging me, 'Will you pour out a glass of wine for Thelma!' I then realized that the young woman next to me, the same who filed in to dinner with me, was my hostess's daughter. . . .

"She was a nice girl, rather the Gretchen type. Pretty too, I should say, in a fashion. She had a fresh rosy complexion and mild blue eyes which looked at you as though to say, 'Here's a man whose meals I'd like to cook, whose bed I'd love to make, and whose socks I'd adore to darn!' You know the kind. Nothing against her, to be sure. . . ."

"I hope you put her in her place!" the irrepressible Captain could not help interrupting again.

"Not I, thank you," said Henry, while the company tittered.

"Ha-ha! That's a good one!" began the Captain again. "Well, I. . . ."

"Captain Jordan!" once more exclaimed his wife peremptorily.

"Pray forgive me, Mr. Thorley, do go on. You see, my wife's here to put me in *my* place!"

Again there was tittering, while the narrator resumed.

"During the whole dinner, it was, 'Mr. Thorley, see that Thelma gets enough *hors d'œuvres!*' Or, 'Mr. Thorley, will you help Thelma to some salt!' Or, 'Mr. Thorley, Thelma's glass is empty, would you be so good as to fill it again!' Or there was the good Frau, in a whisper, close to my ear, 'She's an awfully smart girl, Thelma is. She's graduated from the gymnasium!' Or, pathetically, 'She's my only daughter. It's a pity that girls must some day leave their mothers!' Or, 'I've brought her up carefully, Mr. Thorley. She'll make someone a good wife one day!' To all of which I agreed quite readily and friendlily, thanks to the assistance of some really good Rhenish wine.

"I was beginning to see the drift of things, and rather to enjoy the joke, though I wasn't sure if it was on my hosts or on me. Anyhow, by this time I decided that it didn't matter. Now that it's gone so far, I must see it through!

"There was an end even to this long dinner. A few toasts were made. There was one proposed to the 'distinguished Englishman in our midst.' So, of course, I was expected to do my part. I proposed a toast to 'the exceptional hostess, to be met with nowhere in or out of Weimar, and to the worthy daughter of a remarkable mother,' and even to the portly Herr Weingartner, 'who deserved better recognition from the community!' Indeed, in spite of his being easily the bulkiest member at the table everybody seemed to have forgotten him at the other foot of the table, and I rather enjoyed getting that dig in."

"You rogue!" laughed Captain Jordan.

"Sh-h...." The sibilant interjection came from his wife.

"Then the indefatigable Frau Weingartner commanded the guests to file into pairs again, and to the tune of music we all marched to the large room and into a still larger one, which had been prepared for dancing, Thelma all the while hanging on my arm. I was her chief dance partner for the evening. Between dances we sat it out, usually on the broad stairs ascending to the next story.

"About the middle of the evening there was a longish interval for refreshments. It was during this interval that Thelma suggested that we go to the top of the stairs where they curved towards the landing and were out of sight of the guests. 'It's cooler there!' she said. We sat down there and, to my astonishment, Thelma—very shyly, be it said to her credit—let her head rest on my shoulders. . . . I let it rest there, seeing I could do nothing else. For a long time we sat thus, saying nothing. I was not particularly encouraging, I must admit. 'You are the handsomest man I've ever seen,' she said at last. I said nothing. 'Ever since you came here,' she went on, 'I have watched for you mornings on your way to the university.' Still I said nothing. 'I told mother she *must* make your acquaintance, and get you to come to the house.' . . . Well, I could have scarcely suspected her. I had been inclined to blame it all on her meddlesome mother. This time I replied very politely, 'It's very kind of you to have taken the trouble.' Then, raising her head suspiciously, she asked, 'Have you a sweetheart at home?' 'No,' I said quite innocently, though a moment later I wished I had said 'Yes.' 'You must come here often,' she said, 'we are a hospitable people!' 'That's quite obvious,' said I. 'I'm glad you think so,' said she.

"Well . . . luckily for me, it wasn't leap year. All the same, I feared she was on the verge of making a proposal.

Just then, in the nick of time, the orchestra came to the rescue. So seizing her by the hands—and the bull by the horns, so to speak—I said, 'Come, let's dance! Or else the music will go to waste!' And so we danced. For the rest of the evening I had to use every stratagem to avoid being inveigled up the stairs again, and I succeeded!"

"You're a cruel man!" said his attractive neighbour, but her voice sounded pleased.

"I've been called worse things. But to finish my story. I received further invitations to the Weingartner house, but always on some pretext or other I managed to elude the good people. Then one day, one of the professors asked me to his house. I went. He took me into his study, gave me a pipe of tobacco, and started to tell me all about the Weingartners, what nice respectable people they were, how much money they had, and how Thelma, their only daughter, was the apple of their eye, and would come into a fortune.

" 'What's all that to do with me?' I asked, pretending not to know the object of his talk.

" 'Don't you know?' he asked eagerly. 'Thelma has fallen in love with you at first sight, and her good parents can refuse her nothing. They want you for their son-in-law!'

" 'But I don't know them, and they don't know me!'

" 'It's a wonderful chance, young man!'

" 'But I don't love the girl, Herr Professor!'

" 'You don't?'

"That seemed to provide a poser for him, but after some deliberation, he said:

" 'H'm, young man. I am sorry. That's a poor sort of end to a good story. . . .'

"I suppose he was right. And I am sure it will seem a poor sort of end to you!"

CHAPTER EIGHT

God's Humour

THAT was in Germany. It couldn't happen in England!" said Meg.

"Couldn't it?" said Henry, smiling whimsically.

"Do you mean to say that a decent Englishwoman would demean herself to propose to a man?"

"I won't say if it's demeaning or not. A woman can tell best as to that. But an Englishwoman will find a way to propose when her heart's set on a man!"

"Have you ever been proposed to?"

"Perhaps I shouldn't say it. But I have—and more than once!"

"Isn't it just like a man to boast about it!"

Henry shrugged his shoulders. "You asked me a direct question, and I answered it. . . . In any case, why shouldn't a woman propose if she's found the man she wants? Why should men have the monopoly of the proposing game?"

"I quite agree with Mr. Thorley," said the attractive stranger. "As it is, men have had it too much their own way."

Henry glanced at her appreciatively; and something about her head suddenly arrested his attention, something reminiscent of someone he had known. Then, in a flash, it came to him. Of course, there was something about her that reminded him of his mother in the portrait painted by Priestley.

"*You* haven't proposed to anyone, have you?" came meanwhile from Meg in a horrified voice.

"No," replied the other, with a quiet smile. "You see, I've never had any occasion!"

Henry laughed. That was rather neat, he thought. He enjoyed seeing the charming woman getting the best of the other. And it was nice having her take his side. He had observed with what interest she had followed his story, how she had maneuvered her chair around so that she might see the expression of his face. And he was fully aware how really expressive his face was, when animated; like an actor's, but without an actor's obvious tricks and petty deceptions. There was no deception. It came quite naturally to him. Every gesture, every movement of the brow, every smile however slight had something to say, with grace and restraint; every word had a nuance of intonation, of meaning. Inspired as men of his temperament could be by the presence of a charming woman, he was in his best mood; and with that keen clairvoyance he enjoyed in relation to the other sex, he was not insensible of the effect he was producing on the inspirer of his mood.

When two human beings who are in perfect accord with one another meet they have no need of direct words to convey the sympathy they have in common. Their moods are complementary and exclude misunderstanding. There is that quickening of their bloods which gives tenderness and warmth to their slightest action and slightest word and endows them with especial meanings for each other not inherent in the words themselves.

It was but the evening before that Henry had cursed God because his life had ceased to have any meaning. But tonight every little thing had its own meaning; and the total of meaning, the quintessence of all these little things, had in the twinkling of an eye transformed life from the drab tedious affair it was for him to one radiant and resplendent with a vital force which made living worth while.

Was it love he felt for this woman? Was it love she felt for this man? Why, they scarcely knew each other. They had met that evening for the first time. He did not even know her name. How should one explain such a phenomenon? One thing could not be in doubt. They took the intensest pleasure in each other's nearness, and they were able, without a direct word, to convey to each other the knowledge of this pleasure. Some invisible bond was drawing them together, and they, the others in the room, had no share in it, nor the slightest inkling of this communion. They were, one and the other, like Macbeth, who saw Banquo's ghost, though the others saw it not. Only what they saw was no ghost, but a happy fairy-like being joining their hands and bodies with a benediction. Fancifully, with no thought of evil, they undressed each other. And why not? For there was a special dispensation for two bodies as beautiful and as perfect as theirs; male and female they were, and there was an abiding beauty in the thought of two such beings joined together which is its own justification. Thus thought Henry, stirred for the first time in a way he thought he could never be stirred. Thus also thought the lovely stranger, her innermost being for the first time in her thirty years moved to a curious adoration she had felt only in her girlhood before the multiple-candled altar when she had prayed for a miracle to happen, which never did happen, unless—unless—But she must wait and see. He

too must wait and see. They were on the verge of something—fresh, strange and fabulous. This much they felt,
and were miraculously elated. "Oh, God! Let it come
to pass!" he prayed silently; then remembered how in
despair, in vexation of spirit, he had cursed God, the God
whom he now entreated. A shadow crossed his handsome
face, and there was someone there who yearned to know
why the shadow was there when she was all exultation;
why the shadow? why the shadow? She had no way of
asking him then? They were all talking, still discussing
the silly question as to whether women should propose or
not. What did it all matter, anyhow? But suddenly she
became interested. Henry was speaking. She heard him
say:

"What is pride—pride in a woman? There is no pride
in love. Love burns up everything, consumes all that
dross we call pride and vanity and self-interest! There
are women in the world as proud as those of Spain, yet
the Spanish woman deems it her prerogative to choose the
man who may make love to her, to indicate to him that
he may pay her advances. How infinitely wise she is in
this!"

These words, melodiously spoken, filled her with a
strange consuming pride. His presence, exuberantly male,
hypnotized her, persuaded her, engendered a curious desire
in her to fling herself at his feet, inspired her with a femaleness which yearned to yield and submit.

As if sensible of her mood, his awareness energized him
with a potency, which diffusing itself through his blood
like a strong wine made him speak again, ostensibly to
the company but in reality to her:

"There is a common superstition that woman must be

pursued. Indeed, most women like being pursued. That is, perhaps, because, as things are, pursuit is pleasurable both to the man and the woman. It no doubt furnishes a deal of excitement in an otherwise tedious world. But realization, the attainment of the goal, gives little pleasure or excitement to either man or woman. But when men and women truly love one another, which is rare, the hunt loses its meaning; for love itself, the great mystery, the complete merging of one in the other, is in itself a continuous excitement and pleasure, which nothing can dim! Love becomes the great all in all!"

The others—even the irrepressible Meg—were silent. They could not understand Henry in this mood. They knew him to be queer and odd; such words had no meaning for them and remained words. They preferred him in a lighter mood, as when he told of the amusing episode at Weimar. Women were willing enough to listen to him in any mood, to be persuaded by the passionate nature of the man which expressed itself in the quality and tone of his voice vibrating tenderly and melodiously; if reason failed them, they could fall back on their feminine intuition which told them something if not all, and that something of an essence infinitely precious to a woman's heart.

Lady Brinton, observing the quiet demeanour of her guests, thought it time to call a halt by inviting them to the refreshments in the alcove at the further end of the large room. The company simultaneously rose. Talk became general as the guests moved towards the alcove. Henry walked by the side of the lovely stranger. A vigorous attack was made on the table, covered with sandwiches and cakes and an assortment of bottles containing wine, whiskey and liqueurs. A maid brought in a tray with coffee. The men helped the women; and when everybody had been served, Henry wholly devoted himself to the woman who so enchanted him. They detached themselves from the rest and, moving away from the table, sat down on a sofa within a bay window.

The rest of the company formed their own group round a small refectory table piled with the latest books. In a restrained voice, Lady Brinton was telling them what a wonderful man Thorley was, and what a pity it was that he was being wasted. "He should have been born in a more romantic age," asserted his champion. "He is a man of many parts, but full of thwarted energy. You have no idea what a fine mind he has! But though he could, if he only would, do almost anything, he does literally nothing. It's as if he were under a spell, paralyzed. . . ."

While the good Lady was expatiating on the virtues of the wonderful Henry Thorley, Henry himself was making the most of his opportunity with his charming vis-à-vis.

"Why haven't I met you before?" he began, scrutinizing her face, which was smiling half tantalizingly, half shyly.

She laughed. "That's a question I've been asking myself with regard to you!"

He went on simply and frankly: "When two beings like ourselves are in a place, though that place is as large as London itself, it seems to me that we should seek out each other and like two magnets draw one another!"

Again she laughed, a tintinabulous laugh, which charmed him. "Well, aren't we here together? What more can you want, you exacting man! Perhaps, it will please you to know that I but arrived in town this very afternoon?"

"At what time?" he asked eagerly.

"At two." She looked puzzled. "Why do you ask?"

"That accounts for it!"

"Accounts for what?"

"Everything!" He laughed.

"You speak in riddles!"

"It's very simple."

"Pray explain yourself!"

"I felt depressed all morning," he said, laughing. "Then, suddenly, about two, I shed my burden. There was nothing to account for it then."

"What a superstitious man! As if I could have had anything to do with it!"

"I know better," he said, with such conviction that she believed him.

"Do you always feel things happening or about to happen?"

"Often. But they have mostly to do with me. I can't always tell about other people. . . ."

"I am glad of that. I shouldn't like to know what's going to happen to me! I always imagine such dire things. . . . But tell me more!"

"I generally know when a letter containing bad news is on the way. . . ."

"Really?"

"That is, I can't definitely say it will take the form of a letter. But I do know when bad news is on the way!"

"What happens?"

"I dream about it. Or else I feel so sad, and have such a definite feeling of something impending. Not so long ago I went out to tea, when suddenly, without any reason at all, I felt so sad and so depressed that I wanted to run. At last I could stand it no longer, and had to beg my hostess to excuse me and let me go. I went out and walked the streets for hours. The next morning a letter reached me informing me that a very dear friend of mine was dead!"

"Why were you depressed this morning?" she asked half teasingly. "You must have anticipated some dreadful misfortune!"

"No, it was because of something that happened last night!"

"A secret?"

"Yes. I may tell you about it—some day!"

The phrase "some day" sounded strange. It was as if he expected to know her for the rest of the days.

"It's wicked of you to keep secrets from me!" she laughed, retaliating in kind.

"Not at all!"

"I shall suspect the worst!"

"I doubt it."

"Is it as bad as all that?"

"It's far worse than you can ever imagine!" He spoke half earnestly, half in jest.

"You are enigmatic."

"Life is enigmatic."

"I know it has nothing to do with a woman!" she said, with some assurance.

"You're right there! If it were only about a woman. I might tell you!"

"Only about a woman!" she mimicked him.

"I mean. . ." he began.

"This from one who tonight has championed my sex so charmingly!"

"I'm prepared to do so again! But remember: I championed women not in the rights they were taking, but in the rights they were denying!"

"In short, you love women as you think they ought to be, rather than take them for what they are!"

He laughed. "Well, I suppose that about describes my attitude. You are certainly clever!"

"Thank you. But you were about to go into detail."

"No. . . . But I was about to say that I sometimes felt as though I were Pygmalion who had created a statue of an ideal woman, only to find that on coming to life the confounded female walked off the pedestal, thumbing her nose at me!"

"You are delicious! Simply delicious!" She burst into the bell-like laugh so characteristic of her.

"Now I call it rude, downright rude of the lady!"

"No doubt. What else could you expect?"

"A creator has a right to expect different treatment from his creation." His assertion, spoken in jest, quite suddenly made him think seriously of last night. It seemed to have some bearing on it. But he was diverted by his vis-à-vis.

"The lady was probably bored standing on the pedestal. If I were in her place, I should have done the same, un- less——" But she tantalizingly left the sentence unfinished.

"Unless what?"

"Unless—no, I shan't tell you. I too shall have my secrets!"

"I can guess!"

"You are clever. And I dare say you're right!"

They obviously enjoyed this duel of words, which dimly veiled a duet of sentiment.

"You've known many women," she said suddenly, with earnestness.

"A good many!" Then added, with a laugh: "By far too many!"

"You are frank."

"Yes. I don't believe in lying. . . . Leastwise, not to you!"

"Thank you."

"You have yourself to thank."

"Were these women all so horrible?"

"No. They were charming. At least, they seemed so at the beginning. But in the end they were all horrible. . . . And we could not get on together!"

"You must have been very hard to please."

"Yes—and no! It was all very well until they thought they wholly possessed you and began to make impossible demands."

"You couldn't have loved them!"

"Perhaps not."

"There, you see. And, perhaps, it was you who made demands on them!"

"In a way, yes. . . . I'm really a very simple man, and my demands were simple. . . ."

She laughed. "Simple things are fundamental, and come high—like the expensive simplicity of women's dress!"

"I loathe whining. The weeping of a woman kills all romance, all affection!"

"Were they all like that?"

"No. One or two were regular furies. But I prefer anger. That shows some spirit!"

"You deserve a termagant!" She laughed.

"I've had that kind too. There was one who threw a

tea-pot into my face. I dared her, to be sure. Here's a slight scar, a souvenir of the occasion!" He pointed to a spot on his upper lip.

She searchingly scrutinized the spot indicated and burst into laughter. "What happened then?"

"I pushed her out of doors!"

"How ungallant!"

"There's no weapon against whining. But when a woman becomes physically violent, one feels less compunction in being violent too."

"I should think you've had enough of women!"

"Too much—and too little! I agree with Byron: one can't live with women, and one can't live without them!"

"What then do you want?"

"Cleopatra!"

"To have Cleopatra, one must be Antony!"

"Antony demeaned himself," he replied. "But for the sake of a Cleopatra, one might be willing to be Antony. Anything rather than this humdrum existence with its petty lusts!"

He was quite serious now, and she took on his mood.

"You must be a very unhappy man. . . ."

"Generally speaking, a tormented unhappy man. But at this moment an ecstatically happy one!"

"I am like that too."

"I know. . . ."

And then both lapsed into silence, fraught with meaning. It had come over them both that they were suffering from the same malady, the malady of romantic persons in a romanceless age. And this silence, following on the words just spoken, drew them into closer intimacy.

"God!" he roused himself suddenly. "Here we've been

all the while talking about me, when it's you I'm dying to hear about!"

"What is there to say about me?" she smiled. "I was born, am alive, and shall some day die!"

"No, no! I want to talk about life, not about death. . . . First of all, tell me: is there any Spanish blood in you?" And he scrutinized the dark eyes in the pale face, its natural pallour intensified by the frame of black hair.

"Perhaps. I come from Cornwall. It's quite possible one of my forebears was some lusty Spanish sailor!"

"Highly probable, I should say. Certainly, no one would take you for a pure Anglo-Saxon. I myself have Russian blood. My mother was a Russian. But tell me more!"

"I've been married twice," she said with an odd smile. "And I fear I've sent both my husbands to an untimely grave."

"Fortunate men! To have had you, and died!"

"You uncharitable man to take me so seriously!"

"I can quite believe it!" he persisted, with a smile.

"Perhaps you're right," she mused. "At least, I'm sure people who know of me will tell you so. I made life hard for those who loved me. But life's not been easy for me either. I demanded too much of my men. They didn't demand enough of me! . . . So beware!"

She spoke with the assurance of one who took it for granted that an alliance with Henry was a foregone conclusion. And Henry was delighted with the frankness which met his own frankness.

"I am prepared to have my head decapitated in a good cause," he replied gallantly, and his manner was half earnest, half gay.

"You see," she went on to explain, "I was young when I

married the first time. I was only eighteen. My husband was thirty-five. I left him on the marriage night. I just felt I couldn't live with him!"

Henry gave an understanding nod.

"It was as if he took me for a vulgar woman. Yet before that he had been charming and behaved like a gentleman. You see, I had had so little experience of life at the time, and expected so much of it. . . ." She paused, closing her eyes, as if she were re-living the episode in her memory, evoking distasteful images.

"And what happened to him?"

"He implored me to come back, pleading that he couldn't stand the humiliation of it—as if I myself hadn't suffered the most terrible humiliation!—and on my refusing, out of sheer chagrin, he put an end to himself. The papers were full of his death at the time. He was a man of some prominence. Of course, there were hints . . . I was blamed. . . ."

"Naturally. That's the way of the world."

"For years afterward, I had a distaste for men. I feared them, yet went on dreaming in the way a little girl goes on dreaming of Prince Charming of the fairy tale. How was one to know if one found him? Men have such a way of being charming at times. They pursued me, yet feared me too. I could be so cold to them, and I acted so warily, and some of them had heard of the marriage episode!"

"And gave you a wide berth?"

"Yes. . . . Then, just as I was becoming reconciled to a life in which no man took part, I met a man who completely bowled me over. I met him on board ship returning from India. . . ."

Henry started. "Was the man's name Hopkinson?" he asked abruptly.

"Yes . . ." she replied, startled in her turn.

"First name Jerome?"

"Yes. . . . How do you know?"

"And your name Elaine?"

"Yes. . . . So you've heard about me! Was it all so awfully bad?" She laughed.

"It wasn't exactly flattering," he admitted, with a smile. "So it was you who killed the charming fellow Hopkinson!"

"Did you know him?"

"Heavens, no! I heard about him for the first time last evening. I envied him!"

"Envied him?"

"Yes. Even the scandal-mongers admit he had six months of happiness. That's surely something!"

"Yes, it's true. I'm not quite sure it was six months, though. I suspect he was happier than I. I was very fond of him. I hated to have to hurt him. He was a good sort, a mere boy in his way. He'd have been better off if he'd never met me. Meeting me was a tragedy for him—for me too! He deserved a better fate. It's terrible to have to hurt nice people. Yet how can one avoid hurting them?" Distress crept into her handsome features and enveloped them in a penumbra of sadness, which touched Henry in a vulnerable spot.

"I understand," he made haste to say. "Don't speak of it if it brings back something you'd rather forget! In any case, I've done the same thing myself. I've hurt women when the last thing I wanted to do was to hurt them. But human beings are quite unreasonable. They sometimes invite injury. They give you no alternative. Let's not talk about that!"

"Isn't it strange? Here we've been talking away as if we've known each other always!"

"We have known each other always," he rejoined, with emphasis. "We have known each other, perhaps, in the only real life either of us has had—in our dreams!"

"Reality is so much more satisfactory," she said, with a woman's definiteness, casting a frankly admiring glance at him.

"Yes . . . that is so. . . ." He laughed.

At this juncture they saw Lady Brinton detach herself from the group and approach them. She had observed their interest in one another from the beginning, and had done valiantly to hold her other guests interested, but now she thought that it was time even for so considerate a hostess as herself to interfere and bring the too happy couple into the more normal social orbit.

"Children," she said, with an apologetic smile, addressing herself to Henry and Elaine, "aren't you being rude to your hostess and her guests by getting off in a corner all by yourselves? . . . I'm sure your conversation has been interesting, and I'm sorry to cut it short," she added not unkindly, but in a tone of voice which as much as said: "Well, I know what you've been up to! I'm not such a fool as you may think!"

They in turn apologizing to their hostess reluctantly rose and joined the other guests, who were at the moment discussing the plays of the day. They seated themselves near by and vaguely listened. What were the plays of the day to the play this pair was enacting? And as yet they had not gotten beyond the Prologue. What an idyl was in prospect at the next rise of the curtain. It occupied the thoughts of both.

All parties end, and this ended also. The guests rose. The usual words of farewell were said. Promises were made to come again. Lady Brinton herself saw her guests to the door. Elaine and Henry, who left together, were the last to shake her hand.

Lady Brinton looked after them, and wondered. Had Henry Thorley, so difficult to please, found his long-sought affinity at last? A secret elation filled the charitable Lady's soul. She felt affectionately toward Henry, and she had scanned the social horizon for a woman who might please the curious man. She liked to feel that she had been the instrument for furnishing the happiness which eluded him and was his due. And now, at last—But doubt mingled with her elation. Of all women, Elaine! Would his love for her go the way of the others? If it did, she would never forgive herself—never!

"Elaine!"

"Henry!"

Each name thus spoken came naturally from the other, and sounded to them like lovely music heard for the first time.

"Which way are you going, Elaine?"

"I am stopping with friends in Soho Square!"

"That's quite near!"

Nevertheless, they got into a hansom, and Henry took Elaine's unresisting hand.

"It's all so very strange," he said, after a short silence.

"Strange . . . strange . . . strange . . ." she echoed after him.

"Yes, strange. . . ."

"Strange . . . strange. . . ."

They were overcome with the strangeness of it.

Everything appeared so unreal: the London night fantastically veiled with the thin mist, from behind which peered street lamps like dimmed moons, and in which, phantom-like pedestrians moved hither and thither like but two-dimensioned figures in a shadow-play: everything was strange.

Were they—Henry and Elaine—alive?—real? Henry pressed Elaine's hand—to reassure her—and himself.

"I love you!" she heard a soft whisper on her ear.

Had her ears lied? Her own words seemed to her as unreal as his. She said: "Are you sure? You're not sorry?"

"Why should I be sorry?"

"After what I've told you—about myself?"

"Oh, that!" There was such a gesture of contempt in the tone of his voice as to leave no doubt. He did not believe, or if he believed, it did not matter.

"You've known me so short a time," she pursued her thought.

"I love you!" he said, excluding argument.

The hansom paused before a handsome arched Georgian door. Henry sprang out, and helped Elaine. Then he paid the driver, discharging him. He saw Elaine to the door.

"What time tomorrow?" He asked the question as naturally, as though they had been lovers who had met scores of times.

"I have a luncheon engagement tomorrow—worse luck! Come, and take me out to tea!"

"It will seem like aeons of time. But I'll try to hold out until then!" He laughed out of sheer exuberance.

Then, as they stood framed in the deep doorway, he suddenly embraced her, and, with passion pressed his lips to hers. She did not resist, why should she resist? She felt that they were both in the power of a force too strong for resistance, that they had met in a predestined moment of time when love burns up all usual barriers and hindrances, all precautionary deliberations. . . . Only love, a pure force, free from all dross, was left.

Her flexible body, yielding, fell in with his; the aroma of her was sweet. And in that prolonged kiss, their long pent-up souls rushed to their lips and met. . . .

When a few moments later he had parted from her, the thought, like a hammer, suddenly struck him: last night he had cursed his God, and tonight God sent him a precious gift, the best of all his fair creatures. . . . He felt terribly repentant, terribly contrite, and—somehow—terribly afraid.

CHAPTER NINE

Woman Who Wanted the Moon

ELAINE HOPKINSON ascended the dim lamp-lighted stairs to her room, with unaccustomed flutterings in her heart.

She quickly struck a match and lighted the shaded table-lamp; then, pressing her hands to her temples, paused in the middle of the room, stock-still, like one dazed by an extraordinary occurrence. Yes, a most extraordinary occurrence. She caught a reflection of herself in the full-length mirror, between bookshelves, against the wall. How pretty she looked, how flushed her cheeks, which but a little while ago had been so pale! Will-less she stood there, and dream-rapt, and the vision she glimpsed resembled herself and was yet someone else.

Suddenly, she laughed. And as suddenly, she stopped. Heavens, she thought, what ailed her? Why did she laugh? What was there to laugh at? "I am hysterical," she murmured. She must not laugh again. There were people in the house, her friends and hosts, sleeping in the neighbouring rooms. If they chanced to be awake, what would they think? It was absurd, of course. Utterly absurd. Why had she laughed? She was like one who had lost her wits. What had happened? A strange, extraordinary thing. A miracle. . . .

Yes, a miracle. . . .

She started, shook herself. Then relapsed into her trance-

like reverie. Held by its delicate fetters, she slowly removed her hat and coat, and laid them on a chair. Then,
with startling impetuosity, she flung herself on the bed, and
lay there so still, her large motionless eyes fixed on the
penumbral ceiling. She could scarcely catch her breath.
Unfamiliar feelings possessed her, she felt tremulous under
their all-persuasive hypnotic spell; ready to submit, if need
be—to perish!

What had happened, then? What? What? Oh, God!
. . . She uttered what words came to her lips, and she had
no control over them.

She lay there, her head flung back, her arms under her
head, trembling with profuse ecstasy of long-restrained,
suddenly-loosed passion, scarcely dreamt of, hardly hoped
for, but blindly desired, and dimly felt. . . . It was as if
something, infinitely precious, which had slept so deep, so
deep; something which she had thought dead or non-
existent; in the twinkling of an eye, had come to life,
awaking from a long, long sleep, into which it had been
plunged by an evil spell. A strange man's hand had
touched her, a strange man's lips had come in contact with
her own, and lo!—she flamed into life, as if at the touch
of a magic wand, as in some legend or fairy tale.

"Is it possible? Is it really possible?" she cooed, in a
hushed voice, which did not sound like her own.

A thousand tremors shook her. Her heart beat fast,
troubled by delicious torments. She closed her eyes, the
better to let her charmed fancy play on this new incomprehensible something which, without warning, had
danced into her lately eventless life; she had not long
since given up all hope of anything its like occurring to
stir her out of her despond. She had been a cobwebbed

captive, a prisoner of humdrum life, and now she was suddenly free—free! Free for what? She, who was so proud, wanted to fling herself at a man's feet, and adore, adore!

She was mad, utterly mad, she thought. What indeed had happened to make her so utterly unlike the cool possessed self, who could not eye a man but with suspicion, with reminiscent disgust, born of bitter experience?

The answer was clear and simple.

Here was a man who was different from any she had known. There was something so intensely alive, so infectiously alive about him. Life seemed to emanate from him in waves, in distilled essences—shut in—seeking egress. Here she felt was life which was the very soul of life. And he conveyed the sense of it to her. There had been this instantaneous recognition between them.

She began to recall the things he had said. She thought him especially amusing in what he said about Pygmalion and the ideal lady he had created who walked off the pedestal, thumbing her nose at her creator. "Yet," mused Elaine, "it is as if this man had really created me tonight, or rather re-created me." That a human being, a stranger to her before that evening, should have cast such a spell of enchantment over her, who had thought herself impervious, seemed incredible. "Heavens!" she cried. "Why, it's inconceivable. If he wants me, I must not fail him!"

"But does he want me?" she went on musing, qualms assailing her. "What can he want of me, he who's known so many charming women before? Yes, many. . . . He's said so himself. I am but a poor woman who's made the lives of a few men wretched. . . . But he's so different from them, so different from any man I've met. In his

presence I feel as if I'd never known a man before. . . .
And I love him; really, truly love him. . . ."

For hours and hours she kept awake, musing. She
heard the church clock chime four. . . . Then, impetuously, she sprang from her bed, and flung her clothes off.
Naked she paused before the mirror, and surveyed her
reflected form. Critically, with eyes which sought for
faults. But no! She was lovely, incomparably lovely.
She knew it, if it was herself. . . . After all, if one has
an eye for beauty, one *knows*. . . . What lovely woman
does not know that she is lovely? . . . And she was sure,
he had an eye for beauty. He could not help seeing hers.
He would see her loveliness, and he would embrace it; she
was impatient for him to embrace it. Unbearably sweet
was the thought of his handsome body so close to hers,
loving her. Her heart gave a flutter, her head grew light,
she put a hand on a chair to keep from falling. . . . And
suddenly, she wanted to sing, to dance. There was a
piano in the room, and she wanted to play it. Something
passionate and tender and sad, like the *Moonlight Sonata,*
something which would relieve her of her pent-up joy,
almost as hard to bear as sorrow.

Oh, why couldn't one dance or sing or play when one
wanted to?

All around her there were human beings, her friends,
who were asleep, and they would be vexed if they were
disturbed. The whole world around her was asleep. Even
in daytime it was asleep. Or rather sleep-walking. Presently, from the neighbouring room she heard at first light
but gradually loudening snores of her host—a nice genial
man was Mr. Trent, and a comfortable liver—and these

snores intruding on her own idyllic mood, she broke into
a suppressed low laugh.

"Dear me!" she cried half amused, half abashed. "What's
come over me? I'm truly as bad as a cat wallowing in
catnip!"

And she blew out the light and snuggled into bed, and
imagined such things as never could be put on paper.

It was not until the first light of November dawn that
she dropped into a deep sleep, troubled by strange dreams.

On the next day, to the surprise of her hosts, she awoke
late. They had always known her to be a regular sleeper
and an early riser. She had a slice of toast and a cup of
tea in bed, and when she flung the bed-covers from her
to rise it was nearly time to keep her luncheon engagement; why did she ever make it? she asked herself, as if it
were unusual for her to make one. But she heartily wished
she hadn't made this one. Neither the day nor the person
with whom she had made it suited her. She wanted to
look her best for a person very dear to her, but a stranger
yesterday; she wanted time to rest, and time to visit the
hair-dresser. But she couldn't very well back out of it
now. Her host's son had asked her so often, and she had
always put him off with one excuse or another.

He was a "nice boy," was young Phil; not a boy either,
but a man of at least her years. He was a "nice boy" in
the way certain people refer to a man of a certain type,
whatever his years. Philip Trent *was* a nice boy, and
sooner or later you were bound to call him simply Phil.
Phil, who was in his father's business but lived in bachelor
quarters off the Strand, had on the first day of meeting
become enamoured of his sister Jane's twice widowed

friend. Jane had warned him how foolish it was, and Elaine gave him no encouragement, but as happens in such affairs Phil persisted; he having read somewhere that God helps those who help themselves, and that if you don't succeed the first time, try and try again. And he did. He badgered Elaine with attentions, letters, invitations, and at least once a week proposed by correspondence if not in person; and the consensus of opinion was, as is usual in such a situation, that Elaine, or for that matter any woman, would ultimately surrender, provided no more desirable cavalier appeared in the interval and snatched the prize.

And, really, Elaine had been often on the point of yielding to Phil's importunities. He was, after all, a "nice boy," whom you couldn't possibly dislike, and if she married him, she was sure to have her own way. He had pressed her for an appointment the moment she arrived in town, and she had so often repulsed him before she said Yes, half dubious if she ought to; all the more as she had been seriously considering yielding. That was, of course, before she met Henry. And now she was loath to keep her appointment, yet saw no way of getting out at such short notice. As for marrying Phil, that was quite out of the question now. Not even if Henry didn't want her. Like goes to like, and a "nice boy" must go to a "nice girl," and wed her and bed her. Not a woman like her. That was how Elaine thought, with that final assurance which comes of unlooked-for, God-sent experience, settling all argument. One could not harness a race-horse with a dray-horse, and a spirited woman could not live with Phil. "Never!" It was unthinkable. And, once and for all, she must tell him that. She was not looking forward to the luncheon with any exhilaration. But he was a nice boy, and she must be nice to him. It was so hard for a woman not to hurt a man's feelings, if he insisted on having them hurt. It was particularly hard to have to hurt Phil, who, apart from being Jane's brother, was so attentive and devoted at all times. Last night's conversation at Lady Brinton's recurred to her; how nice if women could only propose for a change! Then men would see if they liked having to refuse a lady!

There was little time for reflection. Phil soon arrived, bringing a large bouquet of red roses, splendid hothouse specimens, which must have cost a small fortune on this foggy November day. Philip Trent was a fairly good-looking man of twenty-seven, but younger in appearance. He was tall and lean, with broad shoulders, long but not too virile face, slightly receding chin, clean-shaven but for a tiny toothbrush moustache. He had the good-natured smile of an easy-going young man, his eyes were brown and docile, and he walked noiselessly with a somewhat shambling, indeterminate gait. Young women thought well of him, but since meeting Elaine three years before he had no eyes but for her. He had been to Cambridge, though to talk with him you'd scarcely have known it, except for allusions to his having been a prize bowler on the Varsity cricket team. He was singularly shy, like a young girl, and, perhaps for this reason, not much given to talk, though upon occasion he displayed a quiet, unobtrusive wit, such as you may see in Punch; Elaine liked him in such moods, and would have oftener encouraged his company but for the fact that at any moment he was likely to switch to the subject of his tender regard for her.

"How lovely!" she greeted him, taking the bouquet, and burying her face in it and drawing a deep breath.

"Would that it were my head of hair!" said Phil, smiling superciliously.

"If your head grew roses like these, I should cut them!" Elaine retorted.

"Delilah!"

"Don't flatter yourself!" And she again thrust her face into the roses, and thought of Henry.

"Flatter myself?" he asked, puzzled. Then, grasping the implication, a light came into his eyes, and he laughed. "Oh, I see. . . . No, I'm not Samson—worse luck!"

He presented so rueful a face that she could not help laughing. "Wait a minute for me!" she said, disengaging her face from the flowers. "I must put these roses in a vase!" And lightly she tripped up the curved, carpeted stairs.

He could hear the swish of her silken petticoats, a sound which never failed to touch him emotionally. He was going to have it out with her today, and he felt nervous though determined. He had felt encouraged by her acceptance of his invitation to lunch. But no sooner he saw her than he felt in her the presence of a new, an alien element, he knew not what, which did not ·augur so well. It seemed to him that she was labouring under some perverse secret excitement. She was flushed, looked almost feverish, and, if anything, even handsomer than usual, and, without doubt, more desirable. The sight of her filled him with that desperation which is born of despair. But outwardly he continued to present the manner and appearance of one who was merely concerned with the prospect of a very pleasant luncheon in the company of a very charming woman.

Elaine presently reappeared, all in readiness to go out.

Phil at once marked the absence of the single rose he expected to see pinned to her bosom. To pin a single rose out of the bouquet he brought her had always been her way in the past; and he now accepted its absence as a certain token of disfavour. What had he done to deserve it? For the time being he concealed his chagrin.

A hackney carriage brought them to Verrey's. They found an uninhabited corner and, ensconcing themselves, ordered soup, steak and kidney pie and golden pudding. Elaine refused to drink, but Phil, to fortify himself against the ordeal he expected and to reinforce his courage, asked for a pint of the oldest ale, intending, if the situation demanded it, to follow it with another.

"Elaine dear," he made an approach to his subject, between vigorous attacks on the steak and kidney pie, "why didn't you pin on one of my roses, as you always do?"

She laughed. "You're observing, Phil. I must give you credit for that."

"I'm not asking for any credit! I was curious, that was all."

"Well, if you must know, it was because I didn't think of it!"

"But you always do think of it," he said, with peevish persistence.

"Well, this time I didn't!" she countered, resenting the possessive tone of his voice, and suddenly remembering that she might have lunched with Henry. "I'm not obliged to think of it, am I?" she chided him.

He laid down his knife and fork. "Of course not, my dear," he said in a manner meant to be conciliatory. "Only you see, seeing the rose there made me think you cared for me a little!"

"And so I do! . . . Just a little," she said, softening. "But there's no use of encouraging you, is there?"

"Of course, there is," he said, failing to grasp the true meaning of her ambiguous question. "I'm ready to marry you. Will you marry me, Elaine? At once, I mean. . . ."

"Sh-h. . . . Can't we remain friends, Phil?"

"Friends? . . . But I love you, Elaine!"

"You're infatuated with me. Not in love. You'd like to possess me. . . . But you'd never be really happy with me!"

"Of course, I would!" he said eagerly, and she thought, rather pathetically.

"Then let's put it this way: I should never be happy with you. You'd not want to see me unhappy, would you?"

"But you would, dear. I would do everything to make you happy!"

"I have no doubt you would," she said gently. "But happiness doesn't altogether depend on having things done for one!"

"No? . . . What does it depend on?" he asked sullenly.

"It depends, Phil, on my loving a man so that I can give myself completely without feeling that I demean myself in any way. And I don't feel quite that way with you. The man I love must be a sort of god to me!"

"Yet you used to give me some hope," he said, doggedly.

"I am sorry. If I did, it was very wrong of me, Phil. Perhaps, I didn't know my own mind. Women have such fuzzy minds at times. I've decided to reform!" She laughed, and took his hand. "Phil dear, don't hold anything against me! And please don't think that I don't appreciate you! You're the bestest man that ever lived.

Really, you are! And I'm a wicked, wicked woman. . . ."

He opened his mouth to protest.

"No, no! Hear me out," she went on. "I've been married twice. I've never hidden that from you, have I?"

"No. That's why . . ." he began.

"Well," she said, interruping him, "those two men might have been alive and happy today but for me! I'm honest with you. They were good men, as the world goes. But I couldn't go on living with them. And they couldn't live without me. Ask anybody. People will tell you that I've killed them. Do you understand?"

"I don't believe these tales about you!"

"You're a dear not to. All the same, they are true! I've been a very unhappy woman."

"Unhappy? I don't understand. You're young, beautiful, not in want. And you've enchanted men. Why should you be unhappy?" he asked, his humanness overcoming his maleness.

"I've always wanted something I couldn't have. I dreamt such dreams!"

"Dreams?"

"Yes. And I wanted them in reality."

"We all dream dreams. . . ."

"Don't you understand? I wasn't satisfied that they should remain dreams! I wanted to hold the moon—in my hands!"

"No, I don't understand," he said, at last. "Reality is jolly good as I see it. You're jolly good. I don't want the moon. I want you. Or if you like, you are my moon!"

She laughed, and released the hand she clasped. "That's just it! I am the moon to you, and you can't have me.

Now you know what it is to want the moon and not have it. It's a bitter thing!"

He watched her suddenly flushed face; but it was not flushed with sadness. A secret happiness suffused it with a rich rose; the loveliness of joy super-imposed itself ·on the loveliness of sadness. What had happened to her?

"Elaine!" he cried suddenly, with the abruptness of discovery. "Do you love someone else?" He narrowly watched her face. "I know you do! You do!" And his heart grew heavy, even as he spoke.

"What if I do!" she said, bristling with challenge; attacking in order to defend.

"Nothing!"

She softened. "Don't you see, Phil dear? You and I are no pair. I tell you, it would be a mistake to marry me, even if I consented! Be sensible! Choose a nice simple girl who'll keep house for you and look after you and love you!"

"I don't want a nice simple girl," he said sulkily. "I want you!"

"Let's be friends," she pleaded.

"There's not much choice left me, is there?" he smiled ruefully, feeling very much as many another man feels in similar circumstances: that is, not as a man at all but as a dog slinking away, head down, tail between his legs.

"I should have thought there was a great choice left to you—a whole world of girls to choose from!"

"There was—before I met you!"

"Why not now?"

"How can I tell you? . . . Only I know I shall never be happy again in this life!"

"Oh, yes, you will!" she comforted him. "You'll see

things differently in the long run. I'm not really worth it, Phil. No woman is. But we are what we are, and we want the things we want, and no man can be happy if the woman he loves is unhappy, and no woman can be happy if the man she loves is unhappy. Can't you see, it hurts me to say No!"

At this point the golden pudding was brought; they ate it in silence. The pudding disposed of, he suddenly sat up, and said rather brusquely, it seemed to her:

"It's all bally-rot!"

She poised her lovely dark brows into a question, and waited for an explanation. As he offered none, she demanded:

"What do you mean?"

"I mean," he said, in a strained yet determined voice, "it's all bally-rot—this talk about the soul, the moon, and all the rest of that rigmarole!"

She drew away from him in resentful astonishment, while he went on:

"You said something about my wishing to possess you. What's wrong in that, I'd like to know. When a man loves a woman, he wants to possess her. Of course, he does! The point is, he doesn't want to possess anyone else. That's where love comes in. He wants and must possess the woman he loves, and he wants to give the woman he loves, his woman, good food and shelter and pretty clothes. And once or twice a year he wants to give her a decent holiday. And, of course, he wants a baby—his and her blood mixed—to carry on, as it were. That's life! And what's wrong with it? I'd like to know. There's what you call soul too, to be sure. But to my way of thinking, if you take care of the body, the soul will take care of itself!"

He paused, taking a long breath, as if talking at length were an effort for him. He was indeed making a supreme effort, his last effort.

But his peroration only met with a gay tinkling laugh on Elaine's part. "You are a dear," she said. "But can't you see, that wouldn't be enough for me—or too much—as you like! If life were only as simple as all that for me! But it isn't. And what you say only convinces me that you and I are as far apart as the poles, and we can never pull together in a single harness. Why, I'd die of sheer boredom! I want life, life! I want someone who will give me joy, romance! Yes, the moon, if you like!"

"It all comes of reading books," he said doggedly.

"No, no!" she asserted positively. "Books come out of this burning desire for life! Men write books because this life doesn't suit them, and they want to show us something different. But books are not enough for me! I want life—life!" Again she laughed. "I'd make you a poor helpmate, Phil. A few weeks with me, and you'd wish you'd never been born! Really, you would! We want such different things."

He hung his head in defeat. She was in the wrong, he thought. But there seemed to be no way of arguing her down. Thwarted, feeling desperate, he wished he lived in a world in which a bludgeon was permissible as a weapon of argument. But this mood passed quickly. They sat on in uncomfortable silence.

She looked at her watch. It was three o'clock. "I must be off," she said.

He bestirred himself, and called for the bill. "I suppose,"

he could not refrain from saying, "you're anxious to be off to see the other chap, who's waiting to hand the moon to you!"

She resented his words. "Perhaps, I am," she retorted defiantly. "Have you any objection to offer?"

"None that would do any good. Only let me warn you to be careful. For when you expect the moon, you may be sorely disappointed if you get only a hunk of green cheese, pretty mouldy at that!"

Elaine laughed, gayly, unrestrainedly, and had to resort to a handkerchief to wipe the tears from her eyes.

"You're getting positively brilliant," she said, taking his arm as they rose. "If you were to make many remarks like that, I might regret my bargain after all!" She did not say this in sarcasm. She was genuinely pleased.

Against his original inclinations, he joined in her laughter. Suddenly appreciative of her point of view, he was, in some unaccountable way, touched.

"All right," he said. "I hope it's for the best. And the best of luck to you. Only make me a promise. It's nothing unreasonable, I assure you!"

"But I like being unreasonable!"

"Well, it's this. If you ever get tired of the moon, do come back to earth again! I mean—to me!"

"I shall consider it, Phil," she said solemnly, and, for no reason she could see, small tears appeared in her eyes. She applied her lace-trimmed handkerchief.

At the sight of her tears, Phil felt like crying himself. He put his hand on hers, and said:

"That's quite all right, Ellie dear! The devil won't take me! Go and have your moon! I'll be patient. I'll wait. If you ever need me—" He found it difficult to proceed.

But he braced himself, and concluded: "Remember me, Phil Trent, your friend, always at your service!"

"God bless you!" she said.

"The same to you!"

He pressed her hand until it hurt; then, abruptly releasing it, strode away.

She looked back at him, but he did not turn. There was something furiously energetic about his stride. Sensible of his mood, she felt sorry for him; for she also knew something of the driving power of unshed tears.

CHAPTER TEN

A Lyrical Interlude

O N TAKING leave of Elaine, Henry felt an exhilaration scarcely less intense than hers. Like a
mariner who was at last in sight of land, just as
he had been on the verge of abandoning all hope of seeing
land, he exulted in the discovery as in a miracle, and his
heart was overflowing with gratitude and prayer,—and
with remorse, only a little less intense than his joy.

Had he not but the night before, Lucifer-like, in a mood
of mad despair, cursed his God? And here, for his
blasphemous malediction, was a reward, so expeditiously
and so felicitously meted out as to appear incredible. God's
ways were surely inscrutable, His humours not to be
grasped by the human mind.

Henry saw his good fortune, so contrary to what might
have been expected, and was afraid. Had his senses deceived him? Had he dreamt it all?

It had always been thus. Reality for him had a way of
taking on appearances more unreal than dream. The very
street he walked in, with its steady rumble of nocturnal
traffic, its mad din as yet unstilled at an hour past mid-
night, its restless phantasmagoria of indeterminate, shape-
less figures scurrying hither and thither, its inarticulate
cacophany of voices, its endless flow of hackney carriages
and hansoms and trucks, following one another in order-
less procession: all this took on for him the form of a

diabolic invention scarcely less staggering than the imagined scenes of Dante's Inferno. And to himself he seemed
as unreal as all the rest of this mad fantasy.

What was he, then, in that unutterable active chaos?
Hardly human, but a titan stuggling in darkness, a moving
energy, a propelling flame, a blind force pushing its way
to some mysterious goal not vouchsafed him to know.

A lovely face revealed for the first time that evening; a
lovely face emerging from the vast unformed chaos, floating as it were upon drifting fumes of incense; a lovely face
smiling a subtle smile; led him on through this kaleidoscopic maze, lured him on to unglimpsed paradise, or—
well, he did not much care. All that mattered was that,
at last, he had found a fair face which had the power to
move him, to stir him out of his slough, to stimulate his
senses to new life.

This fresh contact of the evening revived him, made him
feel as he had not felt since those remote days eleven years
ago when for the first time a girl's face charmed him to
distraction. The girl was a dream of loveliness, of nymph-
like grace; her features were classic without being rigid,
her skin was marvellously white with a tinge of rose, her
hair jet black, her eyes a dark silken brown of a pansy-like
softness. She was a Greek, and she was sixteen. He met
her in an Alpine village in Switzerland.

It was in the Spring. He and his father were walking
along a narrow path between fields of narcissi. The flowers
stretched for miles along the slopes, and on either side
these flowery meadows were flanked by armies of tall erect
pines rising in serried rows to precipitous heights. The
ten o'clock sun, obscured by the ridge, cast upward its rays,
and their ambient soft glow reflected on the slopes shed on

the narcissus-decked, dew-moist landscape its delicate tints, enchanting the eyes. The air was soft and blithe, redolent of youth and of youth's ardours.

God, how good it was to be young, and merely to live, to draw in this clear air, Spring's breath, the odour of the earth, the scent of flowers. Life had no other meaning but this. The sensitive boy walked by his father's side slowly, breathing in deeply all that life had to offer; and it was good. Just ahead, round the bend of the path, the village would presently come to view, a jumbled group of low-gabled chalets scattered along the slope, and on the top-most part of it a largish building, their hotel. There was another hotel, but that was at the farthest end of the vil-lage, and, owing to the configuration of the landscape, quite invisible from here.

Just as they were approaching the end of the path where it merged with the road, they saw a tall lean oldish woman and a young girl coming towards them in the path. This necessitated walking in single file. The boy withdrew be-hind his father to allow the women to pass, while the girl drew behind the older woman. As they passed each other, Henry was so struck by the girl's singular beauty that he could not resist glancing back, only to encounter the eyes of the girl; for she had also glanced back. She was very lovely in a delicate pagan way, and she smiled so bewitch-ing a smile that Henry, smitten at once, smiled back and made a bow. He had never done such a bold thing before. It all happened so naturally, without any aforethought. Then he did a still stranger thing. He bent down, picked a narcissus, and impetuously flung it towards the girl. The girl smiled, in tacit acceptance of the offering.

All this happened so quickly that neither Henry's father nor the girl's companion saw anything.

Forthwith, for the rest of the day, and during the waking hours of the night, the girl's handsome face floating as it were in an aura of its own smile's diffused light, tormented him; try as he would, he could not banish from his thoughts the vision of the graceful girl who fitted so well into nature's embroidery and was a part of it, that field of narcissus bathed in the morning sun's mellow rose glow.

Strange that he had not seen her before. His father and he had been staying here for over a week. She must be staying at the other hotel, the Beau Rivage, he thought. Moved by a strong desire to see her again, he had reconnoitred the neighbourhood that afternoon. Several times he passed the garden terrace of the Beau Rivage and scrutinized every door and window, every human figure to be seen near or in the remote distance. But never once did he glimpse anyone who had the slightest resemblance to the divine image he so ardently sought.

On the next morning, which was fully as lovely as the morning that went before, a wild fancy seized him. Why hadn't he thought of it before? He would appear at the self-same hour and the self-same place at which he had first caught sight of the charming girl. He nursed the mad hope, which almost amounted to certainty, that she would be there. He rose before eight and had his breakfast. Then, with fierce impatience, waited for the hour of "assignation," in which terms he thought of a possible meeting. Only now and then doubts assailed him: "Suppose she won't come!" It was an agonizing thought, and he could scarcely bear it. No, no! She would be there! She surely would be there!

And she was. As he turned the bend of the path, the first sight he caught was of her standing on the same spot he had seen her on the day before; she was contemplating the meadow of sun-bathed narcissi and the majestic pines rising in serried triangles against the precipitous slopes. Her back was turned, but he would have known anywhere the graceful contours of the girl. He paused for an instant to take in the sinuous loveliness of the form in the flowered frock outlined against yet lost in the vast narcissus design. She stood motionless, and only now and then swung her wide-brimmed hat on its neck-ribbons, betraying, he thought, a restlessness, a nervous impatience. After drawing a deep breath, he wended his way up the path, and not until he reached her did she turn her head. This time she did not smile but, as he paused in front of her, she turned on him a grave, questioning gaze. She appeared to wait for him to speak, to explain this extraordinary intrusion on her reverie.

"Mademoiselle," he began falteringly, in French. "Forgive a stranger's temerity in presuming to address himself to you without the formality of an introduction. But there's no way that I can see of getting an introduction, and since seeing you yesterday I've no other wish in the world but to know you. Allow me, then, to introduce myself, Henry Thorley, son of William Thorley, gentleman, of Ravenford Manor, Ravenford, Sussex, England!"

To his chagrin, the girl burst out laughing, and her laugh sounded like a lovely silver bell. However lovely a girl's laugh can be, no enamoured young man likes to be laughed at by a charming girl on whom he had set his heart. Still, even her laugh was better than an outright repulse. And this gave him hope.

"Why do you laugh?" he asked in an injured tone. "You laugh very prettily, to be sure. But I didn't come here to be laughed at."

"Why did you come?" She fixed on him her large, grave, pansy-like eyes, no longer laughing.

"I came here because I knew you'd be here!"

"You knew?"

"Yes . . . I had the notion you would."

"That's strange!"

"Why strange?"

"Because I also had an idea you'd be here. At least, I hoped you would!" she replied, the intent look in her eyes becoming transformed into a faint smile of pleasure.

"There! . . . Why, then, did you laugh?"

"Why shouldn't I laugh? You were so funny making that long official speech!"

"Oh, that! It was natural in the circumstances, wasn't it?"

"No, not natural! If one of those flowers could speak," —she pointed to the narcissi—"it wouldn't address me in that formal manner!"

He was astonished at the answer. "You are right," he said, after a silence. "If I were a flower, I should have spoken quite differently. But I am not a narcissus, and I spoke as a gentleman has been trained to speak to a lady."

"To a lady he doesn't know?" she asked, laughing.

"You are right. I'm not supposed to speak to you at all!"

"There, you see! You shouldn't have spoken to me."

"Yet you say you came here because you'd hoped to find me here!"

"I'm not criticizing you," she said, thoughtfully. "I

should have hated you if you had not spoken to me. Only I didn't expect to be addressed as a public meeting!"

"Oh, I see!" he returned, mockingly. "You'd have preferred to be addressed as a Princess!"

"I fancy I should have liked that! . . . But as no ordinary Princess, mind you. Perhaps, as a Princess in a fairy tale. Princesses in fairy tales are not addressed like Princesses in life. There's too much ceremony in real life!"

He was charmed by her speech, uttered half seriously, half nonsensically. "Very well," he said, "I'll do my best to play the part, which I suppose is that of a Prince in a fairy tale. I shan't say, Your Highness, or Your Excellency, or Your Majesty. I shall call you—heavens, what am I to call you?"

"You may call me Ilyana," she prompted him.

"Ilyana? What a pretty name!"

"I think so myself. Indeed, I prefer it to Marie, which is the name by which my aunt insists on calling me. And that reminds me, we'd better go to some more remote spot where Aunt Julie is not likely to look for me. Aunt Julie is the lady you saw me with yesterday!"

"Is she so severe?"

"What do you expect? It is wicked to talk with strangers. If she should see me with you, I don't know what would happen! She'd surely die from the shock! Whatever her faults, she means well, and I don't want to see her die."

And having said all this, she unceremoniously took his hand, sending a multitude of tremors up and down his whole being, and led him up the path.

"I know just the place," she said.

Henry was enchanted with everything she said and did. She held his hand trustingly in hers, and their perfect bodies, close to one another, because of the narrowness of the path, moved in perfect unison, step in step. It was wonderful.

"Come, let's skip!" he suddenly cried, and, without waiting for a response, clutched her hand.

Then, without much ado, they skipped up the path, both laughing. They skipped on and on, madly, irresponsibly, tirelessly, as if life held no greater joy than this, as if it were justified by this spontaneous motion, by freedom from deliberating and willing. At a point where the path bifurcated, Ilyana gently pulled Henry's hand, and they swerved to the left, and, nothing disturbed, they went on skipping at a rhythmic pace, first up an ascending path then down a descending path, until they reached a small declivity where the tall pines cast faint shadows on the sunlit flowers.

Here, of necessity, they paused, and, somewhat out of breath, burst out laughing in sheer delight of one another. There was a tiny grass-plot here free of narcissi, and, protected by the narcissus-clad hillock they had just crossed, they were invisible to anyone on the main path. The grass being still wet with dew, they sat down on a grass-surrounded rock, and looked at one another half guiltily, like two culprits suddenly become conscious of their wickedness. Ilyana's pale cheeks were flushed, wisps of jet black hair played about her face, and she looked even lovelier than before.

"What would your aunt say?"

"What would your father say? That was your father with you yesterday?"

"Yes. Anyhow, I asked you first!"

"Well, my aunt wouldn't say anything. She'd be speechless."

They laughed.

"What about your father?"

"My father," he replied evasively, "is quite used to my ways. He thinks I take after mother, and is ready to forgive me anything on that account."

"Oh," she laughed. Then, suspiciously: "Do you make it a practice of skipping with girls you don't know?"

"You are the first!"

"Are you sure?" She looked intently into his eyes.

"Quite!"

"I believe you," she said, looking pleased. "I wonder why you skipped with me, and why I allowed myself to skip with you."

He reflected for a few moments. "I'm sure I don't know. I felt like skipping with you, and I suppose you felt like skipping with me!"

"That sounds simple enough! But I'm sure that's how the flowers would act!"

"If they could act!" he corrected her.

"Don't be so literal!"

"Still, I agree with you. People are strange not to follow their impulses. They miss all the fun in life!"

"I've been brought up in a convent. I've been taught to behave. Yet it's quite true, I felt like skipping with you. I wouldn't have missed it for the worlds!"

He admiringly observed her. She talked so earnestly and so honestly yet so lightly too; and when she lapsed into reverie, her large dark eyes glowed so softly, and seemed more than ever like marvellous pansies. Suddenly, a faint, odd smile relaxed her classic features, and something in the expression of her eyes for a moment startled him.

"Why do you look at me like that?" she asked, observing the strangeness of his look.

"I was admiring you! Just then you looked extraordinarily like the portrait of my mother. She was a very beautiful woman!"

"Thank you. I like to be liked for myself!"

"I do. Only I couldn't help remarking the resemblance!"

"Did you love her very much then? From what you say, I should say she's dead!"

"Yes. I love her more than anything else in the world!"

"There's not very much hope for me then?" She looked teasingly at his handsome tousled head, with its longish wisps of soft brown hair falling in disordered array over his forehead and temples and giving emphasis to his live brown eyes. Impulsively she reached out a hand and ran her fingers through his hair. His body trembled from the contact, and he became inwardly animated with a thousand little spurts of fire.

"I love you," he said simply.

"Come!" she cried suddenly, springing to her feet. "My aunt will be wondering where I am." And, seizing him by the hand, she led him quickly the way they came. They walked rapidly, in silence. When they reached the spot where he first addressed her, she paused, and before he knew what she was up to she leaned forward, planted a quick impetuous kiss on his lips and ran in the direction of the village, crying over her shoulder:

"Tomorrow, at the same time, and the same place!"

And vanished.

"Ilyana!" he cried, wondering if he ought to pursue her;

but, heedless, she ran on. Like one stunned, he stood there, watching her gracefully swaying form, until it disappeared round the bend. Then, slowly, thoughtfully, burning inwardly with a thousand little spurts of flame, he turned his footsteps toward his hotel.

He saw her again the next day, and the next. And the intimacy grew, in spite of all efforts, without his succeeding in finding out much about her. Who was she? He knew a little. She was a Greek, and her father and mother were dead. She was in the care of her aunt, her guardian. That was the sum of his knowledge. He wrestled with the mystery, tried to ferret this or that out of her, but to little avail.

"Don't ask questions!" she said. "Isn't it enough that I love you?" And to put an end to further questioning she often stopped his mouth with kisses.

Sometimes she would grow sad, but never would she explain her sadness; then, in the midst of it, she would grow the more ardent and embrace him and press his head to her heart and passionately whisper in his ear:

"How I would love to give you everything—everything! Of myself, I mean! Everything! But I daren't! Simply daren't!"

She spoke these words as if something portentous hung over her head, something which belongs to doom itself, a doom which was very near.

"I know what it is, I know!" he once cried in his sympathy with her distress. "Your aunt has promised you to some ogre in marriage, and you don't know how to get out of it!"

She made neither murmur nor protest, but he knew with that certainty which demands no proof that he was somewhere near the truth. Her sadness slipped from her quickly, like a coat, and she skipped and danced with him, up the path and down the path, as if life were lived just for that, as if there were neither yesterday nor tomorrow, but only the ever present Today, with all of Today's limitations and demands. She was a little pagan, gay or sad according to the moment, or both gay and sad at the same time, like the Neapolitan songs she sometimes sang to him in her low sweet voice. And the thought that this girl, so dear to him, so irrepressibly charming, so life-possessed, might fall into the hands of some railway magnate, some faded sophisticate or roué, awakened all of Henry's fierce pity.

As the irresponsible days went one by one, he felt more and more conscious of the nearness of their parting. How could this go on? Life gave him something, and snatched it away again. Life was like that. Excessive joy and excessive sadness marked these days for him, and also showed the inevitable tokens of the uncomfortable knowledge of penultimate days.

He was long to remember one of the last conversations he held with her. She had begun:

"Human beings are so unhappy! It's because they've lost paradise, and the memory torments them!"

"I thought they were looking forward to it!" he made the teasing rejoinder.

"No, no! I mean the paradise on earth, the one they had had and lost! In a vague way they're conscious of their loss, and they're searching, seeking. . . . They are so unhappy!"

He was astonished to hear such words from her. Under her masking joy he had not suspected her depth. But she was not speaking with her mind. She appeared half somnolent, somewhere in a remote world of dream. She went on:

"Not that they know what they've lost! They don't! But they're so distraught and distressed, and they're always looking for happiness, which seems to elude them. . . . And to have happiness is so easy, yet so hard! They snatch at a little happiness here and there, but mostly they meet with misery. . . ."

"Don't think of these things!" he said, softly, taking her hands and fondling them.

But she went on, as if she did not hear him: "Someone once told me about some island which disappeared under the sea. But though the island has disappeared, every year migratory birds journey hundreds of miles to get to it, and when they come there they circle round and round over the waters where the island had been, until some of them drop from sheer fatigue into the waves, while others fly back to where they had come from. . . . And human beings, seeking happiness, seem to me like those birds. . . ."

These words made a deep impression on him.

The break came sooner than they had expected, and in a fashion humiliating to them both.

They were reposing in the grass. She was sitting up, and his head was in his lap. She was fondling his hair, and he sometimes caught at her fingers and kissed them. Sometimes, he held them, and cried, "I shall never let you go!" while she, bending low, murmured on his ear, "My darling, I love you! How I love you!" His body was aflame with the nearness of her, and a thought, like a wounded bird, struggled within him. How might he keep her? How might he run away with her?

The sun was on the descendant curve, almost hidden behind the pine-clad summits. A soft and ever softening glow warmed the narcissi, endowed them with strange, magical, flame-like tints. A sense of evanescent life possessed the lovers, filled them with the sadness of dying things.

Come what may, thought Henry, flaming with desire of happiness for them both. Convulsively, with flaming fingers, he clutched at her shoulders, drawing her down. Her long hair, loosened, fell, enveloping his face. Its aromas, assailing his nostrils, seemed to enter his body, filling him, in a subtle way, with the essence of her. . . .

Oh, God! Great God! They both started up, suddenly, their blood stilled by the sound of a voice. It was a woman's, pitched in shrill anger, threatening.

"So this is where you are, you miserable hussy!" cried the voice in French, while the embarrassed lovers sprang to their feet.

Ilyana hastily made efforts to straighten out her skirts, which done, she cast her eyes on the ground, and remained standing, motionless, numb.

"Who's the wretched boy with whom you've been carrying on?"

The woman, who was beyond middle age, tall, lean, sharp, with a thinnish beak-like nose, which barely separated her at-this-instant malignant eyes, fixed a glare on poor Henry. She appeared to him like some terrible carnivorous bird, a vulture; but he proudly stood his ground, returning her glare with a dignified still gaze, which at last made her avert her eyes. As Ilyana was still silent, he quietly volunteered a statement, though he was aware how hopeless it all was.

"Madame, I am not a wretched boy. I am a gentleman, and the son of a gentleman. Your niece is not to blame for anything. It's been my fault entirely. I spoke to her first. I pursued her. I'm in love with her! I'm ready to marry her!"

She gave Henry a withering look. "Nice sort of gentleman, aren't you, to pursue a girl betrothed to another!"

"She doesn't love him!" Henry suggested, breathing hard.

"Doesn't love him?" the woman shouted. "Demetrius is worth a dozen of you, and he'd know how to handle you if he were here!"

"Perhaps, madame," he said more quietly. "I am not disputing it. I'm only suggesting that your niece is not in love with him. It is cruel to force a girl to marry a man she doesn't love!"

"You're a nice one to talk!" she turned fiercely on Henry. "You who have tried to seduce a defenceless girl! How long has this been going on! . . ." As she received no answer, she suddenly glanced with suspicion at the pair, and, shaking the girl, blurted out: "Nothing has happened yet? . . . Tell me!"

A well of tears gushed from the girl's eyes.

"Let me reassure you, madame, nothing has happened which shouldn't happen! I told you I was an English gentleman!" He stood there helplessly, longing to take the girl in his arms and kiss away her tears. How terrible it was to feel so helpless, so impotent. And he had brought all this on poor Ilyana's head. He felt the need of doing something drastic to soften the older woman's malignity. He had once offered to take a school-fellow's punishment. Could he not do something to take Ilyana's? "Madame," he said, softly, trying to appeal to the woman's pity. "I tell you it's been all my fault! Really! Please spare her! She's not to blame! Go to my father and tell him to punish me! Only please don't punish Ilyana!"

"I am to blame! I entirely! And I'm not ashamed of it!" suddenly burst from Ilyana. "I wanted him to speak to me! I smiled at him! I made him speak to me!"

"No! No! No!" protested Henry. "I . . . ."

"You shameless hussy!" the woman cried, incensed by the girl's passionate speech. "The more shame to you! Come! No more nonsense!" And she seized the girl forcibly by the hand, and dragged her away, giving no heed to the youth who, uttering protests, followed a little of the way. There was really nothing to be done.

He never saw Ilyana again, even though she managed, by means of a hotel servant, to smuggle a letter to him, washed by her tears. It was very brief:

"I must bear my cross, since such is my lot. But I shall never forget you, never. I love you and always shall. "Your poor Ilyana."

With the letter was enclosed a crushed flower.

Henry wept over the letter, and made efforts to see the girl, but soon thereafter discovered that Ilyana and her aunt had left for parts unknown. His father, knowing nothing of the matter and not realizing what was the matter with the boy, who had grown gloomy, set out with him on further travel.

And now, ten years later, Henry recalled the whole touching episode, which had come and gone like a dream, with extraordinary vividness. And it seemed to him that after a lapse of all these years, Ilyana—Ilyana grown up—had come back to him in the form of Elaine. With superstitious awe he ruminated on the fact that both Ilyana and Elaine in some way reminded him of his mother. The three women stood for perfection to him, and each represented to him that coordination, that balance in life, which seemed to be lacking in the life around him.

And was it not curious, he reflected, that their names should have such a likeness to one another?

"Olga—Ilyana—Elaine!"

He repeated these names to himself, formulating them into a rhythm, a rhythm of infinite meaning to him.

"Olga—Ilyana—Elaine!"

How proud, how lovely, this combination of names sounded! What meanings they conveyed to him!

Yet how terribly sad, how transitory, had been his early intimate experience. His mother he had scarcely known except for the portrait painted by Mr. Priestley, Ilyana had come and gone like a figment of extravagant fancy, vanished, as it were, into the thin air. As for Elaine, he had only just met her; would she, like Ilyana, slip from his grasp before he had tasted of beauty-begetting delights, of the perfect life he had been hitherto hopelessly seeking, like those birds seeking the blessed isle lost under ponderous waters? Overjoyed as he was, he was trembling with fear, lest the fates once again snatch the prize he had long sought and now found.

Last night he had cursed, this evening he blessed; and he looked forward to tomorrow with trepidation and joy.

CHAPTER ELEVEN

In Which An Old Dream Is Continued

HENRY and Elaine were comfortably ensconced in a corner seat in a little alcove in a tea-room off Piccadilly. They had the alcove to themselves, and they talked in pleasant low voices, charged with barely audible ecstasy. After last evening, they were shy, as lovers often are after first avowals.

They felt the need of being "properly acquainted." And so they began by talking commonplaces. Where did she live? Where did he live? Did he often come to London? Did she? What sort of books did she like? What sort of books did he like? They marvelled when their tastes coincided, as when they found that they both loved Shelley and were terribly fond of Browning. Wasn't it wonderful that they should like the same things! And they really did like the same things. Travel? Of course, she loved it, though except for her journey to India and back she had never been anywhere to speak of. How fortunate he was to have seen so much of the Continent! She envied him. How she would love to go to Italy! It had been the dream of her life. Why didn't she go? She had thought of it often, but always something prevented her. And it wasn't the sort of thing a woman did alone. He agreed. There were obstacles if a woman was young and handsome as she was. She ought to go with someone, he obliquely hinted and smiled significantly. On the other hand, he jocularly added, it must be a terrible hindrance to a man to be travelling with a living work of art, for it undoubtedly hindered him from doing justice to the masterpieces in the galleries. Whereupon, pleased, she said he was a terrible tease, which he admitted, adding the extenuating circumstance that one teased only those one liked. They went on chattering in circumlocutions, indulging in generalities obviously intended to have a personal application. They were, indeed, in their simplest statement, violently lovemaking. This method of indirect allusion was deliciously pleasant to both of them. There was a hide-and-seek air about it; perhaps, the sense of the chase. They alternately ran from and after one another. They came to the subject of dreams.

"Yes, I often dream," she said, in answer to his question. "And sometimes it is the same dream. Curious, isn't it, that a dream should repeat itself?"

"Yes, it is odd. Though I've heard of such cases before. But do tell me your dream!"

"I don't mind. Perhaps, you'll interpret it!"

"I can try!"

"I dreamt," she began, "that I was walking in a curious maze of narrow streets, with rows of little grey houses on both sides. The houses were all close-shuttered, and there seemed not a sign of life in any of them. I had a feeling that there were corpses lying in them, and that at any moment anything might happen. The narrow street was winding, and here and there was a blind alley, with just the same sort of houses, and no matter how often I tried, I could not find my way out. The sky was at first grey and loury. Then it changed, became more forbidding. There was a faint light, as the light of an unseen moon, hidden behind clouds. This light grew dimmer and dimmer, and the shuttered houses on both sides looked terrible, uncanny, full of ghosts and secrets, as it were. It was perfectly ghastly. How to get out, was my one thought. I ran this way and that. And no matter which side turning I took, I always found myself back in the same street. I wanted to cry for help, but my lips refused to utter a syllable. I felt as though a terrible calamity were impending, as though the doors and the shutters would suddenly fling open and an army of ghosts and monsters would issue forth. . . . I was on the point of swooning. . . . Just then, the sky suddenly became a bright suffused red as of a gorgeous sunset, and I was filled with a sudden overwhelming joy, almost too great to bear. . . . I felt as if I would burst with it. . . . Then, I awoke both shuddering and happy. . . . Now, Joseph, explain my dream!" she concluded, laughing.

"It's your romantic temperament," Henry smiled. "That maze, those narrow winding streets, those dark shuttered houses—full of corpses and ghosts, those blind alleys which offered no escape—all that is life, life as you and I see it, or rather feel it. You go through a whole gamut of emotions awakened by this life. And at every step, you meet with despair. But the red sky all ablaze like a marvellous sunset is the hope of relief, the hope of a life you wish to have and find unattainable. It is your heart's desire, and the mere hope of it fills you with joy!"

"You're a facile interpreter," said Elaine, with a pleased smile. "Joseph himself couldn't have done better! ... And what do you dream?"

He laughed. "As it happens, I had a dream last night. Not so long after I left you."

"I hope it was a nice one!"

"I don't know that I ought to!"

"But you must! It isn't fair. I told you mine!"

"I won't tell you this one," he teased her. "I'll tell you another!"

"No, no! I must hear last night's dream. It will interest me most, I'm sure."

"Very well. But it's really too. . . ."

"No excuses," she interrupted him. "I want that one!"

"Anyhow, it was a short one. I dreamt I was patting a tiger. I . . ."

Elaine burst out laughing. "A nice thing to dream about after meeting me!"

"There, I told you!"

"Go ahead! You were patting a tiger. . . ."

"Yes . . . I was patting a tiger. And I went on and on patting it. And I had the terrible feeling that I daren't stop patting it. If I stopped, the tiger would turn on me and kill me. . . ." He paused, and looked at her roguishly.

"Well? What happened?" she asked with amused impatience.

"Nothing. I went on patting it. I patted it until my arms began to ache. And that woke me. I don't know what would have happened, if it didn't!"

"What an absurd dream!" she said, laughing. "It doesn't sound auspicious. Except they do say, dreams go by contraries."

Her observation, with all its tacit significance, gave him courage, inspired him to attack the present problem boldly.

"Elaine," he said, taking her hand, and pressing it between his two. "We've been beating about the bush. If I lived to know you a thousand years, I shouldn't know you any better than I know you now."

"Don't flatter yourself, Henry!" she warned him, with a caress in her voice. "Remember the tiger of your dream!"

"I'm willing to take the chance! Better a tiger than a dray horse!"

"Thank you!"

"I trust my feelings. And there's something natural and spontaneous about my feeling for you. . . ."

"I shall demand eternal patting!"

"I would not have you demand less!"

"I am serious!"

"So am I! . . . But as I was saying, I hadn't the least doubt from the moment I laid my eyes on you."

"You've loved women before."

"True. But always with a reservation. Not quite sure of myself or of them. Never fully confident that my feelings wouldn't change!"

"You're an egoist! You speak of your feelings. What about the woman's feelings? They might change, you know!"

"They might, but they haven't yet," he said with a simple assurance that impressed her.

"You think well of yourself," she teased him.

"No. But I don't always think well of women. I'm a woman-hater of sorts!"

"You a woman-hater?" There was genuine incredulity in her voice.

"Why not? The majority of women are so apt to disappoint one!"

"I wouldn't deal with the majority of them," she said double-edgedly.

"You're right there!" he said, amused at her clever rejoinder. "But having a wide experience has its advantages."

"How, pray?"

"It enables one to recognize the real thing when one meets it! Only once before in my life have I experienced feelings similar to those I am experiencing now. But I was very young then. . . ."

"Do tell me about it!"

And he told her the story of his meeting with Ilyana. She listened, fascinated, and when he finished his narrative, he said:

"That was the one idyl of my life. It was my one and only experience unspoiled by any doubts, by caution or by second thoughts. We lived for a while in a world uncorrupted by commerce, in a kind of paradise on earth. And to this day I feel like one of those birds she had spoken of, circling round and round a water spot, seeking the happy isle one feels should be there. . . . It was thus until I met you, my dear!"

"You loved this Ilyana very much?"

"I've never quite forgotten her. In this dark world she's always reminded one of something which everyone forgets; that the first object of life is happiness, or should be!"

"I am jealous of this Ilyana," said Elaine, making a wry face.

"Elaine should not be jealous of Ilyana!"

"Perhaps not!" She laughed. "I could skip as nimbly as any girl with such a handsome boy as Ilyana had fallen upon!"

"I'm afraid the spectacle of you and me skipping in Piccadilly Circus or down the Strand would provide a public sensation, if not actually land us in Hanwell!"

"That's because we should not be attuned to the setting," she observed.

"Perhaps. All the same, I have an idea it's the setting, not we, that would be all wrong!"

"I think I know what you mean," she said.

"I mean," he explained, with some warmth, "that it is hard to have inner harmony when there's so much outer discord. A drab street or drab surroundings set all my feelings in revolt!"

"I sometimes want to do the maddest things!" she said, finding his mood in sympathy with her own; then added: "Only the opinion of the world prevents me from putting them into effect!"

"You mean," he corrected her, "you are possessed of the sanest feelings, and only the madness of the world prevents you from acting on them! For who's mad, we or the world?"

His voice, until now pitched low, rose at his own question. It was clear that the matter was very near his heart.

"It's a vital question," he went on, with some warmth, "and needs answering. And who's more capable of answering it? The man who worships mammon, or he who worships God? The shopkeeper, or the authentic priest? The material man, or the man to whom material possessions don't matter? And, finally, the scientist, or the artist?"

"I suppose," said Elaine, "that depends on how we define life. Life means something different to different people!"

"Precisely. And that's where the root of the trouble lies. For the shoemaker, all humanity, like the old woman, lives in a shoe! But life's neither a shoe, nor a loaf of bread!"

"Science . . ." she began.

But he interrupted her. "Oh, yes! There's biology! It's discovered man to be a superior brand of monkey. But another branch of science has discovered space, so there's nothing for the monkey to do but to jump off!"

"What do you mean?" she asked, laughing.

"Just what I say. What respect has a human being left for himself, now that he's no longer the image of his Creator? As long as he thought that, he was a bit of God on his own! But now he must be feeling small fry indeed! But man has a long memory. Can he go on living, remembering as he does that he had once been a half-god? Science talks of widening man's horizons. But there's no pleasure standing on the edge of an abyss, and to feel that at any moment it may swallow you! Yes, science has taken the ground from under our feet, and it has destroyed authority, and there's nothing any longer that man may cling to!"

"But why should man cling to anything?"

"Because, if he doesn't, he's lost, utterly lost! He becomes like a fragment detached from its sphere and, without rhyme or reason, goes hurtling through space!"

"That sounds exciting! How thrilled he must be!"

"It's exciting enough, I grant you! But for how long? What when he finds the velocity increasing, and that he can't stop! For it's a terrible thing to find out that you've no control over movement, that you're moved without a say in the matter!"

"But surely," she argued, "you have no say in the matter where authority exists either!"

"No, that is a mistaken notion. Authority merely limits movement by creating order in the existing universe, so that the things that move do so in relation to one another.

There's a difference between anarchic movement and movement in an orderly system! This is possible in a small world, such as the Greeks acclaimed. Perfection is possible in a small space. That's why the Greeks were so perfect a people; at least, as perfect as the world allows. They went further than limit their space. They limited their time too! They had no memory—and therefore no mind for recording history. Memory is a pest, because it's the source of regret and remorse! And the future is an illusion. But the present is ever with us, and the Greeks tried to make the most of the present. And so out of their limitations they were able to work for coordination, balance, perfection! They could encompass the conception of their world—a world of beauty, intelligence and emotion—in a small block of marble! They had the genius of synthesis! A Greek could be a soldier, a poet and an athlete, all in one! And there was no excess in any direction at the expense of harmony!"

"I see. . . ." she said, beginning to grasp the meaning of his words.

"But we deal only in fragments!" he went on, with warmth. "We analyze, we study life under a microscope. Every man sees only the fragment that immediately concerns him. And if he sees more, he sees a vast chaos, with a million fragments flying through space. How can he hope to make order out of it, to create any sort of harmony? Yes, there's but one thing left for him to do: to jump off into the space he's envisaged!"

"Are you, then, against science?"

"Yes—and no! I believe in science only to the extent of seeing it as a part of life, and not the whole. If we allow science to control us, it will destroy us like any poison does, taken in its purity; though as an ingredient in a medical prescription it may prove to be a very efficacious thing!"

"Do you consider yourself a balanced man in the sense you mean?" she asked, with some curiosity; fascinated and impressed by the conviction and passion with which he spoke, and mentally comparing him with the prosaic Phil.

"No," he said, with decision. "I might have been a balanced man in a balanced age. But in an age like ours, I am forced to kick against the pricks of life. I am one of life's rebels, a follower of a lost cause! And, most of all, I'm a rebel against the growing arrogance of science, which has destroyed God, and will end by driving men to commit murder and self-murder. . . .

"I am drawn to you," he added more softly, "because I think I see in you a being who, perhaps without knowing it, belongs to another order of things. You want to live life fully and abundantly, but, as in your dream, you are struggling through a maze of streets with shuttered houses full of corpses and ghosts, and your valiant efforts, like my own, seem to end in blind alleys from which there's no egress. . . ."

"That is true," she confessed. "But do go on! I love to hear you speak!"

"It was Blake," he said, thus encouraged, "who said, 'Art the Tree of Life. Science the Tree of Death.' That is a profound statement!"

He paused, but he saw that she was waiting for an explanation.

"It's clear enough," he went on. "Science decomposes life, sees life in multitudinous fragments; as one sees cheese under a microscope! Art synthesizes life, pulls it together, makes an effort to see some unity and pattern in it! But perhaps the time is coming when science, increasing in scope and power, will conquer art, which also will make its function the study of fragments of life. Unless I am mistaken, it's already beginning to do so. When Science, which was once the handmaiden of art, becomes fully Art's master, then good-bye to completeness, abundance, good-bye to beauty, perfection! God! The prospect terrifies me!"

She laughed. "You see things darkly. But you are making the Bible clear to me!"

He looked astonished. "How? What do you mean?"

"You're illustrating to me," she explained, "the story of Adam and Eve in the garden of Eden. They apparently were tolerably happy until they plucked the apple from the Tree of Knowledge!"

"That is so!" he exclaimed, delighted. "Intelligence was the most fatal gift God has given to men! Yet I would not have it away! What a pity they hadn't tasted of the fruit of the other tree first! They probably hadn't the intelligence!" He laughed at his own jest, then went on: "Intelligence is good. Its abuse is what I'm rebelling against. Who can tell? If man uses it rightly, he might regain Paradise! Is not earth a potential paradise?"

"Yes, and a potential hell, too!" Elaine laughed.

"That is so," he agreed. "A potential hell, too! And man chooses to make it the latter. Man is a dual nature. Leonardo da Vinci is the best illustration of this. In him both science and art found an abiding place. He was, if you like, the meeting place of the parallel movements of the Renaissance, which contained the germs of the modern world. Only since then has the world lost its balance, so perfect in him, and developed one side at the expense of the other. It's been watering the tree of knowledge and quite forgotten the tree of life! . . ." Henry paused, and, suddenly, without any ostensible reason, and to the astonishment of his companion, broke into an irrepressible guffaw, which, subsiding, left him giving vent to a series of chuckles, like a series of narrowing ripples on the surface of water.

"What's up? What's the joke? Don't keep it to yourself! I want to know." She urged him to speak, to explain, and again she thought: "What a strange fascinating man!" How different from the men she had known! How different from Phil! "Come, tell me," she said, tugging at his sleeve.

"Forgive me," he spoke at last, and again took her hand between his two. "I am a queer sort of lover! You surely have the right to think me odd. I've started to tell you something important, and here I've gone off on a rampage! It's not science and philosophy I want to talk to you about. I had not planned anything of the sort for today. Indeed, I had intended to devote myself wholly to the more pleasant function of whispering sweet nothings in your charming ear! You have a charming ear, you know. And it deserves to have charming things poured into it, not learned dissertations and dry-as-dust sermons. Songs and words sweet as honey and all sorts of lovely music should be poured into your precious little ears, oh, charming syren!"

"You were discoursing so charmingly!" she said, with mock pretense of not liking his new mood. "What's come over you, my dear man?"

"My dear woman," he gently mocked her, in his turn.

"Don't you realize that as a man of intelligence I am fully aware of the fact that I've discovered a treasure? Am I such a fool as to doubt—and, doubting, procrastinate? Shall I, like a vain peacock, go on spreading my marvellous tail, and strut about this way and that, exhibiting my wonderful accomplishments, to awaken the admiration of an observing female?"

"Fool!" she cried, good-naturedly enough, captivated by his gay nonsensical mood, as previously by his learned mood. "And I took you for such a serious person. I never suspected of finding such a fool and a tease!"

"The worse is yet to come, my dear," he went on, oblivious of her strictures. "If I am a fool, Elaine,"—his manner became somewhat more earnest then before—"then I intend to make the most of my folly. "I began to define life, and never finished my definition. Well, what's life but a preparation for death? Let us not burden ourselves with wasted years, as some people burden themselves with quite useless possessions, which they can't take into the next world with them! Elaine! Why waste time, the precious moments of life? Don't be startled! But will you marry me—now—at once?"

CHAPTER TWELVE

An Astounding Proposal

RAPTURE filled Elaine's heart, as she listened to her lover's words. His quickness of decision, his impetuosity, appealed to her, overwhelmed her. Everything, to this last touch, had seemed perfect in her eyes. Her life, when it was not filled with grief or pain or torment, appeared empty; except for isles of illusion, she could not remember it otherwise; and here was one, at last, who by some personal enchantment, promised to fill the vacuous cup of life to the brim and overflowing.

Although she had no reason to be surprised by his words, they actually came upon her ear like a thunder-clap. She reeled a little under them, and closed her eyes. "Don't be afraid," she smiled, opening them and seeing a look of distress in his. "I'm not going to faint!"

She pulled herself together and made some effort to act with restraint. In token of this, she took her hand from between his two, and put it on his arm.

"Listen to me," she said, in a half earnest half playful tone of warning. "You ought to know the whole truth about me before you embark upon such an undertaking as marrying me. I'm a terrible woman, you know. . . ."

"I know all about that," he cut her short, with a laugh. "You've killed two husbands! That's what you were going to tell me! I don't care if you've killed a dozen! And haven't I injured any number of potential wives? We are quits, you see. And I don't intend being killed by you, but brought back to life! After these years of wandering in a desert, you're living water to me, my dear."

"Listen to me," she repeated. "Neither you nor I are what you'd call the marrying sort. I'm afraid if I consent to marry you, you'll feel sorry afterward!"

"You run the same risk!"

"Perhaps. I'd hate to hurt you. You're rather sensitive, and if things don't go right between us, you'll feel hurt!"

"There's only one thing that can hurt me," he rejoined, "and that's being thwarted by the woman I love. And there can be no thwarting where both parties are really in love and are as frank and honest with each other as you and I appear to be. You can see for yourself. I've hidden nothing from you! One may tell things to you. You are the first woman I've met of whom this may be said. Explanation? I have none. I just feel. I follow my impulse, my intuition. Isn't that enough? I trust you entirely. And I don't want particularly to hear your story!"

"You're generous not to question my past," she said, giving him an appreciative glance. "But I want to tell you, and I must tell you! I don't want anything held against me later. Not that you will! Anyhow," she smiled, "I feel in a confessional mood, and, henceforth, I appoint you my father confessor."

"Fire away, then, if you must!" And he leaned comfortably back, to listen.

"As I told you," she began, "I came of Cornish people. My father and mother died early, and I don't remember them. At their death, my aunt became my guardian, and took charge of my education. She was well-intentioned enough in her way, but she was an Evangelical person, very staid and strict and strait-laced. I was a lively, mischievous little girl, and I dare say quite a handful for the old lady. She used to lecture me a lot about morals and that sort of thing, but I think I took an especial delight in disobeying her. I showed a precocious interest in boys and got into a number of scrapes; and, at last, on the advice of friends and against her own principles and inclinations, she put me into a French convent to teach me French and make a proper lady of me. I stayed at the convent for some years, and, indeed, I liked it so well that to the chagrin of my aunt I seriously thought of becoming a nun and devoting myself to God. She took me out. I was eighteen then and as proper and well-behaved young lady as anyone could desire. I was absolutely without any experience, and was as pure and as innocent as a lily, as aunt would have said. And I was regarded as quite handsome.

"My aunt rigged me out in pretty clothes, and took me to London, and, as it were, launched me into society. I became strangely popular at once, and young men of means appeared to be greatly attracted to me, and paid me a great deal of attention. I rather liked the attention, but did not much like the young men, and, to the chagrin of my aunt, rejected more than one advantageous offer.

"There was one older man, a Mr. Handby—he was thirty-seven or thereabouts—who was greatly devoted to me. He had an office in the city and lots of money, a house in London, a cottage in the country and a villa in Florence. He was considered a particularly desirable match. He was very urbane, and attentive, and had all the manners of a gentleman, and while I was fond of him, I was not exactly in love with him. But the villa in Florence was a great temptation to me. I had always wanted to go to Italy, and the idea of a Florentine villa appealed to my imagination. This, together with the urgings of my aunt and her friends, who painted my future as Mrs. Handby in the most glowing colours, finally caused me to succumb.

"I was married in church before a multitude of envious friends and acquaintances. The wedding was a lavish affair, indeed quite regal, and the gifts filled the large reception room. The honeymoon was planned on an equally lavish scale, and by my wish it was to be spent in our Florentine villa. The thought that I was at last to behold my beloved Italy, Rafael's Madonnas and Giotto's tower, which I had seen only in pictures, quite excited me, and I temporarily forgot that I had to go through the closest intimacy with a man for whom I did not particularly care.

"As my husband's London house was closed, we were to have spent our marriage night in a London hotel, prior to our departure on the morrow for the land I had so longed to see. Forgive my speaking of it, but I often wonder if men ever have an idea of what young romantic girls have to go through with on their marriage night with a man who, to all intents and purposes, is a perfect stranger to them! Mr. Handby, as I learned only later, had had quite an experience with women, which, in a bachelor is generally winked at in society, and is even considered a virtue. As for the girl, she's expected to come ignorant to a man, and this too is regarded as a virtue. She's expected to come spotlessly clean to the man who confers the privilege of making her his wife."

Henry nodded sympathetically. "More marriages are

wrecked on the marriage night than at any other time," he said.

"So it was with me," Elaine went on. "I'll not go into detail of the shame a girl experiences while she sheds her finery and her new owner stands there regarding her appraisingly, and contemplating with relish the dish about to be served to him. It's different, perhaps, when people really love one another, and the shame they experience in common is a joy and delight. But what was I to this man who stood there regarding me with hungry, lustful eyes, eager and impatient to wreak his lust upon me?

"Once alone in the room with him, I experienced the most intense shame and humiliation, which made me forget Italy, Raphael's Madonnas, Giotto's tower; I no longer looked forward to living in a Florentine villa. And the man I married appeared different from the man I had formerly known. Where was the quiet urbane gentleman who plied me with tender attentions, with all those great and petty devotions a man shows a woman before marriage, before he is sure of the ultimate possession of her? All that vanished, as if it had never been. I felt myself blushing furiously, I wanted to cry, to run, anywhere, anywhere, only as soon as possible out of the presence of the hungry beast impatiently waiting to devour me!

"Then I thought: I had made a contract with this man. I suppose I must go through with it. I submitted to him. He possessed me, not with the romantic seductiveness which a sensitive romantic girl has been educated to expect from a man, but with the brute hunger of a man about to attack a steak and kidney pudding! . . ."

Henry, astonished at this plain speaking, laughed at the descriptiveness of her last phrase.

She, momentarily joining in his laughter, then resumed. "That sounds rather strong, I know. But it's no exaggeration. I was to that man only another kind of steak and kidney pudding! But my whole education had prepared me for seduction, not rape! Forgive this plain speaking. . . ."

"I like plain speaking. We shall get on!"

"To me it was an intolerable torment. I experienced no sensation whatsoever short of disgust! Was the man so dense that he could not see that I was suffering, or was it that, seeing, he did not care? I was on the verge of hysterics. . . . At last, I could stand it no longer. I sprang in fury from my marriage bed, and hurriedly began to put my things on. . . .

"Only then, for the first time, did the man awake to the realization that something was wrong. He actually asked for an explanation, wanted to know if I thought it a decent thing to leave a man on his wedding night. In anger I replied that, in the circumstances, I thought it an indecent thing to stay with him. . . . 'What d'you mean?' he asked. 'If you don't know yourself, I shan't tell you!' I replied."

"He had no imagination," said Henry.

"He had a very nasty one," Elaine corrected him. "Seeing that one tack failed, he tried another. He put his hands on me, and ordered me, as his chattel, to desist from my foolish course. That made me only the more furious. I'm a little spitfire when aroused. So beware!" She held up a warning finger, and laughed. "Well, I stamped my feet, and asked him how he dare put hands on me. 'You are my wife,' he said. 'If you don't take your hands from me, I'll scream,' said I. I was quite in earnest, too. I really meant to scream.

"Seeing I was serious, he first tried to argue, then to plead. He got down on his knees to me, said if I left him his life would be ruined, and he would not be able to show his face again for shame. I retorted that apparently he didn't care if he ruined mine, and that I too, if for different reasons, would never again be able to show my face again without shame.

"He kissed my feet, wept bitter tears, but though I was beginning to feel sorry for him, his contrition now aroused my disgust as much as his brute arrogance had before. I thought him a coward. I was angry, and merciless. I felt myself deceived, outraged! And I was so young, and so inexperienced! I went on dressing; then, packing a small bag, I left him. . . ."

"You appear to have begun where Nora, in 'The Doll's House,' ended," interjected Henry.

"I've read the play, and frankly I don't see why Nora hadn't discovered her husband earlier. . . . Well, perhaps if I weren't so young and so inexperienced I should have left him in a different fashion. But I was so furious, so incensed, after my romantic dreams, at the trick the fates played me, that I saw nothing, except that I must get away! I scarcely thought that he would take his life. . . .

"Anyhow," she concluded, defensively, "I never heard the last of it. Everyone was ready to blame me. I've been even called a murderess!"

"It's the way of the world. If I were you, I shouldn't lose any sleep over it!"

"It has made me rather wary, though! And because I am, people have come to regard me as something of a man-hater!"

"That sounds auspicious," Henry laughed, "all the more,

as I have an equally valid reputation as a woman-hater. Only what does it mean, being a man-hater or a woman-hater? Nothing more than that one loves the opposite sex so well that one can't stand the idea of being let down by man or woman, especially as one has already been let down once or twice, as you have!"

"That's true. . . . But I was going to tell you about my second matrimonial venture. Hopkinson was a very decent man. I really feel terribly guilty about him. I've really killed him, you know. . . ."

"Most people kill themselves. . . ."

"Yes, I know. Let us say then that I've caused him to kill himself. It doesn't alter matters very much. The poor good man is dead, and if it weren't for me, he would be alive today!"

"Who knows?" mused Henry. "Men have their appointed hour in which to die. They kill themselves because they belong to a temperament which, at a fatal hour, sees life as an impossible thing. Sooner or later, such a man will do it!"

"I see you'll not give me one little bit of credit!" She gave an odd laugh, the significance of which he could not quite fathom.

"I have no doubt," he said, with a smile, "that your charms could slay a regiment of men!"

"Please don't!" she said. "You've touched a weak spot. Men pay their devoted attentions to me, and out of sheer boredom of life, I encourage them—just a little—less here, more there—according to circumstance and the man. Afterwards, when they prostrate themselves before me, I both pity them and gloat over them in my power. I'm a wicked, a terribly wicked woman. And you're the first man to whom I could say it, without suffering reproach!"

"Yes," he admitted, "boredom is responsible for many unpleasant things in this life. Many a crime is committed in its name!"

"The trouble was that even though I liked Hopkinson a great deal, there was also a great deal about him I did not like. The first things I look for in a man are that he should be strong and handsome and have some sort of spark. Then I look for intelligence, understanding, decisiveness, energy. I expect him to read good books and to talk well. In short," she laughed, "I expect a paragon, with all the virtues in one person. But what actually happens in life? One man is an Apollo, but a fool. Another is a sage, but physically an impossible gargoyle. A third is a Napoleon of energy, whose one interest in life is to conquer as many armies of other people's shekels as he can. . . . And so it goes. If one could only unite the best bits of different men and make one real man! Oh, dear, I want so much!"

Henry burst into a guffaw. "You are but explaining," he said, "the polygamous instinct in man!"

"How, pray?"

"He finds a different virtue in every woman, just as you find a different virtue in every man! . . .

> ". . . for several virtues
> Have I liked several women; never any
> With so full soul, but some defect in her
> Did quarrel with noblest grace she owed,
> And put it the foil: but you, O you,
> So perfect and so peerless, are created
> Of every creature's best!"

"How beautiful! And it hits the nail on the head, doesn't it?"

"Well, I for one have at last found a woman after my own heart!" He laughed, and added: "At last I can satisfy all my polygamous instincts!"

"How dreadful!" she rejoined, good-humouredly. "But I was telling you about Jerome. I was really fond of him, you know. I was returning from India, where I had spent three months with friends. It was the third day out that he first spoke to me. I had marked him from the first, and observed how handsome and lithe he was, and how much he was pursued by women, though the dears got but little encouragement from him. I must confess that his popularity with my sex and his indifference to them had something to do with awakening my curiosity in him. Also, some feminine, you would call it diabolical, instinct stirred a desire in me to make a conquest of him, all the more because the others were not having much luck. I was determined, too, not to make the first overture. At last, as I suspected he would, he noticed me. It was at a dance. Well, you know how quickly people get acquainted on boats. Before the evening was over, he was simply madly in love with me. . . ."

"Perfectly natural, too!"

"Never mind compliments! . . . Well, I really did like him a great deal. An infatuation, I suppose, it was. Wary with other women, he let himself go with me, without aforethought of any kind. It was that I liked about him. He was so disarming, like a big boy just out of school, or like some big playful dog, entirely trusting, with not a shadow of a suspicion of the unworthiness of his mistress. This was all the more strange because he was, on the whole, very suspicious of my sex—though, perhaps, you really beat him in this respect. He was, really, a simple mind, intelligent in his way. I think I must have been in love with him at the time, though I was to realize later that I loved him as any woman would an exuberant child.

"Anyhow, long before the voyage was at an end, he proposed, and I accepted. We were married by special license soon after we got to England. Never did I have a more attentive lover. I had but to utter a word to have him scurrying off to carry out my wish. Nothing was too great or too small for him to do. I used to tease him by suddenly expressing a wish for something quite impossible, and such a sad look would come into his face because the thing was beyond him, and I would have the greatest difficulty in convincing him that it had all been a joke. It eventually got to such a state that I actually began to be afraid to utter any wish at all!

"His goodness, it's a bitter thing to confess, began to pall on me after a bit. For one thing, it was not what I expected of a lover. Then, you see, it made me feel so wicked, and in the wrong. I could have stood a beating better. I was constantly smitten in conscience by doing this or that, which I knew could not have met with his approval, though he never uttered a word of reproach. But underneath it all, I felt his unspoken censure, and he couldn't understand why I was driven to show my temper, which however didn't help matters any.

"We got into a vicious circle, and, as you may guess, things went from bad to worse. It was perfectly dreadful! He took things very much to heart. He was like a man always afraid of something. Often afterwards I wondered how so good a man could have escaped being netted by a woman before he met me, and I arrived at the conclusion that he was instinctively afraid of them. Why, you will ask, he wasn't afraid to marry me? Well, for one thing, he was genuinely in love with me, and his passion disarmed him.

"Anyhow, to make the story short, this is how things happened. He thought I was cross because I was in need of a holiday; and I thought a holiday would do *him* good! So one fine day in June we went to Cornwall. The weather was simply lovely. There was the sea, and the sun, and the magnificent cliffs. For a day or two matters went well, and I thought we were really on the way to recapturing something of the rapture of our first meeting.

"Then for a day or two I did not feel quite myself. And Jerome, apparently thinking he was in some way responsible, began to fret again, accusing himself of causing my unhappiness. I assured him I was quite happy, but would cease to be if he went on fretting. But no, he insisted that he was making me unhappy, and getting out of temper for the way he tormented himself and me, I retorted that he was quite right and that he really made me dreadfully unhappy. And, of course, by now I was. For the next two or three days he lapsed into gloom and, goaded on by something I could not understand, I tried to rouse his anger by all manner of irritating and, if you like, unjust remarks. I got to the point where I felt that anger was better for us both than this continued unrelieved gloom, which was slowly killing him and me. An outburst may be followed by a reconciliation, but this sort of thing went on forever. I thought, if he'd only do something mean to me, if he'd only scold me, tell me what a horrid person I was, I could stand it better than this injured silence! It was as if a heavy thunder cloud hung over our heads, and one longed for the cloud to burst to break the tension and bring relief. But my wicked remarks only drove him into a still heavier mood. I was dreadfully sorry for him, but my own mood was one of utter despair. And here was the sea and the sun to enjoy and the champagne-like air to draw into our nostrils! God, it was unendurable! . . . I felt like running away, I didn't care where. I was getting hysterical. And as I was on the verge of tears, I told him to get out of my sight !

"He said nothing, but giving me the saddest look I ever hope to see in a face again, he walked out of the house. All at once I felt sorry, and was seized with a most terrible foreboding. He scarcely left my presence than I ran out after him. I wanted to tell him that I was sorry. It suddenly occurred to me that he was but a big boy, a sulky child who perhaps needed different kind of management from the kind I had tried.

"I couldn't see him anywhere. I ran this way, and that, and I ran along the cliffs like one possessed, shouting his name. I returned to my hotel in great distress and flung myself on my bed. When he failed to appear for lunch, I was in a panic, and began to fear the worst. I couldn't eat, and again went out to search. After hours of fruitless search, I returned to the hotel once more, hoping against hope to find him there. Only one thought was in my head: how happy I should be if I found him at the hotel, safe and sound. But no! He wasn't there. And no one had seen him. I went to my room, and threw myself on my bed, where I lay in a state of coma.

"Then the terrible news came that he had been found

by fishermen at the foot of a cliff. There were visible
signs of the ground of the overhanging cliff having given
way, and this fact gave rise to the surmise that he had been
the victim of an accident. But I knew better. He had
quite deliberately, I thought, manufactured this bit of evi-
dence so as not to leave the least stain on me. He was good
to the last. Not that his goodness helped matters any as
far as gossip was concerned. I already had had one hus-
band-suicide to my credit, and people talked as if I in person
had pushed him off the cliff. . . . I suppose, in a way, I
had. . . . I was too much broken up at the time to care
one way or the other. . . ."

Elaine's voice faltered. Tiny tears appeared in her eyes.
But she made an effort to control herself, and succeeded so
far as to smile.

"So you see," she said, softly, "I've killed two husbands! . . ."

"Nonsense! You. . . ."

"And by the way," she interrupted him, "Jerome left
me six hundred a year—on condition that I don't marry
again! . . . I often wonder," she added, with a smile,
"if he made that condition to save me or some poor devil
of a man!"

"I see you take things in the right spirit," said Henry,
and his voice revealed his admiration.

"Are you still, in the face of it all, prepared to marry
such an ill-fated woman as myself? A moment!" she
cried, seeing him about to speak. "You know, I shan't
bear you a grudge if you withdraw your rash offer!"

"Far from it, my dear. What you've told only makes
me the more determined to marry you!"

"Listen to me, darling," she said, laying a hand on his

arm. "And don't be shocked at the proposal I have to make. . . . You know, rash man, I am strongly tempted to take you at your word. Of course, you know it! But my experience in the past has made me cautious—for the man, if not for myself. It gives me the right to act on a whim. Promise me, you'll not say No!"

"Tell me what it is!"

"No. You must first promise!"

"How am I to know it isn't to your disadvantage?"

"On the contrary. It is wholly to my advantage!"

"Shall I consider it in the same light?"

"Yes. That is, if you are sensible!"

"That sounds equivocal."

"Promise!"

"Very well. I promise. Under protest, mind you!"

"Never mind that. You've promised. That's the point. And I'll hold you to it!"

"You're a little tyrant!"

"Call me what you like. You've given your promise. And, as a gentleman, you may not go back on it!"

"Fire away!"

"Lately, as you may know, a new idea has been bruited in the world as a solution of the unhappy marriage problem. Please remember, I've been married twice!"

"Yes. . . ."

"Now this idea. . . ."

"You're not going to propose Meredith's Trial Marriage?"

"Yes. How quick you are to read one's thoughts! Why not give trial marriage a trial? . . . Well?"

She flung her question, and watched his face, which revealed an astonishment too great to insure a rapid answer.

"Well?" she repeated. "Well? . . ."

"What shall I say? You've exacted a promise from me, and I suppose I must abide by it. But before we proceed, let me point out the disadvantages to you of such an arrangement!"

"Let me be the judge of that!"

"Well, then, I agree. But only on one condition!"

"What is it?"

"First promise that you'll not say No!"

She reflected a while.

"Very well, I promise. I suppose it's only fair after I've held you to one!"

"Good. I want to insist that the length of the trial shall not exceed six months. That is to say, if we're still happy at the end of six months, we'll not wait another day to enter into holy bonds of matrimony!"

"I agree!"

"Excellent. You're a jewel. A finer one than I've even suspected. . . . Now one more thing remains to be settled. How are we to avoid a public scandal? You know what England is in this year of Our Lord!"

"I thought of that. There's France!"

"To be sure. Shall we start tomorrow?"

"At your service, my lord!"

"You're wonderful!"

Her answer was to put her hand trustfully in his. It was a token of her submission.

CHAPTER THIRTEEN

Trial Marriage

HENRY and Elaine took the night boat train and arrived in Paris the next morning.

Henry, who knew Paris well, ordered the cabby to drive to a little hotel in the Rue des Saints-Pères. He preferred the left bank not only because of its relative quiet and unpretentiousness but also because he felt more conscious of the Parisianness of Paris here; and of its streets he preferred those which ran into the embankment, facing the Louvre.

It was here that the city presented him with its most fascinating aspects. If you looked up and down the river, or across, you saw the grandeur, but the spot itself on which you stood was on the edge of the human intimacies which either repelled or endeared the place to you. There was the interminable line of bookstalls along the Seine, as it were—a series of ramparts erected from the brains of the ages, too often covered with dust, yet warning the superficial traveller having no respect for such things to keep to the other side of the river; you could not have a more eloquent boundary. All along this main cerebral artery and in its multitudinous byways, resembling convolutions, there were the little curio and print shops, and windows showing artists' materials in great profusion. And there were the numerous tiny cafés, crowding the narrow pavements, with students of all nations and native habitués sipping their coffee or *apéritif*. All this had a peculiar glamour for him remembered since his days at the Sorbonne years ago.

Only now, in addition to the attractions of the old city he adored above all other cities, there was a handsome woman at his side, moreover a woman he adored above all other women and who adored him above all other men. Surely, there was some truth in that "all the rest shall be added unto you." For he was handsome himself, and young, and well-to-do, and full of the ardours of a fresh passion, which promised to last through eternity. What more, indeed, could anyone want?

Even the weather was auspicious. They had left London in fog, and here was a November day as clear and as crisp as the most exacting lover could desire. From the open carriage crossing Pont Royal, they could see Notre Dame and Ile de la Cité bathed in sunlight as they might on a fine summer day. They had already caught the infectious gaiety of the place haunted by the merry ghosts of Rabelais and Molière resident in living men, and, holding hands, they laughed spontaneously and in the happiest possible way: that is, for no ostensible reason at all. . . . Merely to live, to breathe this salubrious air, to know that one loved and was loved, was reason enough. They were both in that peculiar state of exultancy in which the discovery that happiness was really possible was the supreme absurdity, awakening mirth. They accepted everything they saw, and loved and embraced it.

"Look!" cried Elaine at one time, pointing to a long-haired, immense-hatted figure, with a huge portfolio under the arm. "There goes an artist! I'm sure he's an artist! And just fancy—he might have come out of *Punch*!"

"Yes," Henry chided her. "We English are very exact and realistic. *Punch* never exaggerates! . . . Do you remember the Major at Lady Brinton's party? Mightn't he too have come out of Punch—I mean just as he was?"

They laughed at the recollection.

The sight of women emerging from boulangeries with loaves of bread a yard long under their arms especially moved them to laughter. And Henry made a droll jest about it.

"Only here one can understand why bread is called the staff of life. Why, one can readily use a loaf as a walking-stick!"

"You silly!" And she laughed immoderately.

The frequent exchange of caustic pleasantries between their cabby and other cabbies too precipitately crossing their path was the repeated source of considerable amusement. Indeed, everything was amusing, everything contributed to their hilarity.

At last they reached the Hotel Rabelais. A neat and pleasant Madame—Elaine thought her charming—greeted them and offered them a choice of rooms; also asked Henry to enter their names in the book; boldly, to his own joy and Elaine's, he inscribed, Mr. and Mrs. Henry Thorley, adding the word London after the name. Then, a good-natured maid conducted them to their rooms.

The Hotel Rabelais was a modest establishment, run chiefly for persons of moderate means. A foreigner but rarely set his foot within its doors, which circumstance insured real French cooking.

Henry gloated at their good fortune in securing the only suite of apartments the hotel contained. It was on the first floor, and included a large bed-room, sitting-room, and what was very rare in those days—a bath.

"How nice and comfortable!" exclaimed Elaine, and immediately, before the amazed scrutiny of Henry, with a woman's practicalness, felt the mattresses on the bed piled prodigiously high with bedding. "They are quite soft and comfy!" she said delightedly.

"Of course, they are!" retorted Henry. "Remember, we are in France, my dear. It's only in England the hotels still insist on giving you bags filled with cobblestones for your back. Yet we English are supposed to be the most comfort-seeking nation on earth!"

"The wall-paper, you must admit, is a trifle flowery!" she said, laughing, as she indicated the design of pink trellised roses running along the walls, with perching chubby cupids running into the ceiling at the four corners.

"Yes, and you're expected to live up to it! It's all meant to induce cheerfulness, which is every Frenchman's duty. Honeymoons are a specialty here, I should say!"

"Suppose they should find out we're not married!" said Elaine suddenly, turning a grave face towards him.

Henry kissed her and laughed. "My darling, such a discovery would fill them with elation. They take us English for sticks who do not know how to love. What do they care? Indeed, most of them regard with something like suspicion the lonely bachelor who never admits to the precincts of his habitation the brightening presence of the other sex. 'What!' I've heard them say, 'You mean he lives alone? What a nasty man!' . . . I am not sure," he went on, when Elaine ceased laughing at the drollness of his story, "that madame does not already suspect you of being a runaway wife enjoying the embraces of her clandestine lover! Or, perhaps me as some virago's husband escaped for a spell with an infatuated virgin!"

"She does?" Elaine incredulously asked, with a sudden show of shyness.

"Women like that are intuitive, and you and I are so happy today that we wear our hearts on our sleeves!"

"Mayn't we be a regular honeymoon couple?"

"Only we aren't, and I noticed madame looking thoughtfully at your left hand!"

"Oh!" Elaine laughed, casting a glance at her hand bereft of the golden ring of marital servitude. "But you are right. I have no ring there!"

"It was thoughtless of me. I must get you one—at once!"

"No! No! We shan't travel under false pretences. You may get me a ring, and I shall wear it because it's yours— but no wedding ring! Not until we're properly wed, my lord! I've had two before this, yet I've felt that I was wed in the sight of men, but not in the sight of heaven! It's going to be different now. No more deception of others or of myself! . . . You aren't sorry yet?" She looked with coy tenderness at him, and her gay laugh filled the room.

"Sorry? Oh, my dear! My dear!" He flung his arms around her, and fiercely hugged her to his heart. "I was never so happy, never so sure of myself! And you?"

In answer, she took his hand and kissed it. Then, abruptly, pulled him towards the door. "You silly! Here you stand and talk, while your wife before heaven feels hungry for breakfast at one of the cafés I've heard so much talk about!"

"Forgive me! I almost forgot that even those who love must eat! . . . But you must come back afterward, and have some sleep. You haven't had a wink last night!"

"Nor you! But I can't sleep. I am so happy, and so restless. After breakfast I want to see the sights. That is, if you are not too tired or sleepy yourself!"

"It's absurd to sleep, of course! Love murders sleep! . . . Thorley shall sleep no more!" he added with a mock melancholy gesture. "Come, darling! I feel like skipping!"

"Still harping on Ilyana! Nice lover!" she mocked him. And, in this gay mood, they went out of doors.

Late that afternoon she said:

"I'm going out to do some shopping. I'm going to get myself a brand new trousseau. Remember, you abducted me so quickly that I scarcely had time to collect my things in Penzance. I'm sure you don't want a trousseauless bride!"

"How thoughtless of me! Do you want some money?" Embarrassed, he drew out his wallet.

"No! No!" she gayly waved him away. "A bride is supposed to bring her own trousseau, and I intend to live up to some formalities of life. I'll be back in an hour— perhaps two!"

"Good. I've a bit of shopping to do myself. In an hour, then, my dear!" And he bundled her into a cab.

Henry welcomed this diversion. He had been wondering how he might carry out a little surprise he had planned for Elaine. And so he hailed the next passing cabby and started on a shopping expedition of his own. His purchases included a handsome sapphire ring, three bottles of Chambertin of a celebrated vintage, a bottle of Benedictine, three large bouquets of hothouse roses, six tall candles, and a bundle of incense sticks.

Back at the Rabelais, he consulted the proprietress, and,

taking her into his confidence, said he was celebrating his
wife's birthday. Would she not make an effort to prepare
a special dinner to be served in their rooms. He enu-
merated the items of the menu he had planned. Hors-
d'œuvres, of course, with the best caviare—she mustn't
forget the caviare!—as the chief ingredient. Then, soup,—
Saint Germain—her favourite, he had learned. Then, filet
of sole, fried in fresh butter. Then, roast chicken, the
juiciest and the tenderest she could find. For a sweet,
well—perhaps Madame could suggest one? She reflected
for a few moments before speaking. Would Madame Tor-
lee like a *pomme bonne femme* with fresh cream which
would simply melt in her mouth? Or would she prefer
a chocolate or a vanilla souffle "as light as a feather?" The
time was too short to prepare anything more elaborate.
A thousand pities he had not spoken earlier in the day.
She might have—— But Henry cut her short. He had
decided on the *pomme bonne femme*. It sounded well,
and auspicious, if it was only a baked apple! "Only be
sure they're nice, outside and inside. There mustn't be a
worm at the core!" He laughed gayly, but he meant it
seriously. Their nuptial dinner mustn't be spoiled by a
worm at the heart of the apple. He felt almost superstitious about it. Madame also laughed. She would personally inspect the apples and see that there was no suspicion
of a worm about them! This young man's gallantry
pleased her, and, scenting amorous adventure, she entered
with a full heart into the conspiracy. And—he had promised to pay well. "Thank you! And if not too much
trouble, please, madame, round off the feast with cheese
and as a savoury chicken liver on toast, or some similar
delicacy!" No trouble at all. Monsieur could count on

anything he wished. Everything would be of the best, and everything would be prepared in a fashion satisfactory to Monsieur and Madame.

Henry hurried with his purchases upstairs, and set to work to prepare the rooms for his bride. He put the tall candles in the candlesticks, and found places for the incense. He arranged the roses in vases, carefully, and in charming symmetry, and set out the vases so that they were reflected in the mirrors, intensifying the effect of profusion.

He gazed at the remaining bouquet for some time, as if reluctant to put into execution the plan he had formed with regard to it. He laughed, then did an extraordinary thing. With an impetuous gesture, he seized the bouquet of rich, full-blown, red roses in his hands, and strode into the bedroom. He flung aside the down puff and the blankets and vigorously began to divest the stalks of their petals, which, in handfuls, he strewed about the sheets, laughing the while at his own mad fancy, the whim of love.

When at last the stalks were bare and the sheets fairly covered with the velvety petals, he stood contemplating with ardent eyes what he had wrought. Here was a nuptial bed fit for perfect lovers, he thought, and, thinking he heard footsteps on the stairs, he quickly restored the bed-covers to their former neat state, and chuckled. The footsteps continued upward; it was not Elaine. He was glad, for there still remained things to be done.

Presently, he had coal fires blazing in both rooms. The hanging curtains were drawn, the candles lighted. Nothing seemed to be wanting now but Elaine. In impatience he sat down before the fire in the sitting-room to await her.

She returned at half-past six, her arms filled with parcels.

"How lovely it smells here!" she cried, eyeing the roses. "And what a lovely fire! You're surely the perfect lover!" And, depositing her bundles on the table, she flung her arms around his neck, and ardently kissed him. Then picking up her parcels, she retired to the bedroom with a mysterious air, shutting the door behind her, and calling from the other side:

"You mustn't come in until I say I'm ready!"

In the meantime he was not idle. He unlocked his suitcase, and hurriedly set to rig himself out in full dress. After surveying himself in a mirror, and finding satisfaction in his appearance, he lighted his pipe and sat down to wait.

Soon the maid appeared with a table-cloth, and, covering the small round table, she set out the necessary utensils of sterling silver, polished immaculately, evidently out of Madame's private hoard. A vase of roses graced the centre. Henry called for a cork-screw and, uncorking a bottle of Chambertin, hitherto out of sight, poured it into a cut-glass decanter. He then lighted the six tall candles, three of which he deposited on the mantel-piece and three on the table; their light sent glints on the sterling silver spoons and forks. Madame, he thought, was generous, in producing these articles, doubtless out of her private hoard.

He looked around. Everything was lovely, as it should be. Life was simply perfect. The stage was now fully set; it needed but the appearance of the leading lady to lend that ultimate sanction to the enactment of a sacred mystery, of which this was only the beginning.

At last the bedroom door opened, and there appeared a vision so transcendently lovely that Henry could but stare mutely in reverent wonder. Elaine had on a black velvet frock, the upper part of it tightly encasing her to reveal her form and graced round the low neck with a broad white collar of beautiful lace; and from it emerged her shapely head more lovely than it had ever appeared to him before; while from the slender waist there descended, gradually widening, in slightly curving lines, like a bell, the long skirt, from under which small silvery slippers seductively peeped out.

Framed in the doorway, she paused, smiling, her long bare slender arms, snow-white across the black of the velvet, meeting in a clasp of hands. She stood there still, in the statuesque attitude of a woman conscious of her own beauty, inviting admiration.

He, too, stood stock-still, as if fearful of breaking a spell. Then he sprang forward, as if to embrace her, at the same time breaking the silence.

"Galatea!" he cried.

"You impatient man! There will be plenty of time for that!" she answered, as she quickly turned as on a pivot. "Now how do I look from the back?"

"Perfect, my dear, simply perfect!" There was intense, flame-like joy in his cry. "To think that I've found you, and that you're mine! To think that all these years I didn't know you! Poor wasted years, Galatea!"

"You were a long time finding me!" she mocked him. "I can't forgive you that! . . . But suppose Galatea should suddenly step off her pedestal and walk away, thumbing her nose at you, Pygmalion!" Reminding him of his own jest, she turned her face tantalizingly over her shoulder.

"You marked time," he countered, "by taking two husbands to your sweet bosom!"

"Beware! I'll remind you of your experiments! And pray, sir, don't make any experiment of me!"

"This, madame, is an experiment by your own will. Six months' trial, you said. It is so designated in the bond."

"Six months—or less——" she corrected him. "See that you don't abuse the loan!"

"Hardly. The interest on it will be the years to come!"

"That's rank usury, sir!"

"We share the splendid fault in common, madame."

"How, pray?"

"I lend myself, even as you lend yourself!"

"Ah, I never thought of that. You are sharp! I fear you'll get the best of me."

"I trust so. The best of you will be marvellous. In any case, with such loveliness I am sure to get the best of the bargain!"

"Pygmalion grows modest! Or else, he is fishing. But compliments, sir, are not in my line. Galatea left Pygmalion because of the compliments he paid her. But this Galatea would be loath to leave her Pygmalion!"

"Why?"

"It would turn Pygmalion's head to know! So I shall not tell."

"What a pity. . . . Well, Pygmalion invites Galatea to a plate of caviare!"

For there was a knock on the door, and the maid entered with a tray.

Even while they were laughing at this exchange of nonsensical pleasantries, he took her hand and led her to the table, holding her chair for her in a courtly manner until she was seated. Then he took his own chair opposite, and began the dining ceremony by filling the waiting goblets with wine.

"Come!" he said, clinking glasses with her. "Let's drink to the dream about to become a reality!"

Her mood was jocular. "Not the dream you dreamt a night or two ago? I mean the one in which you were patting a tiger eternally, on the penalty of being eaten if you stopped!"

"No, not that one!" he laughed. Then, more earnestly: "I mean the dream of perfect love, which may never be marred by petty vice or a petty quarrel!"

They drank; then tasted of the hors-d'œuvre. "This caviare is delicious!" she said. "But tell me more of this dream of yours!"

"Even since I was a boy I dreamt of the perfect life," he began. "I suppose I inherited it from my mother, and it was further encouraged by my education. I scarcely dare speak of it to anyone; for people would laugh and think it absurd. . . . I was something of a phantast in my childhood, and, looking out of my window toward the sea, I used to imagine a face rising above the horizon-line; a human face, a youth's, handsome like a dream, and smiling a smile—oh, how shall I describe it?—well, perhaps of paradisian bliss. Later, images of ideal women's heads, with enigmatic Leonardo smiles, would appear before me; and sometimes women's bodies of superlative beauty and of graceful line posturing like the figures the old masters drew. Beauty of line always attracted me—indeed, far above colour. Your own lines," he added with a rapturous smile, "are superb! I suspect the Greeks often took a fragment here and a fragment there to create the ideal head or figure. But your head is quite of a piece—every feature is perfect!"

"I thank you, kind sir! I've been told that before, and, would you believe it—by a painter?"

"Who?"

"Mr. Wyndham Priestley!"

"Priestley! I know him well."

"One day he looked at me so curiously that I asked him why. And he told me that there was only one woman he had known and painted who strongly resembled me."

"Did he say who it was?" There was eagerness in Henry's voice.

"No. I didn't ask him. But wait! He did say she was a Russian lady married to an Englishman."

"She was my mother!"

"How strange!"

"Yes, life is strange. It makes me feel there's some fate guiding us inevitably the way we should go. Isn't it strange that you and I who but a few days ago did not know of each other's existence should be sitting here, on the verge of a great adventure?"

"Oh, dear! How solemn you are!"

"Yes. Strange wonders fill me with awe. The sight of you here, looking so beautiful and so lovely, and the knowledge that you are mine and that I am yours, fills me with such elation, such unutterable ecstasy, that I can scarcely speak and demand of myself repeated proof that I'm really alive and not merely dreaming!"

Just then the maid entered and, removing the hors-d'œuvre plates, placed the steaming St. Germain before them.

"How lovely! My favourite!" she exclaimed. "This

ought to move you to even greater eloquence," she chided him.

"And why not?" he replied. "Food is a part of life, and by no means an ignoble part. In a perfect life one must have perfect food also. One could not think of putting tripe and onions before a goddess!"

"You *are* the perfect lover!" she said, half in earnest, half in jest. "I've never met anyone before so intensely in love with perfection. You attach great importance to perfection, don't you?"

"Everything, my dear. Or rather, as I should put it, to balance, perfect balance."

"Where's the difference?" she asked, puzzled.

"There is a difference," he asserted with emphasis. "Don't you see, the object of life should be happiness. You agree to that, don't you?"

She nodded in the affirmative.

"Well, then," he went on. "Don't you see, it's clear that people's ideas of happiness differ. Your first husband, for example, tried to use you as though you were a steak and kidney pie. They are your own words." He laughed. "Now, isn't it clear that he might have been happy if he had married someone who was a steak and kidney pie?"

She smiled. "You have an odd way of putting things."

"Now," he went on, "all Utopias are based on certain laws, usually economic laws, on laws assuming that all men are equal. But that's tackling the problem by the wrong handle."

"Tell me the right one!"

"Political economy ignores the human factor, and equality does not exist. But there should be an opportunity for everyone to be happy. There always will be servants and kings, and the assumption is that in a perfect Utopia the servant should be as happy as a king. This involves a perfect balance of human relationships. A servant's perceptions may be more limited than yours or mine, but shouldn't the servant, within the limitations prescribed by his nature, be as happy with his maid as I with you—completely happy, though in a different way?"

"But surely," she said, "that implies different degrees of happiness!"

"Quite. That is the merit of my Utopia. Everyone would get as much happiness out of life as he or she is capable of; just as a good player is sure to get more out of a poor violin than a poor player out of a good one. But the poor one gets his pleasure just the same!"

"I should say it would be hard on the person with a good ear who has to listen to him."

"You are bent on contradicting me," he said good-naturedly. "But I like it. I don't want a poor stick who will agree with everything I say. This is a good beginning. We shall get on!"

"I was only teasing you," she said, laughing. "Of course, I agree. Haven't I been unhappy because I, too, have been a mad romantic seeking perfection which is not in this life? I've been contradicting you just to make you talk. This is so delightfully different from what I've been used to. My aunt always predicted that one day I would do some such foolish thing as to tie myself up with someone as scatter-brained as myself. She was right. But I rather like it, you know—I've always wanted someone quite mad——"

"Like myself——"

"Yes, like yourself. And I'd about given up hope of such a lunatic existing!"

"But I'm not mad," he remonstrated. "Nor are you. Not really. Quite the contrary. We are abnormally sane. It's they who are mad, who are addle-pated. They— who mock at us. To be happy is to be sane. To be deliberately unhappy is to be utterly mad. Look at the world, and see how unhappy it is! Men seek power, and are destroyed by it in the end. Men seek wealth, and do not know what to do with it after they have secured it; they can take it neither to heaven nor to the infernal regions with them. Men profess religion, and think it consists in singing hymns and making the other fellow behave. . . . Of course, there are armies of unhappy who can't help themselves. They are, for the most part, victims of the great conspiracy of those who sit in the high places and spend their time, consciously or unconsciously, in devising miseries. Oh, yes! We could do with fewer politicians, fewer generals, fewer bishops, fewer princes of commerce —yes, even with fewer scientists. We could do with more genuine holy men, more philosophers, more artists, more men of faith, more actors, more adventurers, more clowns, more good chefs—in short, with more men who make life interesting, pleasant and diverting!"

"In short," she mocked him, "with more people like ourselves!"

"Even so," he agreed. "Let's be happy!" And he refilled the glasses with wine. "Let's be happy in the way the Greeks were happy!"

"But we can't be like the Greeks," she remonstrated. "That would be going back, and we can't go back!"

"That's a fallacy! It's true, we're not like the Greeks, but we can emulate something of their spirit, something of their balance; translate their peculiar temperament into its modern equivalent. We have so much more than they in many ways, but we lack the one essential thing they had, and without which it is impossible to live—balance! We are experts, specialists, one-sided, maniacs! We are fragments—pieces—bits—never whole!"

"Why don't you do something?" she asked. "A man of your ideas should be active, should——"

"Dearest," he interrupted her. "I've been waiting for you to say that. But let me make a confession. I've been seeking for you. I've felt incomplete, but a half being without my complement. How could I do anything without feeling whole? And how could I be whole without you, my darling? I have felt such a discontent, such a nostalgia, such an inner ferment, such a void, which only you could fill. But now that I have you—and that I have created, at all events for myself, the necessary balance—what will not you and I do together, my darling—you and I? I have my own little spot in Sussex, where, by virtue of inheritance, I am landlord to many. I intend, first of all, with your help, my dear, to make this spot and all who inhabit it as happy as may be allowed to us. You'll help me, my dear, won't you?"

"Of course, I'll help all I can!" she said, touched by the earnestness of his plea and infected by something of his fervour. "My darling, I can do little enough, but what little I can do it is yours to command."

"Thank you," he said, and, reaching for her hand, kissed it fervently.

"I love you, I love you," she said, "and I'm afraid I may disappoint you. I don't want to do that. And may heaven help me!"

"May heaven help us both!" he echoed her.

"You're a strange man," she said quietly. "You are in love with me, and I am in love with you, and we have both partaken of red wine, and yet—" She averted a shy gaze, hesitated.

"I've not taken any liberty with you!" he finished the thought for her. "No! I don't want to snatch at you! There's so much of this snatching in life. I hate snatching——"

"So do I. Other men——"

"I want our love to be beautiful," he went on. "How can anything snatched be beautiful? Decorum is a part of life, and an essential part, too, I think. This is our nuptial supper, and after that shall come our nuptial night——"

A reverential glow lighted up her eyes as she listened, and within them both a deep fire sending forth shoots in all direction was gradually enveloping them in an all-possessive flame, which, reaching out towards the other, yearned to merge, only as fire merges with fire, and water with water.

Thus the moments passed, long eternities of sweet agony, of lingering expectancy. . . . Flame yearned to leap to flame, to die together in embrace, in one irresistible conflagration. No man and woman were here, but two flames of equal ardour, in which personal sex was consumed and became as cleansed of petty thought and petty emotion as anything does which passes through fire. . . .

At last, the last crumb was eaten, the last word said, the last liqueur drunk. They rose to prepare for the night.

The fire in the bedroom grate flared, and the candles flickered; the vases of roses were distributed about the room, permeating it with a hypnotic aroma. Outside it was cold and damp, but here it was snug and warm, exultant with a repressed happiness. The flares from the fire in the grate caused shadows to dance on the walls, and something danced in the hearts of the lovers. They were happy in one another, and the little wine they had drunk, and the wine-like words they had exchanged, intensified their lovers' mood of intoxication. As if they wished to prolong the sweet agony of expectancy, they undressed slowly, with great deliberateness.

Henry had put on a beautiful new blue corded dressing-gown, which made him appear even handsomer than in the evening-dress he had been wearing; its long straight draped lines lent added height and grace to his figure. He now sat at the farther end of the room, while he watched Elaine standing before the fire divesting herself, one by one, of her several garments, all such pretty filmy ones, of silk and lace. She did this, unflustered, naturally, seemingly without shame. At last, her final garment slipped from her, falling round her feet; and he gazed at her graceful, sinuous figure, warmed and tinted by the flame, in adoration. He rose to his feet, and stood as in a dream. And it was as if he were in a dream, a dream he wanted to prolong, lest he wake and find the vision gone.

At last he bestirred himself, found his voice. "One of the graces come to life!" he cried, and walked rapidly towards her. He extracted the sapphire ring from the pocket of his gown, and slipped it on her finger, saying: "Before God, before the sacred mystery of the universe, I, Henry Thorley, take thee, Elaine, for my wife! . . . With my body I thee worship!" And, flinging off his dressing-gown, he picked up the lithe graceful figure and bore her to the nuptial bed.

"What's this?" she cried, in astonishment, as her skin, petal-like to his fingers, touched the rose petals with which he had strewn the white sheets; then gave way to a gay ripple of laughter. "You are simply perfect!" she murmured, and, with the perfumes of the rose-petalled bed encompassing her, without shame she yielded to her lover, flame to flame.

The sweet moments passed, followed by a quiescent exultancy. They lay in each other's arms, merging even as flame with flame. Where did the one end, and the other begin? Which was the man, which the woman? They were not as two, but as one. In the beginning, sometime in the remote past, they must have been one; then split by some resentful god's lightning into two, male and female; and now some propitious fate had brought them, after a long seeking, together, and they were one again: as in Plato's myth of the androgynes.

"I'm absurdly happy!" cried Elaine.

"Happiness is always absurd, always irrational," said Henry. "Certainly, people would think us absurd if they could see us now! And they're afraid to be happy, lest they appear absurd. From the sublime to the ridiculous is but a step—so it is said. And so you rarely have the sublime without the ridiculous! And so, darling, if we are to remain happy, we must live in our way, as though the outside world did not exist. And does it exist for us now? Does anything exist but you and I?"

CHAPTER FOURTEEN

Trial Honeymoon

IT SO rarely happens in life that reality exceeds expectation. Yet this happened in the lives of Henry and Elaine. The fondest dreams they had had before their meeting were as a shadow to the exultant reality which followed. Every great thing and every little thing made its own happiness for them. Whether in the sharing of some simple pleasure or in the ultimate embrace, they found that joy and oneness which belongs to lovers of legend and fairy tale.

"Henry," said Elaine, walking at his side in Rome, some weeks after their meeting, "do you know, I used to think that 'walking on air' was merely a phrase. Yet here am I really walking on air!"

"Elaine," he replied. "Every moment I'm with you I ask myself the question: 'Am I alive, or am I merely dreaming?' I have the horrible fear that I may awake and find that it has been a beautiful, a perfect dream, but alas, only a dream!"

"No, Henry darling! This is the only real life. I now know that before I met you I had not lived! Call our life a dream, if you like. But if this is a dream, then what went before was a nightmare!"

"Elaine, my dear heart! You are right. Yet our happiness *is* an island dream surrounded by a world of nightmare. All around us is strife, traffic, beggary, thievery, the conflict of ambitions, the clash of hatreds, the eternal pursuit of the will-o'-the-wisp. But these things touch us not. Elaine and Henry are a world in themselves. . . ."

"But, my dear," she interrupted him, pressing his arm tighter, as if for protection, "I am afraid, horribly afraid, of the large world outside! Even the happiest of islands, may, you know, be submerged by the sea!"

"Yes," he agreed, "this external world is frightening. It's only this that can hurt us!"

"I don't think anything can ever really change our love," she said, defensively, seeking for corroboration in him.

"I'm not afraid of that! And as a proof of my faith, I would be only too glad to marry you at once!"

"No! No! I don't mean that at all," she hastened to say. "I know our love is not a thing of the moment. But I'm horribly afraid of being a burden to you, of hindering you from developing and exercising your gifts, your vocation in life!"

"I have none!" he laughed.

"You know you have," she asserted with emphasis. "There's that little spot in Sussex you so often talk about. You know you love it. You know you're anxious to transform it into an earthly paradise!"

"Oh, that! . . . I'm not thinking about it. Not now. When I do, you'll help me. We'll do it together!"

"Oh, my dear, my dear, suppose I should fail you!"

"But you won't!"

"Suppose I do!" she persisted.

"Why should you?"

"I may be jealous of it!" she laughed.

"Jealous?" He glanced at her uncomprehendingly.

"Yes, jealous that other people should share in my Henry."

"Ah, as for that, they'd share in my Elaine, too!"

"But I shouldn't want them sharing in me! 'I am my beloved's, and my beloved is mine!' That's how I feel! So there!"

"You darling!" he cried, feeling a pride in that she loved him so much.

"If we could only limit the world—our world—to us two!"

"Perhaps you are right," he agreed. "Perfect happiness lies in limitation, not in spreading out. We ought to be like those Tanagra figurines, happy in their petty intimacies, and not like those gigantic Michelangelo figures in the Medici chapel unhappy in their contemplation of space and eternity and the endless sorrows of a vast universe!"

"Don't you see," she said, with feminine realism, "you are going to ask the outside world into your parlour. And you'll be too busy to notice poor me!"

"No! No! When they go, I'll be all the gladder to see you. I'm a man, and I'll grow ashamed if I don't do my part in this world. I'd like to bring our happiness into the lives of others!"

"You want to set up as a teacher unto men!" she teased him. "As for me, I feel quite happy in your arms without the world looking on!"

"Certainly an original way of putting things," he chided her. "Perhaps you are right! But I can go further. For in holding you in my arms I hold my true world to my heart. Yes, my very own world. A world to love, to wreak my tenderness and my passion on, a world to mould and create according to my fancy. When I am so close to you, I feel like a god and a creator!"

"I'd love to have a baby by you," she murmured, "your baby!"

"I'd love it," he said.

"I'd have it to look exactly like you," she went on. Then, after a pause: "It would be a pity if you died without leaving your likeness!"

Yet something within him called upon him to spread tidings of perfect living, perfect loving, to the rest of the world. That, perhaps, was his vocation. He imagined his self-respect demanded something of the sort from him. Was it enough that a man should be perfect in himself— if he was perfect!—without bearing any relation to the world around him?

He had a power over Elaine, he was aware. Would he not ultimately—and this was the ultimate test of the power of his love—mould her according to his desire and his conception of a helpmeet to a god and a creator? Every man, he thought, could be, within limitations, a god and a creator. She was malleable, as a woman should be; and spirited as she was, she was so much plaster in his hands for love to shape within and without: a Galatea in life playing up to Pygmalion.

Their tender words led to tender actions, often to the ultimate embrace. They were like children playing; their innocent play led to the repeated discovery of one another; they never approached the love act with deliberate intent. Spontaneity guided their actions; there was no calculation, no suspicion of what was to come. They always desired one another at one and the same moment. No "evil" thought contaminated their relation; always pure joy animated it and inspired it to common ecstasy. Again and again they marvelled at the apparent innocence of their simultaneous desire, at the balance and coordination of body and spirit, on the part of one and the other, working in unison. It was really as if they were one; in their most perfect moments there was neither maleness nor femaleness, but a rounded flow as of one, a ring of fluid flame, joining them, merging them in a pulsating oneness, a mood strangely akin to a mystical experience. It moved them to worship, to adoration. For Elaine, in particular, with her woman's capacity for wholeheartedly absorbing passionate experience, life with her lover assumed the nature of unceasing revelation.

"Why haven't I met you before?" she repeatedly asked Henry in moments of intense loving. "I wish I could have come to you a virgin untouched by any man!"

"But you have!" he would reply with convincing earnestness. "No man has really touched you, for you have responded to no man's passion but to mine!"

"That's quite true. I can't understand it. Not even poor Jerome ever awakened the woman in me. Do you know, he actually asked a doctor to examine me to see if anything was wrong with me!" She laughed at the recollection. "Do you know what the doctor said?"

"Haven't the least notion."

"Well, he was a plain, blunt sort of man, and he told him that the fault lay wholly with himself. 'You're not the man for Elaine!' he said. Wasn't Jerome in a rage when he heard that!"

"I suspect the number of men and women in your and Jerome's shoes is legion."

"I never understood the full significance of the doctor's words until I met you!"

Henry laughed.

"Do you know," she went on, "I had really at one time thought there was something wrong with me. And because I could not respond in a way a woman should, I used to feel such utter shame in receiving my husband's embrace. But with you, I feel no shame at all, but such naturalness, such joy, and such pride! The very memory of my earlier experiences fills me with shame and horror. That is why I wish I had come a virgin to you!"

"I wish you had," he said solemnly, "though, somehow, every time I come to you, you make me feel strangely virginal, as if I had never known a woman before. Each experience is a new experience, and every delight is a new delight!"

"I feel much the same way," she said fervently. "Each time you love me, it seems as if I've never been loved before. Or rather," she laughed, "it is as if each time another man loved me. You are, you must know, so many men to me. Variety, they say, is the spice of life. That's why I shall never leave you. And don't you try to leave me. I shall pursue you to the ends of the earth!"

He laughed. "Have no fear of that! I find myself in the same boat. In loving you, I feel as though I were being a terrible polygamist! For you are several kinds of women to me."

"Mind you," she resumed, "though I should feel mad with jealousy—I mean emotionally—intellectually I could scarcely blame you if you wanted other women. You are so wonderful! I sometimes feel as if it were your duty to fill the world with your babies. For they would be sure to be beautiful. And heaven knows, the world has need of beauty!"

"That sounds very well," he replied. "But I'm not in this world to act as a stallion on a stud farm. Quite apart from that, I am so constituted that women as a race don't move me! But the mere touch of your hand never fails to awaken such deep tenderness that in the end every particle of me cries to join with you, and when severed from you I seem to myself but as a half being desolate without the other half of myself!"

She was delighted at his words, and glowed with pride at the thought that she meant so much to this man; and was filled with joy because he meant scarcely less to her. What a man he was at loving! When he loved her, her whole being seemed attuned to his pulsating tenderness. In such moments—her romantic imagination lingered on the reiterated fancy—she often likened herself to a singing violin whose too sensitive, vibrant strings, touched as it were by a master player, burst into resonance rich with exquisite nuance; plaintive notes mingled with gay, tears and sighs lost themselves in elfin laughter, ineffably merging; a culminating crescendo of emotion flooding both with an overpowering sense of oneness, that sense of complete accord which swept man and his instrument into whole-hearted surrender, each to each. When one night, she conveyed the thought to her lover, he laughed and said:

"Of course, darling. You're a Stradivarius! And I feel as though I were Paganini!"

And together they laughed delightedly at the whimsical fancy.

Not that the lovers always indulged in such imaginative flights. They often descended to earth, to earthly ribaldry

—"the Rabelaisian touch," as Henry termed it. Elaine was astonished to find herself entering into the spirit of bawdy banter, hitherto unfamiliar and unthinkable.

"Dear, dear!" she once said. "If any other man had ever said that to me, I should have been furious with him and had had nothing more to do with him. Yet I accept everything from you, and I like it! When you say such things, they don't somehow sound wicked, but merely funny!"

"I'm glad," he said, "for I'd hate to discover my Elaine to be a little prude! Rabelaisianism, in a measure, has a place in life, and no balanced human being will reject it. The Greeks, the best balanced people that ever lived, accepted Aristophanes as well as Euripides! It is only when Rabelaisianism becomes an obsession that it is the vile thing that it can be. But when it makes us laugh heartily . . . well, in laughter is its justification! Wit, and wit alone, may excuse even vulgarity!"

Occasionally, to her own astonishment, Elaine found herself indulging in bawdy talk. This delighted Henry, who liked the addition of the earthly flavour to her naturally romantic mind.

"Splendid! Splendid!" he once cried, laughing. "You are daily becoming more and more a fit helpmate for Henry Thorley!"

"You mean," she retorted, "you like the idea of being Pygmalion creating a statue to your liking. But if I remember aright," she warned him, "you said on the night of our first meeting that any lady you were likely to create would walk off the pedestal thumbing her nose at her maker! Do you remember?"

"*You* wouldn't do that, Elaine?" he teased her, with the

assurance of a lover who knew himself to be loved beyond all mischance.

"Wouldn't I, though? You don't know what I would do! Or any woman, for that matter!" She grimaced.

"You couldn't do that, Elaine," he repeated firmly, with emphasis. "Without you, I would be as nothing. Without me, you would be as nothing!"

"I'm afraid it's only too true," she yielded. "At least, as far as I'm concerned. But if ever I get old and ugly, you'll——"

"No, no!" he protested. "We'll grow old together. And you'll never grow ugly to me!"

"Oh, yes, I will!" she insisted. "And when I do, I shall run away. I don't ever want you to see me ugly. I can't bear the thought! When I grow old and ugly, I shall run to my friend, Phil, who's promised to take me in when you've grown tired of me."

"Phil?"

"Yes—the man who proposed to me the same day you did. Phil's a nice boy. He has seven razors, each marked for a different day of the week!"

"And excellent testimonial to his sense of order, I'm sure. But can he manage to keep in order one exacting wife?"

"He would be kind," she said gently. "I might have married him, if I hadn't met you."

"I can't imagine you married to a merely kind man."

"You're right, I'm afraid. But you are also kind. . . ." Then, after a pause, she added: "Yet interesting, too. You're a strange combination of virtues. There's a little bit of everything about you. You're simply perfect!"

He smiled. They were approaching the Coliseum, which already showed its haunting contours and shadows in the moonlight. "Balanced, perhaps; but not perfect," he corrected her, pressing her hand.

"I don't understand. . . ."

"A man may have but one virtue," he explained, "but because that one virtue is complete, that man stands perfect. You spoke of Phil's kindness. But Phil's kindness was not great enough to conquer you. The perfect good man would be he whose goodness, inherent as a force in his personality, is great enough, perfect enough, to overcome temperaments apparently antagonistic. Such a personality, human or divine, must have belonged to Christ, and that was why the Magdalens and the sinners followed Him. The radiance of His supra-goodness was enough. . . ."

"I wonder . . ." mused Elaine. "He must have been attractive . . . I imagine Him . . ."

"No, no!" he abruptly interrupted her. "His traditional appearance as a handsome being is all a surmise, because we like to imagine that such beautiful thoughts could have come from none but a beautiful body. I do not say that such is not the case. But I do say that the power of His attraction lay not in His physical beauty—the Apollos are usually beautiful and cruel—but in the perfection of His goodness, in the radiance of which men basked and were happy. Balance, in the Greek sense, would have ruined this perfection!"

"I don't follow," she said, perplexed.

"I mean," he went on, "there was a single virtue intensified to the Nth degree, just as in Napoleon the lust for conquest was so great that its mere force created that magnetic force, which attracted men and made them willing to follow their perfect general to the death!"

"Well! Go on!"

"In a well-balanced personality this is impossible. Any man possessing it might become an artist—a Shakespeare or a Goethe—never a Drake or a Nelson! For balance is harmony—a coordination of parts—and how can there be cordination where one fault or virtue dwarfs the others?"

"You are contradicting yourself, Henry!" interrupted Elaine. "Surely, Christ did coordinate His perfection of goodness with perfection of action. For did He not drive the money-changers from the Temple?"

"Yes, He did," retorted Henry, "but even then His action was dictated by His sense of goodness. But He wouldn't have, let us say, stopped on the way to admire the appearance of the Temple! His sense of goodness—active goodness, if you like—became a force, a flame, igniting men, calling upon them to let the world go and save their souls. He was the supreme Romantic!"

"But we, too, are romantics, Henry. For we live but for one thing—our love!"

Henry contemplated her for a few moments with a meditative air. "Perhaps you're right," he said at last. "But that rather knocks my idea of being a balanced man into a cocked hat!" He laughed. "Indeed, what you say gives me the notion that I may be merely a discordant man. The elements of balance may be there, but—" He gave a helpless shrug of his shoulders. "Consider me," he went on. "I've inherited impetuosity—the romantic temperament—from my mother. What would have I not dared to do if I had this virtue—or fault—alone! But I also possess common sense, inherited from my father. And what's the result? Nearly every wild impulse of mine is nipped in the bud, simply paralyzed! Pardon the mixed metaphors! But you know what I mean. It's like being

Don Quixote and Sancho all mixed up in one person, with Sancho too often holding the leading reins! Yet Don Quixote in himself is perfect, and Sancho in his way is perfect. . . . To coordinate them is my . . ."

"Look!" Elaine suddenly exclaimed, for they had entered the ancient amphitheatre.

The circular old walls, pierced with a multitude of black gaping holes, presented an eerie appearance in the light of the full moon, and, deserted as the enclosure was at the moment, it seemed haunted by a thousand sinister memories. Hand in hand, they stood silently within one of the gates, gazing in awe at the immense ruin, upon which life long since gone by had left so dark and so indelible an impress.

They slowly circled the enclosure, pausing before the two companion gates which had once released lion and Christian for the edification of a multitude which had to be diverted. This engendered in Henry a new train of reflection.

"There's one thing I've tried to understand, and can't," he began. "And that's cruelty—cruelty of any sort. Think of it, dear heart! If you'd been living in the old days, you, a frail beautiful thing, might have been pushed through this gate to face a powerful lion! And all because you were a good little Christian!"

"Silly man!" She laughed. "I wouldn't have been a Christian in those days. I would have been the same little pagan I am now!"

"But, my dear," he went on, argumentatively. "Suppose you were a Christian! What pleasure could men and women have in seeing you torn into bits by a ferocious lion? That's what I can't understand. Granted there is in life a measure of unavoidable cruelty, what of the deliberate and needless cruelty practised on all sides? Think of the instruments devised by man from the beginning of time for the torture of fellow-men! Men have killed each other in defence of their country, and for sheer glory, and they have killed each other in the name of faith and in the name of love, and for power and for property—and there's the worst cruelty of all, because most unreasonable, and that is cruelty for the sheer pleasure of it, cruelty for cruelty's sake! What does it mean? I have asked all sorts of men about it in the course of my travels, and those who could explain everything else could not explain the meaning of cruelty. It's a ghastly and insoluble mystery!"

Henry frowned from perplexity, and his frown gave a fantastically intense appearance to his face because of the lights and shadows engendered by the lurid moonlight. His face seemed ponderous with questioning, and the frown appeared fixed as on a sculpture.

Elaine gazed at her lover quizzically and with apprehension. He appeared tortured. And at this moment it was as if he had retreated from her, were not altogether her own, and she felt some deficiency in herself. Happiness was in limitation, in keeping the outer world outside the bounds; he had said so himself; and here he was trying to transcend boundaries beyond his reach. She could not pursue him there; he was not hers while in this questing mood. It was even as if he were not on earth at all. "Why? Why?" his face, dimly hidden, in penumbral shadows seemed to ask, and it also seemed to give the answer: there was no answer. She, alive only to the lover, to the romance of the place and moment, wanted to shake him, shake him vigorously, shake out of him his distress-

ing bundle of thoughts; but finally resorted to more insidious devices which she had never known to fail her
before. She would try the magic of her fingers. That
too—magic—was his word. Effortlessly, at will by sheer
desire, she could generate a gentle wanton warmth, which,
suffusing her fingers, she would by mere touch, potent
hypnotic touch, transmit her own mood, like a charmful
current, to her lover, who, suddenly, with warm desire
coursing in his awakened blood, would turn to thoughts
of encompassing his love, of embracing his world contained within the graceful bounds of a woman's shape, and,
in the embrace and complete merging, sink and lose that
vast tormenting world which but a little while before
threatened to draw him into its boundless chaos. It was
to him a repeated miracle that the outer world, just as it
was on the point of engulfing him, should itself, with all
its burdens and woes, be engulfed in the mysterious chaoses
of a diminutive woman. And strange it was that the
woman he then beheld, the woman he loved and no other,
should be the instrument of so fabulous a miracle. Those
tiny fingers, tingling with warmth, had the power of drawing a circle of enchantment round them; and all that vast,
illimitable, external world, for all its strength and clamour,
could not pass the line they traced. It was so at the beginning of their intimacy. It was so now.

"You goose!" she laughed, smoothing out his knitted
brows with those same fingers. "You yourself have said,
happiness is in limitation. You have me. I'm your world.
We love each other. What does anything else matter?"
And she went on smoothing his brows and kissing his
hands, and he was all afire with tenderness for her. He
would have fain lifted her in his arms and borne her to

the lair where the lions had been confined or where the Christians had been incarcerated in preparation for the slaughter of the innocents. But the gates were locked, and the place was cold and damp. The ghosts of rent sacrifices seemed to stalk about the desolate arena and to conquer its romantic glamour.

"Let's go home," she said, laughing.

And "home" they went to re-enact the sacred rites of love, which rooted the vast outer world out of their thoughts, exorcising it as effectually as the seven devils were exorcised out of the body of Mary Magdalen.

CHAPTER FIFTEEN

Legal Tie

THUS they journeyed the length of the Italian peninsula, stopping here and there to consider the highlights of picturesque and romantic charm, places now seemingly dead but rich in ghostly memories of life once lived intensely under pressure of great events and conflicting movements. Of all the cities they saw, Naples alone appeared alive in the way the old pagan cities must have been alive. It was as if its people gave no thought to past or future. There was neither yesterday nor tomorrow, but the ever-present today, calling upon one and all to make the most of it and not mar the day by vain fretting. And, in spite of many cross-crowned churches and the illumed images in the corners of the little dark shops, the people were pagan and lived paganly, lazily enjoying the languid day, plunged in the hypnotic mood of *dolce far niente*.

In this mood, in constant sight of smoking Vesuvius presaging weather, they lived in acceptance of what life had to offer. Only the beggars whined, but their whine was professional, abstract as the art of the actor or the melodious chant of the itinerant vender of lemons. As they walked along the narrow pavements, barely wide enough for a loving couple to pass, Henry and Elaine had to make way for handsome women with swinging ample hips and soft smouldering eyes betraying heat of blood. Elaine eyed them admiringly, with eyes of romance; but she marvelled

206

that the men who accompanied them should be so diminutive and, in many instances, so foppish; she saw nothing romantic about them; they appeared to be just males, males before anything else. But how adorably they sang, with what melodious tremulous voices they performed their nocturnal serenading chants, one voice succeeding another to execute impromptu variations. Nowhere was singing as universal and as lovely as here. With horror she heard Henry say that the Neapolitans pierced the eyes of their canaries that they might sing the more beautifully.

"How terrible!" she exclaimed. "Perhaps that answers your question about cruelty. Men may be cruel to create more beauty. . . . But how terrible to pay such a price!"

"Yes, terrible . . ." he echoed her, and grew pensive.

This question of cruelty obsessed him. For the sake of the coordinating principle of life, he was willing to grant a measure of cruelty as one of life's ingredients, yet he could not wholly reconcile himself to it. But there was no doubt of it: Cruelty did play a function in the creative processes of life. There was cruelty in the sexual embrace, there was cruelty in the begetting of life. A virgin was destroyed to make a woman, a piece of marble had to be hewn to make a statue. And the labour of hordes and hordes of slaves, under the lash of exacting task-masters, went to the making of pyramids, erected stone upon stone, in groans and agony. The pyramids he had once glimpsed in the moonlight appeared romantic, but the making of them was not romantic. The thought stung.

Again, he reflected: beautiful women were generally conceded to be cruel. He glanced at Elaine. How thankful he was that she was beautiful, yet not cruel. Not cruel? Not cruel to him. Yet—according to her own confession—

she had been cruel to others. This troubled him with a great troubling. There had been justification, he was willing to grant. They—the young men—had bored her; she had not really wanted them. But that was not it. What troubled him was that, not wanting them, she "led them on," encouraged them to desire her, and watched their love antics, which amused her and tormented them. It had been a kind of pastime, a game of feeling one's power. Her beauty and her aliveness had given her the power, and she was cruel in the use of it. But he was not free from this fault, if fault it was. He was like her. He had, in his day, been cruel to women, and for the same reason. They had bored him, and he had not really wanted them. He had "led them on," in his own fashion. He was like her. Cruel like her. Yet here was the miracle. . . . Neither he nor she was cruel to the other. Each was capable of being cruel, yet neither thought of being cruel to the other. There was no need for it. For they were on equal terms, coordinated like perfectly related halves, incomplete without the other, and having no real existence without the other. They still, like children—when no strangers' eye was upon them—skipped along the pavements of nights; they still enjoyed their animated repasts together at exotic tables, under which their knees or their feet met, stirring the blood with the delicious tingling of first meetings, while they looked at each other meaningfully, as if there were no other meaning in life but their love. People often glanced at them with strange, wondering eyes, as if there were something peculiar, of an unworldly nature, in their behaviour. Henry and Elaine were not unconscious of these glances, but they were impervious to the whole outer world and did not seem to care what people thought of them. Life was a continuous love game to them, an eternal honeymoon; and everything they did was as a deliciously lingering prelude to the inevitable embrace—oneness, physical and spiritual oneness: that oneness which we attribute to light, air, darkness, water, fire. In the dark of the chamber he would hold his world, now of a molten softness, wreaking on it his active gathered passion, churning it from within, moulding it from within and without, animating it with a flame consuming all dross, all petty thoughts, angers, irritations, all feelings and moods which make life unbearably trivial. Elaine would lose herself in his arms; and in the first instant of their fusion that which in every-day life was Elaine precipitately left her; it was as if the body itself had become transmuted into pure rapture, pure spirit.

Nothing seemed to stand in the way of their legal union; yet, when at the end of three months, he renewed his periodical offer of marriage, she countered it with the answer:

"No, darling. Not yet. Though I know it will always be like this, and we are each other's for eternity. Let's stick to our agreement! It was for six months. And as I am sure of you, and you are sure of me, there can be no real harm in waiting."

She had no ulterior motive. How could she have? Here was a man who loved her with a love surpassing her wildest dreams. He was handsome, he was romantic, he was masterful, he was virile. He possessed her in the manner of a god, and he treated her as a goddess. He accepted the gift she offered him quite naturally, as if it were his right, and he knew how to use the gift. She had no thought of resisting, of making him plead and coax for her favours.

She only desired to submit, submit, submit. By her submission, she conquered him, made him part of herself. And in this whole-hearted submission lay her greatest happiness, a mysterious happiness which was always fresh and spontaneous and never failed her. Above all, it was the freshness of the contact that repeatedly astonished her, held her imagination in thrall. She could not understand the extraordinary power of the man or the change he had wrought in her.

He always acquiesced in her desire for delay, though he saw no reason for putting off the marriage any longer. The present was satisfactory, every day offered its own adventure. There was no abatement of their common emotional fervour; the future appeared altogether glowing.

But even ecstatically happy couples must have some occupation, and their chief occupation at this time was sightseeing. Naples offered fascinating excursions. One day they went to Capri and remained there until the olive groves and Tiberius' villa exhausted their attractions; another day they viewed the Greek temples at Paestum. The harmonious beauty of the Temple of Poseidon, desolate of worshippers, and uninhabited save for armies of green lizards, which crept out of crevices to bask in the hot sun, filled Henry with awe; this magnificent ruin retained that balance, that sense of proportion, which he sought in his own life and had not wholly found. It filled him with an ineffable longing for he knew not what, and he snatched at this unknown something as one snatches at a tune one had once known and forgotten, or at a word which will not come to one's lips.

But nothing impressed Henry and Elaine so much as Pompeii, the city raked up out of the ashes. There was something so extraordinarily real, so palpably alive, about these sad ruins. The grandeur that was Rome, visible in what remained of Caesar's city, was as an artificial stage-setting compared to this. The meandering, narrow, paved streets, so much like those of Naples; the ruts of the wheels in the cobble-stones, over which the carts had traversed as it were but yesterday; the fountain of stone, worn away by hands; the roofless wine-shops, with still intact counters which had once displayed the red juice of Bacchus; the luxurious villas showing emblems of phallic worship—omens of fecundity; the Latin inscriptions written for the day urging citizens to vote for this or that worthy; above all, the little brothel, by some strange irony the one building chosen to remain intact; all this stirred Henry and Elaine in a way that larger and more pretentious ruins failed to stir them. The whole place seemed peopled with ghosts of men who, overtaken by abrupt disaster, had had no time to take leave of this life peacefully and now lingered as melancholy presences around the once living abode of their dreams. Here men had shopped and trafficked, and told amusing tales, and exchanged gossip, and engaged in wit and banter, and loved and exchanged vows, and begot children and buried their dead; the spirit of life but lately lived hovered above this city of the dead.

Inevitably, it made one think of death.

The place had a curious effect on Elaine. For the first time since Henry had known her, she had fallen into a mood of depression, mystifying him. It was unlike her to be sad, though she had confessed to having had sad intervals before she met him.

"What's the matter, my dear?" he asked, as they trudged along the streets of the desolate city.

"Nothing . . ." she said, but her voice did not carry conviction.

"But you are sad, darling," he protested gently. "It's so unlike you!"

She did not reply. Her eyes had a remote expression, as if she did not hear him. At a loss, he glanced at her anxiously, feeling helpless for the first time. He wondered if the strong sun beating down on the shelterless city were making her tired.

"Elaine, dear heart!" he pleaded. "You're unhappy. You know you are. I am here. I love you. I can't bear to see you unhappy. What's wrong, dearest?"

She remained mute, wrapt in a palpable sadness which he somehow felt he was unable to assuage.

"Elaine! Elaine!" he went on pleading. "Don't torment me! Can't you see how I suffer?" He felt ashamed for having to plead, never having done so with her before. "I beg of you, Elaine, tell me!"

"I can't. . . ." The words came faintly, and sounded something like a moan. And she became mute again.

"Let's get out of here, darling," he suggested at last, seeing she was not disposed to talk.

"Yes, let's go," she murmured. "This place gives me the creeps."

They turned towards the exit gate, and walked for some time in a brooding silence. The tender pressure of his warm hand—hers was extraordinarily cold—failed to produce the usual effect. Very much concerned, he walked gravely beside her, while her mood insidiously communicated itself to him.

In this troubled state of mind, the pair of lovers boarded the train for Naples.

It was not until they were half way to their destination that she brightened a little and spoke.

"I simply couldn't stand the place one little minute longer," she said. "It was terrible!"

"Terrible?" He waited for her to proceed.

"You know what I mean," she went on, in some curious way annoyed, because obviously he didn't know what she meant. "There must have been many like you and me—you see what I mean—and to be so suddenly snuffed out like candles! The atmosphere of the place—wasn't it awful?"

He laughed. "You are very susceptible to atmosphere!"

"I am. It gets into my bones. If you don't want to lose me, you must take me to places which are gay and sunny, and full of laughter!"

"It was sunny enough today, I should have thought," he said with a bantering air.

"Sunny enough, yes. But it was a sun beating down on bleached bones!"

"I'm afraid you won't like Ravenford," he said, after reflection.

"Perhaps not. . . . What a pig I've been!" she suddenly became contrite. "Of course, I shall like it! As if I couldn't be happy with you anywhere!" She laughed. "You and I, Henry, will reform Ravenford. We'll transform it into a paradise!"

Their good spirits were restored, and they were again happy; it was as if a dark cloud had passed across their sky, and was gone. But it really had not passed away, but lingered somewhere in Henry's heart, troubling him with hitherto unthought-of thought: that clouds were possible in the most ecstatically happy of lives. Before this day he wouldn't have thought it possible that a cloud could mar their perfect days. He had come to accept their happiness as a permanent state incapable of being broken by anything short of the direst calamity or death. He had had the reiterated assurance that their love had the power of drawing a circle of enchantment round them, excluding dangers lurking in the outer world. And now they had been betrayed; a breach had been effected in the circle, the enemy had broken through. And he who had thought that he was strong enough to protect their love from external assault, he who had thought that the world he possessed was wholly his own to do what he would with it, suddenly found there was a nook in it not his own and that he had been impotent to hinder the enemy from taking possession of it. It was true, the breach was temporarily repaired, but then this was accomplished only by running away. In a subtle way, the episode at Pompeii shook his confidence at the very moment he thought his confidence could not possibly be shaken. He could not get away from the thought: it was not he who had possessed Elaine in the dead city, but the spirits of the dead, who were stronger than he; and he could do nothing to prevent it.

Of course, it was nothing, a mere nothing, he again and again tried to reassure himself. He had no reason at all to feel troubled; all women were prone to moods, and a sensitive woman like Elaine was more prone to them than others. But being of a romantic nature, his heart was stronger than his mind; repeatedly it resurrected for him the moment of his impotence, the moment in which not he but a dead world possessed Elaine, the moment in which he and all his love could do nothing to wrest her from its insidious subtle clutches.

The idyllic days went on, he had almost forgotten the moment of his weakness. It had been a bad dream, a tiny isle of misery in the immense sea of happiness, and with passing days it receded, and, ultimately, as it were, disappeared from the horizon. They continued their itinerant honeymoon, spending their days and nights in dream places like Amalfi, Sorrento, Palermo and Taormina; Greek temples, forsaken but still beautiful even in their ruins, greeted them at Syracuse, Gigenti and Sagesta; and Sardinia and Corsica and the Balearic isles knew their feet. Islands attracted both of them. Were not islands a symbol of their own happiness islanded in a world growing daily more tedious? They liked to think so, they thought of their fabulous happiness in terms of a blessed isle, against which beat a tempestuous sea.

Then, in Majorca, while they were standing on a cliff, looking out to a blue sun-lit sea, she first whispered the sweet secret in his ear: a new life was stirring within her.

He was jubilant. Flinging his arms about in the air, he suddenly began to dance a wild dance before her amused eyes. "Come!" he cried, embracing her, and drawing her into the dance. "Come, let's go to the first civilized port and marry me! We've waited long enough!"

"No! No! Henry!" she replied, gently resisting him. "We must stick to our bargain. The time won't be up for another week!"

"But, my dear," he pleaded. "Suppose I should die before the week was up. You would then have a fatherless child!"

"No, no, Henry. If you should die, I should die too. In any case, death or marriage would not really alter matters.

The child is yours, and I am so proud! . . . And who knows, Henry, you may tire of me within the week!"

"Don't be a goose!" he persisted. "Let's away and get married!"

But she was firm, and would not be prevailed upon. "A bargain is a bargain!" she reiterated.

A week later, at Marseilles, they formally became husband and wife; and immediately after the ceremony began their homeward journey for Ravenford.

CHAPTER SIXTEEN

Ravenford Manor

RAVENFORD MANOR stands on an eminence of some two hundred feet a quarter of a mile to the left of and above the village of Ravenford. It is a large, longish, black and white structure, in the characteristic Tudor style, with two upper overlapping stories and a spacious precipitately sloping tiled roof, both ends terminating in backward and forward projections, giving the building the shape of a capital I.

Perfect in its proportions, and dignified, as must have been the mind of the architect who conceived it; unspoiled by restoration, time has added a lovely mellowness, matching the mellowness of old wine. With its mullioned windows and casements, its delicately patterned vine-clad walls, its matured dark-brown doors with antique bronze knockers, all fashioned by the loving hands of cunning craftsmen, it presents—when looked at through the broad railed gates, the one point of vantage—an appearance of such harmony as to stir the admiration of any prying stranger sensible to such things.

Moreover, the stately beauty of the building is handsomely set off by the matching beauty of the surroundings. Two rows of very erect, very tall poplars flank the straight roadway leading to the gates, from either side of which stretch the seemingly endless stone walls of the garden, lost among woodland. Within the gates, near the small but comfortable-looking lodge, the road curves rightward and leftward, forming a broad loop to allow vehicles to approach and depart, and within the loop are visible motley beds of flowers harmoniously arranged and tenderly cared for. Tulips, gardenias, hollyhocks, poppies, iris, clumps of rhododendron, red and yellow roses, laurel, and other plants, blend into a floral symphony, a feast for the eyes. On either side of the loop are old oaks, yews, evergreens, silver and copper beeches, profuse greens and reds of various shades and textures.

The windows of the front of the house face seawards, and, from the first story, the sea can be seen in all its changing moods. At the furthermost end at the back of the garden are situated the orchards and the kitchen-gardens and the green-houses, and beyond them, invisible for foliage, is the stone wall again. Two tiny cottages, occupied by servants, stand in one of the corners.

The interior of the house contained at the time its own gathered treasures in keeping with the exterior. The broad unvestibuled entrance led directly into the small reception hall, whose low sturdy cracked beams and sober wainscotted walls, and ancient side-board and a long three-century-old refectory-table flanked by a dozen windsor-chairs, gave an old-fashioned but by no means senile welcome to the appreciative guest; and the final touch to this study in the antique is the broad open fire-place built for the reception of logs, with old andirons, old prongs, old bellows, and with cosy ingle-nooks for friendly sitters. The rest is all a matter of detail: old brass candlesticks and copper utensils polished to catch glints of light, old pewter plates, old silhouette portraits and daguerreotypes, and, in a corner of the room, an old disused spinning-wheel. This was the tea- and the dining-room. A door to the left led to the domestic office; another, to the right, opened into a spacious study and library, which was sometimes used for the reception of larger gatherings. This was a high, admirably proportioned room, whose walls were covered with old calf and parchment-bound books reaching more than half way to the ceiling; while the broad deep bay windows recessed between the shelves were provided with cushioned seats encouraging tête-à-tête. An ingle-nooked fire-place, even larger than the one in the dining-room, was topped by an expansive carved mantelpiece, upon which reposed miniatures, photographs, silhouettes, daguerreotypes—likenesses, past and present, of the Thorley clan—and all manner of gew-gaws, all of which were reflected in an immense gilt-framed mirror rising to the ceiling. Large, modern, upholstered chairs, covered with chiffons, a concession to the times and to comfort, were placed about the room; and, at the opposite end of the long room stood a fine old desk whose area was in keeping with the goodly proportions of the room; it was chiefly used to serve refreshments during receptions of guests. An immense Kermanshah rug graced the centre of the room, and at the corners were less flowery examples from Bokhara. In front of the fireplace a handsome white bear reared his head from a spreading soft skin, the whitest of white, a trophy brought back from Russia by William Thorley, together with his exotic bride.

The other rooms were furnished and decorated with the same impeccable taste that belongs to tradition. The things grew up with the old house, and not a thing was added but that the house was consulted, not an article went in but that the surroundings approved of it. The three carven four-poster beds were not the least of the desirable posses-

sions. The largest and most imposing of these, as
far as could be remembered, had been always assigned to
the reigning mistress of the house. In this bed all the
Thorleys of five centuries had been begotten and conceived,
and not a few had died in it. The bedroom itself was the
most spacious and the loftiest in the house, and its three
broad windows, separated by narrow partitions, opened out
superbly to the sea. The master's bedroom, communicating
with it, was only a little less comfortable. Henry's father
had made it serve as a private study as well; and here, over
the fireplace, hung the Priestley portrait of Olga Thorley.
There was a desk at the opposite end of the room, and
William had placed his chair against the wall so as to enable
him to contemplate the portrait from a point of vantage.
Shut in with his own thoughts, he would sit here for hours,
until, after long intense gazing, the figure would seem to
come to life and the smile on Olga's face would become
strangely real, casting upon him a hypnotic spell, so that
he would fear to stir lest the living vision vanish and leave
him bereft. The awakening would leave him sad and
shaken, and the servants at such moments passing his door
would sometimes hear long-drawn-out sighs, and occasionally, they thought, a sob; and they would shake their heads
dubiously and in pity. He was a kind master, and it was
not right that he should be thus troubled. Their thoughts
regarding their former mistress, however, were not warmed
by sympathy, and in confidential moments the bolder of
the servants expressed some unflattering sentiments. "It's
er—my opinion," said the old gardener, Jim Peskett, to
Mrs. Agatha Mundy, the cook, "that that Rooshan woman
was a reg'lar witch" (he had once used a less delicate word
which rhymed with it, for which he was properly reproved

by the respectful Mrs. Mundy), "and she's beguiled the master to his destruction. A downright shame too!" "Yes," agreed Mrs. Mundy, "I wonder what he ever did see in 'er! He should 'ave wed an English lady, for only such as knows 'ow to take proper care of a good, noble man!" "That's a fac'!" said Peskett. "I once 'eard of another good Britisher that's wed a wicked furriner, an' he came to a bad end, and—" And the gardener launched forth into a long story.

Unmindful of what the servants thought or said, William Thorley sat there contemplating the portrait, and musing on possible ways in which he had maltreated the woman he loved. But there were moments, for which he lived, when his eyes lighted up with rapture at some earlier pleasant memory.

Henry, in every sense, made his father's room his own, and did not move the slightest object in it from its wonted place. When at Ravenford, he often would sit in the self-same chair, and study the portrait with admiration, cherishing the likeness of his mother scarcely less intensely than his father had; but there was greater joy in the young man's contemplation.

After the death of Olga, William's maiden sister, Emily Thorley, took complete charge of the household. Tall and meagre, strait-laced and staid, and clear-cut with a sober dignity as a Holbein portrait, she was the embodiment of Victorian virtue; her not insensitive patrician head ("made in England," Priestley laughingly said of it once) bore that impress of integral authority which can belong only to one descended of a long lineage of propertied folk. She refused to engage a housekeeper, and did all the managing of servants and household affairs herself. But there was nothing menial about her person; even the keys which during busy hours hung from her waist did not have the appearance of keys but of dignified symbols, the sacred insignia of a domestic high priestess.

At the time the estate fell into Henry's hands, she was fifty years old and looked it; it was hard to imagine that she had ever been young or that she would ever grow older. She was a fixed type firmly moulded by blood, time and convention; perfect of her kind, she exists in every land and every age, with slight local variations. As a matter of fact, of course, she had been once young and not uncomely. She had even been admired by a handsome young man and accepted his attentions, only to change her mind when, to her horror, she discovered his "perfidy." She saw life in terms of "property," and she was not one to share hers, even when it came in the shape of a young man, with others. Had the young man persisted, she might have ultimately compromised, but the young man did not persist and very soon after his rejection found consolation in a young woman who was not so exacting. This only increased his perfidy in her eyes, and she made a vow to have nothing to do with men. This vow proved superfluous, for she received no other opportunity; the circumstance intensified her detestation of the perfidious male. The mood did not extend to include the males of the Thorley clan, and she was very fond of her brother William; it was a great blow to her when he brought back with him from Russia his alien bride.

From the very beginning there was tacit hostility between them. Emily's sense of decorum was much upset by her sister-in-law's impetuous ways, while Olga regarded Emily

with the contemptuous indifference of the romantic for
one too heavily endowed with the ballast of common sense.
There was no room for Mary and Martha in the same
house, and during Olga's too brief tenancy of Ravenford
Emily's visits were few and far between. She had been
indeed exasperated with her brother for not keeping his
wife under better control, and when, with a woman's
intuition, she perceived how matters were faring between
them, her attitude was one of reluctant contempt mingled
with pity. What good was a man if he could not keep
his wife in order? Such a thing as a wife's insubordination
had not been known before in a Thorley household. She
could not understand it, and had little sympathy with it.
Nor, when death removed the foe, could she understand
William's overwhelming grief. She thought he was well
rid of "that woman," and in her heart rejoiced for his sake.
But as the years went on, and his grief did not abate, she
was very sorry for him, and began to devote herself to
making him comfortable. As she saw him helpless and
apathetic, she took the household in hand, as well as
Henry's early education, and both these tasks filled her life
and gave it a meaning it had hitherto lacked. What little
meaning, however, William's life might have had was lost
in the charitable processes carried out by the well-meaning
lady; for there was little or nothing left for him to do.

Henry's defection at school nearly broke Emily's heart.
She could not understand any young man interfering in
the school discipline; still less could she understand her
brother condoning the caning episode. When, in a more
amiable mood than she had seen him since Olga's death,
he returned home with his son, she was visibly aghast, and
would have remonstrated, had she not detected something

in his manner with which it would have been useless to contend. The dead alien woman had surely bewitched both father and son. She did unavailingly protest against the boy being taken abroad to be educated. Was it not enough that Henry should have a foreign woman's blood in his veins without intensifying the terrible malady with a continental education? She was, at heart, an ardent patriot, and she was insular as any untravelled Briton could be.

William was fond of her, as she was of him, and he was not unmindful of the suffering he caused her, but he saw no way of alleviating it. Once life had become a torment to himself, it was bound to inflict torment on loved ones around one. The aura of pain was even as the aura of joy, radiating its potent light upon all within the circle of its activity, and affecting each person in the measure of his or her susceptibility. The room in which hung the portrait of Olga served as a shelter, a refuge, as a private chapel for his secret devotions. The image of the beautiful woman, who had been his wife, exhaled so much sorrow, so much pain, a whole sea of sorrow and pain, and to immerse oneself in this sea was to lose oneself in it, as a particle is lost in the oblivion of vastness. He swam in this sea of sorrow and pain, and, like a swimmer, he felt not the weight of the sea in which he swam. Its waters sustained him, though it was easy to drown in them. He did not drown. Cleansed and chastened, he would reappear among his household and contentedly attend to his tasks, to his servants and to the management of his estate.

But sometimes, without giving previous notice to Emily, he would order his bags packed and depart for the continent to obtain tidings of his son more direct than could be obtained from the casual correspondence.

As this became a habit, Emily accepted the abrupt departure philosophically, but was amply compensated whenever William succeeded in bringing back his son to Ravenford for a holiday. Then her joy became abounding. For Henry had become almost an obsession with her. She had grown to love the handsome, brown-haired, brown-eyed lad, whose zest for life was revealed in the slightest gesture, the slightest movement of his tall lithe figure. There was something infectious in his animation, and Emily's eyes never were more keen nor did her heart ever glow more warmly than when Henry's presence graced Ravenford. In his own fashion, he appreciated his aunt; for, in the absence of a mother, she had been something of a mother to him. How much of a son he was to her, he never quite realized. After his departure, she would take to her room and have a good cry; then reappear as if nothing had happened. Never did she allow herself to show the slightest vestige of emotion in public. The servants knew her for an equable, even-tempered mistress incapable of open anger or an excess of sorrow or joy.

After William's death, which was due to sudden if natural causes, Emily centred her whole affection on Henry. But putting one's eggs in a single basket rarely proves a satisfactory performance, and this ultimately and inevitably was to prove no exception to the rule.

Aunt Emily had welcomed Henry, but newly arrived from his long continental sojourn with all the love due to her favourite nephew and all the respect due to the new master of Ravenford. Alarmed by his restlessness, and, with a woman's unerring instinct, justly divining its cause, she energetically set about to find him a helpmeet from the numerous young women of her acquaintance, a helpmeet most fitted to carry on the traditions of the Thorley house which had suffered such a relapse during the tenancy of her late unfortunate brother. She found a likely candidate in one Jane Baskerville, the daughter of a celebrated London barrister, who was a great personal friend of hers. On one pretext or another, she asked her, with a number of other young persons, for a week-end at Ravenford. She was a well-formed, comely young woman, with the clearest imaginable blue eyes and an abundance of common sense; and Aunt Emily was gratified to see Henry devote some attention to her. Later she discreetly taxed her nephew with some questions regarding the paragon:

"Well, Henry, what do you think of Miss Baskerville?"

"She's a nice girl, Aunt Emily."

"She's an exceptionally nice girl, I think," she said encouragingly. "And so sensible!"

"Yes, she is an exceptionally nice and an exceptionally sensible girl," Henry agreed and, seeing what was in his aunt's mind, laughed.

"If I were a man, I'd marry a girl like that in a minute," his aunt went on, tentatively, with a casual air. "She'll make some one a splendid wife!"

"No doubt," answered Henry, his eyes twinkling. "What a pity you're not a man!"

"I am serious, I assure you," she went on. "Don't you think her handsome?"

"Quite!"

"And so healthy!"

"She's the very picture of health, dear Aunt!"

"And so modest!"

"She blushes very prettily, Aunt."

"And have you noticed how reserved and lady-like she is? She never speaks but to the point."

"She's a good listener, I'm willing to grant," said Henry equivocally.

"You've observed that, have you?" asked Aunt Emily eagerly. "You're a particularly good talker, you know," she added, significantly.

"And you're a particularly perfect dear, Aunt Emily," laughed Henry outright. "And I'm willing to give your Jane the most excellent testimonials. Indeed, if you can find the right man for her, I shall take great pleasure in offering my services as best man!"

"You're a tease, Henry!" Aunt Emily, realizing his discovery of her plot, also laughed. "The fact is, my dear, the best man is he who marries Jane!"

"Quite!" he readily agreed. "But the fact is, she is not my kind!"

"Not your kind?" she echoed him. "What is your kind, pray?"

"I can't describe the species to you, my dear Aunt. But she must be what you'd call a *rara avis*. I've not met one, but there must be one somewhere. And I'm sure to recognize her the moment I see her."

"By what token?"

"By the light in her eyes! By the light I shall feel in mine! Without a word, she shall know me, and I her. I am afraid she won't seem sensible. And I know I'm not sensible!"

"Henry!" cried Aunt Emily, with a helpless gesture.

"Yes, dearest aunt!"

"I'm afraid for you, Henry."

"Afraid of what?"

"Afraid that one day you will bring some impossible creature home, like—" But she paused, and bit her tongue.

"Like the one father brought home, you mean!" he finished the sentence for her, and laughed.

"I don't want to say anything against your mother," said Aunt Emily softly. "She was a very handsome woman, a very strange, a very remarkable woman,"—she spoke slowly, reflectively, with evident pain,—"and your father doubtless loved her. But she was not one of us, and she never became a Thorley."

"Is it then so important to become a Thorley?" the young man asked, and waited.

She mused a little, then answered soberly: "Your father's house, Henry, was a house divided against itself."

"That may be true," was the reply, uttered with deliberation. "Father was a good man, but he was not the man for my mother. But I am different. I am less like father, and more like mother. And my wife must have a temperament, akin to my own. . . ."

Aunt Emily heard these words with a heavy heart; they fell like a death-knell upon all her hopes. And they confirmed that which she feared most.

"Hen-n-ry," her lips faltered for the first time. "You should marry a woman who would take care of you, who would bear——"

"Don't you see, dear Aunt," Henry interrupted, seeing the effect his words had produced, "I must marry a woman whom I can love, who will make me happy. You don't want to see me unhappy, do you? Now, do you?" he repeated with a desperate intensity intended to touch the deepest chord in her.

She sat in a grave attitude, her long white hands relaxed in her lap, like one in sorrow and at a loss, and her sober face was touched with sadness.

"I don't feel like other men," he went on. "Sometimes I wonder if I'm a man at all. I am like a child, thrown upon this great world, and frankly, I don't feel that I have any need of a helpmate as much as I need a playmate. Simply because one has grown up, the world conspires to make one useful. But let me ask you, what's the use of being useful? Men would be far happier if they did not fall before this idea of utility!"

"My dear boy, what are you saying!" Aunt Emily roused herself. "There's work to be done in this world, and some one had to do this work! Remember the Scripture, Henry: 'Thou shalt earn thy bread in the sweat of thy brow!' "

"Of course, Aunt!" Henry laughed. "But that was a curse pronounced by God upon men for taking too deep a bite into the apple of the tree of knowledge. The Bible doesn't pretend it to be a blessing. On the contrary. The Book clearly states that it was a punishment for man's deliberate foolishness in losing paradise. And those of us who still have some dim memory of the Garden of Eden and would like to see our heritage restored cannot forget that toil is the symbol of our banishment. Besides, if you're going to quote Scripture, what about, 'We do not live by bread alone!' or 'Consider the lilies of the field, how they grow . . . they toil not, neither do they spin'?"

Henry glanced triumphantly at his aunt. This was getting too deep for her, a simple-minded woman. She did not reply at once. When she did, it was to ask quietly:

"Do you love this house, Henry?"

"Love it? Why, of course! Everything in it!" His answer was emphatic.

"Quite so. Well, it was all made by the toil of human hands, and made to endure too!"

"I don't deny it. But the human hands that made it loved their work. This may be readily seen. And when you love your work, it becomes play. I don't think, my dear, that men love their work today. Or they wouldn't make such ugly things!"

"I don't understand. What do you mean to convey by that?"

"Simply this. I acknowledge the good of work only when it's a pleasure. Pleasure exists only where there is love. I don't want a useful sensible wife because I'd not love her and I'd have no pleasure in working either for her or with her."

Aunt Emily threw up her hands in a gesture of despair. "My boy! These are new-fangled notions. What's the world coming to?"

"A bad end, I hope!" Henry laughed perversely. "My ideas, you see, are quite old, rather in keeping, I should say, with this old house and the things in it. What this house wants is a lovely woman, the kind I have in mind!"

"Your father tried it, Henry. The late Mrs. Thorley, your mother, was a lovely woman. I'm not saying anything against her. She suffered as much as anyone. It's simply that she was out of place. . . ."

"But——"

"Don't you see, Henry,"—she waved him aside—"the generations of Thorleys set their mark on this house, and every woman who entered it had to bow to the law of the

Thorleys. They've had to become part of the house even as every object added to the house had to become part of it. It was thus until your mother came——"

"And she upset the house——"

"She came a rebel into it!"

"Perhaps, the house was ripe for revolt."

"What do you mean?" She spoke in a voice of startled horror.

"Just that. The house is old, and may be getting over-ripe. Ready to fall apart, perhaps. Like an over-ripe cheese!" He laughed indecorously.

"How can you say so? The Thorleys have been ever sturdy folk."

"Even the sturdiest folk grow old!"

An uncomfortable tense silence followed. An expression of sadness stole over the patrician features of Aunt Emily and eclipsed the pride visible there a moment before. She was thinking: not thus did the Thorleys of old talk, and it gave her unutterable sorrow to hear these painful words from the nephew she was so fond of, and who was the only Thorley left to carry on the work of the Thorley house. She was about to give way to anger, but she reconsidered. It was not meet for a proper Thorley to reveal a deep emotion. And what was the good of it? But she could not wholly suppress the profound melancholy she felt, and Henry was too much preoccupied with his own thoughts to notice it. There was something peculiarly vibrant in her voice, as she said with a dignity, deliberate and emphatic:

"The Thorleys may grow old, but they never lose their faculties. Your grandmother Amanda died at ninety-three, but she died of pneumonia, not senility. She kept her wits about her to the last, and her final words were: 'It's pneumonia that's killed me, not old age!' "

"She must have been a wonderful woman," mused Henry, impressed by this revealing glimpse of his grandmother.

"She was a true Thorley," said Aunt Emily, with just a shade of asperity.

"How old is the oldest piece of furniture in this room?" Henry asked, glancing round at the antiques of the reception room.

Aunt Emily looked at her nephew, wondering at the seeming irrelevance of his question, and answered:

"Over three hundred years."

"And how old is the newest piece?"

"That side-board is the newest thing here. It goes back to Queen Anne's reign!"

"I thought as much!" There was the triumph of conviction in Henry's voice.

"Why do you ask?"

"Don't you see, my dear aunt, when the last piece was added the house stopped growing. It's the law, when a thing stops growing it's the beginning of the end. A house is like a human being. It has a beginning which is in childhood and youth, a middle which we call the prime of life, and the end—decay—death!"

The old spinster trembled at the words, as if they touched some secret chord in her, and her face grew pale. But she quickly recovered herself, and repeated a former question:

"Don't you love this house? Don't you love everything in it?"

There was a curious insistence, a curious solicitude in

her voice, and she waited eagerly for the answer—her heart cried, May God grant it be the right one!

"Yes. I like everything in it. I've said that before. But I love it as one loves a perfect old man who has lived gracefully and long, whose character lines have a dignity from noble living and whose hair is silvery white with slow aging. What's finer than perfect old age? It's like tonight's twilight—don't you love it, dear Aunt? Just look out of the window! The sun of a serene day has gone down behind the hills, the warm afterglow bathes the landscape, and the lengthening shadows tell us that the night approacheth. . . ."

Aunt Emily laughed. She was amused, but she was also vexed. "Please leave the poetry out, Henry! It only confuses the issues. I am a simple woman. Frankly, I don't see why the Thorley house shouldn't go on until doomsday. Life does not die with the old, but goes on through the children. Every winter's followed by spring——"

"No poetry, Aunt!" came the laughing interruption, which she ignored.

"——and as long as there's a man Thorley left, the Thorley race may be counted to go on!"

"It seems a heavy responsibility devolves upon me," Henry smiled.

"A heavy responsibility, Henry. You have no brother. You must keep the name of Thorley alive!"

"Of course, my dear Aunt," said Henry, with unconcealed tenderness. "But I must do more than keep the good name alive! I must make the next holder of the name worthy of the life I give him."

"I don't understand. You're enigmatical."

"No, I'm not," he protested. "My words have no hidden

meaning. I mean, if I'm to be a father, I don't want to be a father to a figurehead called Thorley. This house has enough furniture. I want a son who will do credit to the name! And to have such a son one must have the woman who is to be his mother. And she must have equal love for the father. Only out of great passion great spirits are born! No! No! Your Jane wouldn't fit the part at all! She's nice, but I might as well marry an extinct volcano!"

At the word, "passion," Aunt Emily's thin lips quivered. She was not fond of the word. It meant so many things to her, all of them unpleasant. It did not sound quite right in the old house with its elaborate array of cracked timbers. There had been passion enough in the late marital episode which had taken place there, and what had it done for the house? Its disastrous effects were not yet forgotten, they deeply impressed themselves on her dry mind, they still rankled in the old breast. The word raised a storm of memories in the usually placid firm brain. She was aghast.

"Passion?" she murmured at last in sibilant protesting accents. "It's not a nice word. It doesn't describe nice feelings!"

"What's wrong with passion?" Henry was clearly astonished.

"You would not have drunkenness in the house?"

Henry broke into a guffaw. "What a comparison! . . . I dare say," he added, after a pause, "passion is a form of intoxication. But, surely, Aunt Emily, it's a grand thing to be drunken with love!"

Aunt Emily visibly shuddered. She did not like her young nephew's attitude at all. And it boded ill to the Thorley house, which needed substantial pillars to sustain it; not light, flimsy columns reeling from the earth's slightest tremors. It was on her lips again to remind him of his father's grave error, of the havoc that flighty Russian woman had caused. But on second thought, seeing it useless, she desisted, and showed the strength of her disapproval by rising from her seat and gliding from the room without another word.

The matter was never broached again.

And now, months later, upon the receipt of a telegram from her nephew to the effect that he was coming to Ravenford with his bride, Aunt Emily became a prey to the most violent agitation. As she recalled, almost word for word, the conversation she had held with him, she wondered what sort of woman he could be bringing home as the mistress of the manor. Was it a foreigner, like his mother? She, doubtless, was. Were they not married at Marseilles? She did not anticipate anything good. But her sense of duty urged her to prepare a welcome to her foolish nephew and the mysterious female stranger, his bride.

The old house became the scene of great bustle and feverish excitement.

BOOK TWO

REALITY

CHAPTER SEVENTEEN

Homecoming

I T was the loveliest of April mornings, when the intimate English countryside, all agreen and aflower, presents its happiest face. The air was soft, the sky blue; a slight haze rose from the dew-wet ground and, like a broken silvery veil, interposed itself here and there, as it were in strips, shadowing but not obscuring the trees. The cocks crowed, the dogs ran about in sheer joy, barking at nothing. There was a ceaseless twitter of birds. Only the imperturbable tabby sat in the grass in undemonstrative silence, at the approach of a bird intensifying its eyes to two points of concentrated watchfulness. The early spring flowers reared their heads, a profusion of fresh colours and odours assailed the passer-by who chanced to glance through the broad railed gates. The old house, its mullioned panes catching glints of the sun, never looked statelier or lovelier than on this blithe windless morning, when nature appeared to hold her perfumed breath, and the trees and the flowers stood still, plunged in a mood of dream. The doors of the house were open, but no voices were audible; nor did a face peer from any of the open casement windows to greet the loveliness without. Only the straight thin ribbon of smoke ascending from a tall chimney gave token of life within. And, indeed, with good reason, the house within was agog with excitement. Was not the master, who had been absent for six months, this day returning, bringing a bride? Could there be a lovelier spot or a lovelier day to greet master and bride?

Everyone in the house had had his or her breakfast early. All was hurry and bustle here, what hurry and bustle for so old a body presenting so quiet an exterior! The maids were running up and down the stairs, or they were cleaning and dusting, or taking up rugs and putting them down again, or rearranging the furniture. Particular attention was given to the nuptial chamber, every detail of which was looked to under the watchful eye of Aunt Emily herself. The four uprising carven pillars of the broad four-poster bed shone, not a speck of dust was to be seen. The sheets had been aired by Aunt Emily, who also arranged the cut flowers in the several vases. A bright fire was blazing to take off the chill; the room had not been used since the late mistress died. Olga died in this very bed.

In the kitchen, the old cook, Mrs. Mundy, was excitedly preparing a meal such as she had not been asked to prepare for many a long day. The master and his bride were expected to arrive in time for luncheon.

But none in the house, not even Aunt Emily, was labouring under greater stress of excitement than Jenkins, the old butler. Jenkins was sixty, and he was excited because he was about to see Ravenford Manor pass into the reign of its third mistress. The old heart was trembling. Jenkins loved the old house, he had spent most of his life there, he was part of it—scarcely less a part of it than one of the cracked old beams. And though you wouldn't have guessed it to look at him—for with strangers he was dignified to a fault—he loved all his successive masters with that love which only dogs can show. He had re-

joiced with them, and he had sorrowed with them. He
did not know why he did one or the other, but to see his
master in a joyous mood was to awaken a like mood in
him—if he had had a tail, he might have wagged it; to
see his master grieve, was to make him sad. The Thorley
tradition was strong in his bones. His father had been a
butler there before him. A good butler he had been, too,
perfect in his art—for who will deny that being a butler
is not an exacting art?—and in the Thorley household, the
circumstance had given rise to the saying that "butlers
were born, not made." The truth of this was further
attested by the additional circumstance that Jenkins' thirty-
year-old son, William,—Jenkins himself was a widower—
was in service in London, and was expected to take his
father's place, in the event of his incapacitation or death.
And there was a rigid grace, one might say a butlerian
dignity, about Jenkins which lent ultimate conviction to
the jest. But rigid as were the contours of his clean-shaven,
lined face and of his tall gaunt body attired in formal
butlerian vestments, inside he was all soft and his heart
pulsed warmly to everything that concerned his master
and his master's household. And how well was his master
aware of it and bore him that tender if unspoken regard
which every kind master bears toward a loyal servant!
Words, indeed, were not needed here. One has but to
record the fact that on the one occasion that the usually
well Jenkins had a serious illness, his master spared neither
effort nor wealth to minister to him and, to the astonishment of the servants and the marvelling neighbourhood,
called in a specialist from London, just as he might have
done for his own kin.

On this day of days, when the master was bringing home

a bride, old Jenkins went from duty to duty about the house like one lost. Hours before his master's expected arrival, he alone of that household again and again projected his grey head through an open window in the direction from which the couple were expected. Each time he drew his head in with a keen disappointment, only to be expected.

Time, however, does pass, and the long hours of waiting passed by, the way of all hours. Suddenly, old Jenkins, standing on a second-story landing, his head craned out of the window, heard the familiar sound of wheels, and in the near distance he descried the familiar two-horsed carriage.

All at once, his heart leapt, gave wings to his old feet. He was eager to be there among the first to greet his master. Filled with unspeakable elation, his gnarled hand snatched at the old curved banister, and he tripped down the stairs faster than his feet had been wont to do of late. Unaccustomed to such rapid locomotion, something happened to the poor old man's brain, which grew giddy and faint, and, before Jenkins could control his limbs—for he tried to pause—his feet slipped from under him, and he clutched at an elusive rail; helplessly, his old body fell and will-lessly slid down a whole flight of stairs, his skull striking each step with a dull thud. The body fell at the feet of the master, who at that very instant entered, with his bride on his arm.

There was a few moments' silence, and there was consternation on all faces. Motionless, as it were transfixed in a nightmarish tableau, everyone stood in a tableaued group, with expressions of frozen horror, where but a few instants before thawing smiles had been. A tiny stream of blood trickled round the old man's temple. On one side his white hair was mottled red.

One maid then screamed, awakening all.

"It's Jenkins! . . . Oh, God!" the heart-rending cry came from Henry, suddenly coming to life. Elaine no longer holding his arm, he tenderly bent down over the prostrate limp body of the servant, whose eyes were closed but for the whites.

"Quick! Call the doctor!" he shouted, his handsome face writhen with compassion. . . . Then he felt for Jenkins' pulse and listened to his heart. He pronounced dejectedly: "I fear the poor fellow's dead. . . . Dead!"

So it was. Jenkins was really dead, beyond all human recall. A terrible dejection, despair, settled upon Henry, as he gazed upon the lifeless features of the faithful servant. For the time being he had forgotten his bride, who stood there, dazed, half-fainting, her frightened, woebegone eyes scarcely able to comprehend what had happened.

And again silence, that audible, terrifying silence, oppressive as the stillness before the clap of thunder.

Even the usually imperturbable Aunt Emily looked on quite helplessly, stunned by the untoward event which spoiled the welcome so arduously prepared for bride and groom. It was not the death of Jenkins that so profoundly stirred her. It was not compassion that was the dominant mood, though compassion was there; it was fear, a strange, nameless fear. It was as if in the moment given to rejoicing, a voice from the secret unknown had struck uncannily upon their ears, and in portentous accents bade them beware!

Suddenly, looking up in distraction from the body of Jenkins over which he was bending, Henry became aware of the presence of Elaine, and he sprang towards her in time to catch her swaying form as it was about to fall. "Water! Water!" he cried, and lifting her in his arms, he bore her upstairs and laid her gently in the magnificent carven bed.

Such was the homecoming of Henry and Elaine who, for six whole months, had known scarcely a moment of unhappiness. And because they had been so uninterruptedly and so blissfully happy, the unlooked-for misfortune struck them hard and with the sudden force and effect of lightning.

And a pall fell upon the old house. For a while, the steady whispers and murmurs of the servants were the only tokens of life; it was like the rumble of retreating thunder. Lifelessly the good Aunt Emily wandered about the house, and sometimes paused before the well-known bed-room hoping to catch the sound of voices which would indicate the return of life.

Henry was sitting at Elaine's side. Her eyes, turned upward, were open but motionless, as of one in a trance. Then came soft moans, uttered at intervals; and for a long time Henry was afraid to speak. He held one of her hands in his; in the beginning it had been cold, but as it grew warmer he took courage and began to speak. He spoke, mumbling comforting words, which did not appear to comfort her, perhaps because they lacked inner self-assurance.

"Dearest," he whispered, "don't take it so to heart. It was likely to take place anywhere and at any time!"

"No, no, Henry," she answered weakly. "We've been happy for six months—so happy, dearest. It was too much to expect to last forever!"

"But we are happy now, darling. I love you, and you

love me. And nothing can change it, nothing! Now, can it?"

"Yes, we love each other," she agreed. "But you know well, my dear, that that is not everything. Love is one thing, but happiness——"

"No! No!" he warmly protested. "When two beings love, nothing—nothing—can hurt their happiness. They should be able to bear misfortune, face blows, poverty, and what not. . . ."

She tenderly pressed his hand, and smiled a sage, sad smile, which seemed to emanate from some sudden memory of ancient experience, hitherto hidden. "Ah, darling! I don't deny that these things can't hurt our love. What I said was that they can and will hurt our happiness. You know it, and I know it!" She spoke with such conviction that a dread fell upon his heart, and the spark of hope went out.

Why should the death of the loved old servant make a difference? The thought troubled, rankled. . . .

"No, dear heart, you can't mean it!" he said, suddenly redoubling the ardour of his words, to banish his own doubts. "It's a pity the old man died, for I loved him. It is as if a pillar of the old house were gone, and he was a friend too. Yet much as I grieve his loss, what is his death against your love and mine? How can it affect our happiness? It's unreasonable to think that it can, I tell you!"

"Unreasonable? Perhaps. . . ." She mused, and smiled a faint odd smile, which was at the same time sceptical and tender. "Life does not exist on reason. You know that as well as I. For that matter, our whole happiness, the happiness you and I have known, is based on unreason.

Don't tell me it isn't so! No, no, let me finish,"—she waved him away, seeing he was about to speak. "Yes, I agree, it's unreasonable to attach importance to external things. But don't you see, my dear, it's not a matter of thinking, but of feeling. I have a premonition, a presentiment. . . ."

"How could the death of the poor old man have given you such an idea?" Henry interrupted her, but his heart was cold with a nameless fear.

She laughed. "You know better, Henry," she said.

"You mean," he said, knowing very well what was on her mind, for it was also on his, "that you are taking Jenkins' death as an omen?"

"Yes," she murmured, closing her eyes.

"But it may be only a coincidence," he argued, with effort.

"Do you believe that?" she asked, opening her eyes wide and looking searchingly into his.

"Yes," he said in a firm voice, resisting her intent gaze, but again his heart faltered.

"Do you really believe that?" she repeated, as if anxious to be convinced.

"Of course, my dear!" he cried, with ardour, seeing her wavering. "I've never yet lied to you!" Which was true, but he knew that he had lied to her now. He must lie, for their happiness was very dear to him. The time had come when truth had become terrible, when for truth he must give her the illusion of truth. "I tell you, it's a mere coincidence," he repeated with firmness, and once more resisted her gaze with his own.

"Perhaps," she yielded to him, and put her hand in his in token of her faith. "You will love me," she murmured, "you won't let unhappiness come!" Her warm hand clutched his, and fired him with a strange tenderness.

Yet his heart was full of misgiving, of unwonted bitterness, for he had won his victory with effort, by lying villainously to her; and somewhere deep within him he resented the use of subterfuge, this enforced abandonment of truth. They had been until now so natural, so effortless with one another, without premeditation they had entered into each other's thoughts and moods, and their culminating emotions had had a spontaneity and freedom which gave sanction to the most rapturous delights, the most ecstatic togetheredness. He had, immediately after the unfortunate episode of Jenkins' death, made a desperate effort to banish from his mind the idea of its being an ill omen, and might have succeeded if Elaine hadn't so persistently tormented him with the same morbid fancy. And now, because she had harped on it, it would not die, but recurred again and again, torturing him with its insistence on life. There was irony in the circumstance that having succeeded in convincing Elaine of its foolishness, he could not convince himself. It was a terrible, a bitter thing, to have to persist in dissimulation. There had been truth between them up to now, and he had never thought that the time would come when he should need to abandon it.

"You will love me," she repeated, "you won't let unhappiness come, will you?" Her feverish fingers, with an almost delirious frenzy, passed over his body, engendering in him a morbid passion, begotten of misfortune.

She wanted him, that much was clear. And he wanted her, this too was clear. But their desire of one another was no longer, as hitherto, induced by pure ebullient joy, but by some strange infiltration of sorrow flooding their beings with a bitter distress seeking relief.

With a frenzy born of despair, he caught at his wife's form rendered by distress supine, helpless and desirous, and with a savage fury, unaccountably welcome to them both, he wreaked his bitter passion upon her, pouring out all the welling bitterness that was in him. Her frail body, the vessel that received it, felt an inexplicable exultation; and sorrow mingling with sorrow lost their common bitterness and, by some unconscionable alchemy, left them both with an unaccustomed sense of shame, which lingered, filling them with confusion, with the sweet agony of new knowledge, such perhaps as was experienced by Adam and Eve after their transgression and expulsion from the garden of Eden; and it was already in their case as if they felt the nearing presence of the flaming sword of the cherubim.

Now, quite free from bitterness and pain, they lay quiescent in each other's arms, and the outer world receded from them into some vast void, and the immediate past appeared as a terrible dream, from which, shuddering, they had only just awakened.

It was late in the afternoon when Elaine, smiling faintly, raised her head.

"I am hungry," she said.

This was a token of life, a token of returned sanity, and Henry welcomed it as Noah must have welcomed the appearance of the first dove after the deluge. He alertly sprang from her side and, donning his blue silken dressing-gown, bent over Elaine's form and whispered:

"My darling will have the best feast available in the house!"

And he rushed from the room.

He presently returned, with the cheering words:

"It'll be here in a jiffy!"

And, indeed, five minutes later, Molly, one of the maids, appeared, bringing with her a white table-cloth and a tray containing plates and other utensils. She removed some gew-gaws from a small table and spread the cloth, and set the table for two. She then left the room, to reappear within five minutes with another tray containing a whole roast chicken, which had been prepared for luncheon, some salad, bread and butter, honey, and a bottle of white wine.

They seated themselves, facing one another, and avidly fell upon the fare set before them. So great was their hunger that they picked up the legs of chicken quite unceremoniously with their fingers and ate as if life offered no greater pleasure. At first, they ate in silence, interspersing a word here and there incidental to the meal. There was an extraordinary intensity in the mere satisfaction of the most crude (and most important!) of all appetites, without which satisfaction none of the other appetites could exist. Love and grief and ill-omens, all the things which had pleased or fretted them, were for the time being equally forgotten.

"I never was so hungry in my life!" said Elaine, finishing the final course consisting of a baked apple covered with thick clotted cream.

"Nor was I!" admitted Henry. "We've consumed a lot of nervous energy, and that always makes one hungry!"

A moment later he was to regret his words.

"Couldn't you avoid reminding of the unfortunate day?" she said, with a shade of asperity.

Unaccustomed to such a tone from her lips, he was too

astonished to reply. He looked at her in the hope of discovering the secret of this unaccountable attitude, and found nothing to enlighten him. She had the expression of a pouting capricious child. It distressed him, because he had not seen it in her face before and could not understand the cause. And now, at this extraordinary change in her, strange qualms seized him. What was wrong? Had marriage changed her? Never during the six months' "trial" had she, as much as by a word, been sharp with him. And now her words sounded unnatural on those lips, they cut him to the quick.

What wicked thing had he done? What wicked thing had he said?

He had far greater reason to feel unhappy over the sad death of the old man; he had known him from childhood and loved him and been beloved by him. He had made what he thought was a perfectly innocent remark. There had not been the slightest wish to give her pain, but rather an intense desire to assuage her grief.

He thought quickly, reconsidered. She was a woman, with a woman's delicate nervous organism, now tense and overwrought; he must be patient and kind. His troubled frown yielded to a smile. He said:

"I am sorry, my dear. I didn't mean to remind you of anything unpleasant. I myself feel rather broken up. I scarcely know what I'm doing."

"I know, I know, my dear," she said, more softly, stroking his hand. But a minute later, clutching fiercely at the pillow with tense fingers, she cried in a distraught voice, like one possessed:

"I wish we hadn't come here! I wish we hadn't come!"

Distressed by this new outburst, he flung himself down
on his knees beside her, and murmured:

"What is it, darling? What troubles you? You seem
frightened. What are you afraid of? I am here, and I
love you, and I shall take care of you. And we are in this
lovely old house——"

"Don't talk to me of this house, *please!*" she cried, visibly
moved by some overpowering emotion which he could not
fathom.

"I shan't if you don't want me to," he said, desperately,
trying to appease her and not knowing how.

"Don't you see," she said, half rising from her pillow,
and eyeing him intently. "I'm afraid of this house. Yes,
afraid!"

"Afraid? Why?" It seemed preposterous to him.

"I wish I knew. But there's something about it that
frightens me!"

"Nonsense, my dear," he said, half relieved to find her
fear indefinite, half apprehensive for the same reason;
the indeterminate nature of her fear inducing unknown
fears in him. He felt a chilling numbness creep over him.
His heart seemed to stand still.

"I have a presentiment, a foreboding," she went on. "A
misfortune seems to be hanging over my head!"

"No, no, my dear. You're overwrought because of what
happened today——"

"I wish it were as simple as that. . . . Are you sure no
one was killed in this house?" she asked, turning a frightened face towards him.

He laughed a reassuring laugh. "Quite certain, my dear!
Quite! The history of the house is an open book. Nothing
untoward has happened here. The Thorleys have been

a just race! They have no blood on their hands." The last part of his speech was uttered in a tone of amused irony. He added: "Really, you've nothing to fear from them! They've not even left a ghost. No, not the Thorleys! You may depend on it."

She appeared comforted by his words and the ardour with which they were spoken. And his hands caressed her, soothed her, frightened away her fears. His hands always acted hypnotically upon her, she grew quiet under their calming spell. She lay there supine, without a thought or a worry, while they stroked her; her eyes open and closed to the steady, almost mechanical motion of the upward and downward strokes of his warm, strength-exhaling hands. An inward purring contentment took possession of her, causing her to forget her fears. She was like an instrument in his hands, her nerves were like strings responding to their harmonious, gentle touch.

He was happy in that he was able to exorcise the devils out of her, yet he was afraid to desist lest they return. He had a feeling that if he desisted they would return. His fingers were getting tired, yet he kept on. He wondered when they might stop. And for the first time in their intimate life curious thoughts and feelings took possession of him, savouring of unaccustomed resentment—resentment of what?—he scarcely knew. It arose from a half-conscious realization of his strength passing from him, of the viaduct-like functions of his fingers by which his life's blood passed into her. It was not the giving, since love is giving, that some secret part of him mysteriously resented. But there was the simultaneous realization that his ceaseless caress was drawn from him not by some common spontaneous impulse as might have happened in the past, but that it was forced as it were by a whim or a caprice, by an imperative insatiable demand exacting proof of tenderness where no proof was needed. And his fingers were getting more and more tired, and because of the steady rigidity of his position, the bones of his body began to ache.

And now, by some curious association of ideas, the dream he had jestingly told her at second meeting, returned to his memory. In this dream, dreamt on the eve of this meeting, he caressed a tiger and had to go on caressing it; the certain penalty if he ceased was to be torn into bits. He also now remembered how she had laughed when he told her the dream and the precise words of her comment:

". . . . It doesn't sound auspicious. . . ."

And a little later:

". . . . Remember the tiger of your dream! . . . . I shall demand eternal patting. . . ."

Inexplicably, the memory now frightened him. After all those months, it seemed for the first time pregnant of ill-omen, just as this very day the circumstances of Jenkins' death presaged their own dire calamity.

He tried hard to crush the mood which increasingly possessed him. It was nonsense, of course! How superstitious he was getting to be. And, gathering all his courage, he said to himself: "No, no! What's come over me? I am selfish to grudge Elaine this caress. Love is giving, giving! Everyone agrees on that. She, poor thing, was badly shaken today, and she needs me, and I must give her everything! . . ." But his consolation was brief. The thought now troubled him: why hadn't such thoughts arisen before? They had seemed in the past to give freely and spontaneously of self, one to the other, and neither had been conscious of either giving or taking, or of responding to a demand. How could they? Together they had been one, and there is no consciousness of giving or taking when two are really one, inexpressibly one.

Under the influence of his mood, his tired fingers gradually ceased their caressing of Elaine.

She, instinctively and femininely intuitive, was not unaware of some thought possessing him alien, if not actually hostile, to his habitual mood. It was as if his caressing hands which, at the beginning, had imparted to her of their strength and tenderness, had at last, in the contact, allowed to convey to her some of his irrepressible doubts. And these doubts touched her like so many cold little shoots of water suddenly projected among the warm currents of his tenderness. She did not know what to make of it. She was tired, so tired; in this hour of nameless grief and harrowing ill-omen, as she felt herself helpless, sinking in a torpor of despond, she clung to him for deliverance. And, under the hypnotic caress of his hands, which had never failed her, she was conscious of being delivered. From the tips of what she called his "magical" fingers there emanated a strength which plunged her into forgetfulness, oblivion. How wonderful to forget, how delicious to float in mystic clouds, protecting her from evil!

And now she was like one awakened from a dream of quiescent happiness and returned to reality. At the withdrawal of his hands, this reality burst upon her with all the fury of a storm delayed. She rose from her pillow and, all distraught and wild-eyed, wrung her hands and cried out with a despair which seemed to come from the deepest depths of her:

"I hate you! I hate you! Leave me! Leave me!"

"Elaine darling!" cried Henry, in his turn, touched by her tragic gesture. "What's the matter? What have I done?"

"Go, I tell you! Go!" There was a desperate insistence in her voice.

Perspiration gathered round Henry's forehead, while he stood there helplessly, his hands to his temples, not knowing what to do or say.

"Go! Go!" she repeated, her cry growing shriller, penetrating to all corners of the old house. "Go! Go!"

Almost bereft of his senses, scarcely aware of what had happened, Henry tottered out of the nuptial chamber, like one who had just seen a ghost.

The cries gradually ceased, but from below excited voices reached him, and they sounded like muffled whispers from the secret chambers of his throbbing brain.

Then—as it were, the doors of these chambers blew open, as before a wild gust of wind, and there came an instant of lucidity, and in that instant an image formed. He saw a deep, dark cleft, a bottomless ravine, illumed by a flash of forked lightning, followed by darkness, silence. And in that same instant, he suddenly remembered: he had once cursed God!

CHAPTER EIGHTEEN

Life's Like That

THE sudden remembrance of the curious episode of six months before in the London fog now strangely affected the hero of this tale. So-called sensible people, if they had heard of his predicament and had had all the facts laid before them, would have said that here there was no predicament at all, that the situation was one wholly of his own making, that there was little cause here for losing sleep. And to do Henry Thorley justice, after the first shock of revelation, such was the attitude he tried to assume. Why blame a woman's hysterical outburst on the spitefulness of a deity engaged in running a boundless universe in which human beings, however, important to themselves, were no more than mere specks of dust or gyrating, fretting, active fleas, trained in the multiple arts of *amour-propre?*

He must try to be sensible, sensible, he went on thinking when assailed by doubts typical of men of his temperament, but he found this scarcely less difficult than it is for sensible people to feel romantically. Sensible people, even those professing faith, did their duty towards God and men in a moderate way; they worked by the sweat of their brows for six days a week, and on the seventh they paid tribute to their God by singing and praying, and leaving shillings and pence on the plate; they did this methodically and in the same spirit as they paid their taxes to Caesar. Such was Henry's notion of sensible people, and the idea of being sensible himself was inexpressibly distasteful to him. Something in him rebelled against an existence regulated by formal rules, conventions and duties, which deprived life of zeal, love and rapture. Life to him meant the exuberance of Mary pouring out rich ointment on Christ's feet and wiping them afterwards with her abundant silken hair, and not the protestations of the "sensible" against such flagrant waste of valuable substance. He could not see eye to eye with the sensible ones of the earth, he could not reconcile himself with their lack of fervour, their indefiniteness as characters who fell into the category expressed in the phrase, "neither fish not fowl nor good red herring." If they were only one thing or the other, and not the miserable compromise, which was neither light nor darkness, but an indeterminate grey, pestilential and deadly like stagnant water.

And, naturally, his deliberate effort at "being sensible" came to nothing. For to Henry Thorley, God was a real entity present in every manifestation of life. There was a human order and a divine order. The human order had its kings and governors, and its bishops and archbishops, graded down to petty officials and police officers and timid curates. The divine order had its angels and arch-angels, its invisible spirits, its hosts of familiars, animating the universe with active, flaming energies, which stir men to joy and sublime deeds. And impinging on both was a third order, the diabolic, with Satan and the devils and armies of imps, all those secret but ever present forces of evil whose tireless assaults so often succeeded in affecting an irreparable breach, enabling these spirits of darkness to roam about freely and at will, usually in some innocent

disguise, say that of lawyer, merchant or tinker; they had
the effrontery of appearing even in the shape of a bishop.

What relation had the divine and diabolic orders to
the human order? This relation, to his way of thinking,
was simple enough. God in man made man human; true
humanity was composed of divine attributes; the more
human a man was the more he approached to a likeness of
God; such was the meaning of man being made "in the
image of God." Again, Satan in man made man inhuman;
true inhumanity was composed of diabolic attributes; the
more inhuman a man was the more he approached to a
likeness of the Evil One.

Henry was far from arbitrarily accepting this order of
affairs as literal truth to which he might witness in a Court
of Law. He merely put it that way to himself because his
mind loved some sense of order, and the allegory which his
fancy devised gave him a point of approach and departure,
a standard of values. By means of sub-conscious channels,
he perceived the presence of forces in conflict, forces within
and outside of human beings, often too in one and the
same person. It really seemed as if God and devil con-
tended for the possession of this or that soul, and between
the two the poor object of these contentions was subjected
to such struggles, despairs and lacerations as ultimately to
leave it wounded and scarred, and craving for rest, peace,
and even death. Such was the existence to which the
chosen of the fates, those marked of God or Satan, were
doomed.

Even as he struggled to be "sensible," he was forced to
return again and again to his original conclusion. And it
was devastating.

What distressed him most about his homecoming with

his bride was that it made him feel that the tenure of his kingship and godship were at an end. For during the six months of their trial marriage, he had led, so it seemed to him, an existence as perfect as was permissible on this imperfect earth. Elaine was his bride, and she was his kingdom and his world. And by the power of love he ruled over his kingdom, and by the power of love he re-created his world, and in the hurricanes and eruptions of love's passion and in the warmth and sunshine of tenderness he shaped his world according to his desire, and this world, grateful and submissive, gave him its adoration. Yes, he was king here, and a god too, and limited as his world was, as far as it went, it was perfect. Perfect. Thus, before this day it had been.

But now—but now——

The invisible enemy had effected a breach. The enemy had waited in ambush, and, at one bold stroke, destroyed his happiness forever. Forever? Yes, forever. Because such perfect happiness as had been his and Elaine's depended on mutual confidence, and on an unbroken continuity of this confidence, on the condition that nothing, nothing, nothing, no circumstance whatsoever, could ever violate the fortress of their love in which they had entrenched themselves. There was no longer any serenity, no longer any assurance that what happened today would not happen again, no longer that sense of permanence which had given such a feeling of the absolute. His world, of which he had been hitherto the master, had gotten out of hand, and that challenging spirit of his which in a moment of incitement had caused him to curse God now caused him to ask: What was the trouble with the greater outer world—had it gotten out of God's hand as his. Thor-

ley's, world had gotten out of his? Was it yet again
Pygmalion creating a statue after his heart's desire only
that ultimately the lady might step from the pedestal
thumbing her nose at her creator?—God Himself, or
Henry Thorley, or whoever it might be that created a
world only to lose it?

He laughed, not without bitterness, at the recollection
of the jest uttered by him at his first meeting with Elaine.
And he remembered her answer: "What else could you
expect? The lady was probably bored standing on the
pedestal. I should do the same, unless—" But, in spite of
his entreaty, she never finished her answer. "Unless what?"
he now asked himself, the question he had asked her.
And as he had hesitated to tell what he had surmised as
regards the enigma, so now again he hesitated to formulate
his answer to himself, and averted his gaze from the face
of truth, a glimpse of which he had caught, as it were,
through the chink of a door, then passed on quickly. "Impossible! It cannot be!" he cried, trying to crush his fears,
which, like birds once driven away, came flitting back into
his heart, pecking there importunately at his heart's substance. For if his secret thought were true, then the answer
was to be sought in his own heart, not Elaine's; in Pygmalion's, not in Pygmalion's creation.

He was reassured on seeing her that evening. She received him in her room with a happy welcoming smile.
She was gentle, all contrite, and her eyes implored forgiveness.

"I was a bad girl," she said. "Really, I scarcely know
why I acted as I did."

"You gave me a bad scare," he smiled. "I thought you were possessed."

"Indeed, I was," she caught at the phrase. "It was really as if something outside myself had gotten hold of me. I felt desperate, as if some catastrophe hung over my head. I wanted to run and scream. I am sorry, my dear." And she ran her fingers softly through his hair.

He felt intensely relieved. And with the suddenly renewed optimism of a romantic, he conceived a wild hope that all his lugubrious meditations of that twilight had no basis in fact and had been born of fears engendered by the nerve-racking events of the day, unlikely to recur again.

"It's happened before . . . long ago," she went on, after a pause. "I was a young girl, and one day, without apparent cause, I threw myself on the floor, and in a most unseemly manner I began to kick with my legs and to scream. . . . I remember how my poor aunt stood over me and tried to calm me. But the more she tried the harder I kicked, and the louder I screamed, and the more terrible were the words with which I abused her. And I had a most terrible desire to do something violent, something destructive, break crockery, tear the curtains, trample the flowers in the garden. . . . My aunt was in tears. Seeing that her appeals only made me act more disgracefully, she left me. And, strangely enough, once I was alone, I grew quiet and was myself again. Really, I don't know what possessed me. . . ."

"Very likely you were possessed," said Henry. "I mean in the sense that people were possessed in the Gospels, when the healing hands of Christ cured them. I have no doubt," he added, laughing, his spirits now fully restored, "in Mather's day, in New England, you would have been burned for a witch. We know so little about these things. . . ."

"Oh, I don't know about that!" she retorted. "Poor aunt consulted a doctor about it afterward. And he said it was most likely just an attack of indigestion!"

"Doctors nowadays have a reason for everything," Henry again laughed. "And being possessed has gone out of fashion!"

"It's a fact, I did feel possessed," she admitted. "But it was due to surroundings. You know how susceptible I am to surroundings."

He nodded in the affirmative, as he thought of the Pompeiian episode. But she was thinking of the old house, to which they had just come.

"Well," she continued, "it wasn't altogether the shock of Jenkins' death that upset me, though that was bad enough. I've seen death before. . . . But immediately I got into this room I felt as if something took possession of me, as if someone had been killed here. I felt most horribly!"

"And have you this feeling now?"

"No, not now. . . ."

The answer reassured him. He was stroking her head with tender hands.

"You have wonderful hands," she said, not for the first time. "When you stroked me this afternoon, it seemed as if a ghost had left me, and I found myself lulled into forgetfulness. It was as if your hands were healing me. . . . And then. . . ." She closed her eyes at the recollection of her experience.

"And then?" he questioned her anxiously.

"And then—your hands seemed to grow alien to me. It was as if I were being drenched with warm and cold water at the same time, and I found myself wondering if something had gotten hold of you too. I could always tell the touch of your hands. If I were blindfolded, and did not hear your voice, I'd know you at once by the wonderful touch of your hands. During all these months I've never once been unhappy but the touch of your hands banished depression, home-sickness. . . . This afternoon I needed your hands as I never needed them before. . . . Yet towards the end, I actually found myself shrinking from them. . . . I couldn't understand it. . . . It was strange, and it was horrible, because only a little while before I found such comfort in them. . . . I don't know. . . . Perhaps, the fault was in me. . . ." She looked imploringly to him for reassurance.

"I think I was too much upset," he explained. "I was tired. My own hands felt cold and dead to me. You are right. My spirit had gone out of my body . . . out of my hands. . . ."

"And I was a wicked girl, my dear. I thought you had ceased to love me."

"No! No!" he protested. "You don't believe that! I've never yet come to you as one tired of your embrace. Today. . . ."

"That is true, my dear," she mused. "Yet you were somehow different today. . . . I don't know how to describe it. . . ." Troubled doubt shaded her words, and again, her big eyes, half curious, half imploring, sought his for reassurance. "When you were so close to me, I almost felt as if it were some stranger. . . . Yet I didn't altogether dislike it. . . . I felt strange too. . . . It was as if two different beings loved one another, and loved differently. . . ."

There was truth in what she said, his heart could not deny; and he was eager to be as candid with her as she had been with him. He hastened with an explanation, to make a clean breast of it.

"We must never doubt each other again," he said gently. "When you thought I had ceased loving you, I thought you had ceased loving me. I had a feeling of being thwarted. My impulses seemed paralyzed. We have always loved each other freely. Neither you nor I have ever withheld ourselves from each other. For to love is not enough, one must be also loved. And when you said you hated me, I believed you. And it froze the very marrow in me. In my turn, I withheld my love because I thought it was not wanted. I felt as if the temple in which I worshipped and had such raptures of happiness had suddenly tumbled about my head, and I did not know why. And I got all mixed up inside. Such sadness and bitterness and confusion filled me, and oh, what despair! And, when at last, I saw you wanted me . . . my love . . . such joy and relief came to me . . . such fury and fierceness too. And I seized you to my heart, my dear, as one seizes one's own world which has all but escaped one's grasp. And in that instant, dearest, I gave all that was in me, my love and my hate, my troubles and my confusion and my rage, all the best of me and all the worst of me—all this I gave you, could not help giving you! Ah, yes, and I was cruel, fiercely cruel, and that I loved too—for that too arose from my love. And for the first time, I began to understand something of the nature of cruelty, in that it grew out of germ of love. . . . No, I don't say I understand it altogether. . . ."

I only say I understand cruelty arising out of love. . . ."

As she listened to this extraordinary confession, her eyes glowed more and more warmly. She felt no displeasure, only happiness. "And you gave all that to me?" she said, in a tone of reproach which she made quite clear she did not want taken seriously. "Ah, but you were fierce! Like a lion making an assault on a helpless prey. But I loved you like that! You were different, and it was as if I saw a new world, a world of which I had been ignorant before. And I seemed to step outside myself, as you stepped outside yourself; and we were no longer in the small world that was ours before. And now I wonder if we shall ever get back into it again! . . ."

"We must, and we shall!" he interrupted her.

But she waved him away. "No, no," she said firmly, with feminine realism. "We might as well face the truth. We've stepped out of one world into another, and it will be hard, perhaps impossible, to get back. For today, when you were with me, I felt the presence of another world, a larger, less perfect, more confusing world, full of confusion and trouble and excitement—yes, and of cruelty too. Haven't you said so yourself? And I took your rage and your troubles and your pain, and felt the happier for it. Why, I don't know. . . ."

"I am glad," he mumbled, her speech shaking him out of his relative complacency.

"Don't you see," she cried, taking his hands in hers, "all that I am I owe to you! I am a different woman from the one you met at Lady Brinton's six months ago. You've churned me all over. Our embraces have been no mere orgies of lust, but a real communion between two spirits. And I've been so inexpressibly happy. Oh, I can't think of hurting you! Please remember, my dear, I was a wicked girl today and, who knows?—I may be a wicked girl again. For things *are* different. And I love you more, not less!"

Her speech affected him strangely. He felt stirred and exulted; at the same time a mood of uncertainty possessed him: life was no longer walled in within an enchanted circle bounding a limited but perfect world: it reached into this direction and that, into an outer chaos, illimitably vast, and full of active lights and shadows and lurking dangers and precarious delights. It was a world not of the eternally static as theirs had been, but of the eternally impending and as subject to the weathers as the earthly earth itself. He was allured, and he shrank back.

For the time being more care-free than they had been since coming to Ravenford, they laughed gaily and happily, and not even the body of a dead man in the house eclipsed their anticipation of renewed happiness. Tactfully, Henry suggested that they should have supper in the bedroom. The day had not left him without apprehensions of further disaster, and he was not anxious for a revival of the day's memories. Besides, he was not sure that Elaine and Aunt Emily would get on together, and that evening was no time for a test. Enough had happened in one day. Quite enough.

For days prior to the home-coming, Henry feared the meeting between his aunt and Elaine. He could not conceive of two characters more diametrically opposed, the one solidly sensible, the other fervently romantic. And, indeed, even though he was not aware of it, in the tragic moment of Jenkins' death, the two women had the opportunity to glimpse the other, and that single glimpse was sufficient for one to take measure of the other. The older woman, who was the more collected of the two, took the more deliberate impression. She was not surprised. It was what she had expected. The day richly reinforced by hysterics on part of the bride left her to meditate upon the folly of men and to ponder her own course of action. As for Elaine, her impression was instantaneous, coming as in a flash of lightning, and in the hours that followed it was remembered and forgotten and again remembered: it arose like the clear image of an austere genii out of smoke and vanished in smoke, this phenomenon frequently recurring.

With the appearance of Elaine, the whole past of Ravenford re-erected itself before Aunt Emily's eyes. It was William Thorley and Olga all over again, was the inevitable thought. For Elaine strangely reminded her of the Russian woman who had brought the first misfortunes on the Ravenford house. And, in seeing Henry and Elaine together, she unwillingly shrank back as if she had seen ghosts.

At the same time, having in mind all that had passed before, she was determined because of the love she bore her nephew not to antagonize the new mistress, but to do everything in her power to maintain the peace of the house against any emergency which might occur. And it would occur, she hadn't the least doubt. She "felt it in her bones." And what Aunt Emily felt in her bones had nearly always a way of coming true. For some reason, which no one has ever explained, it is easier to prophesy evil than good. Is it because evil is so much more positive—should one say, more active—than good?

Be that as it may, in spite of the good lady's amiable intentions, the day came when she made her first remonstrance, much delayed. It was on a Sunday morning.

"My dear Elaine, you never go to church. All the mistresses of Ravenford have been church-goers. There is a Thorley pew which has been in the family for generations. The parishioners expect the Thorleys to set them an example!"

"Can't one be a good Christian without going to church, Aunt Emily?" asked Elaine, sweetly, not without mockery.

"Perhaps . . ." answered the older woman, for a moment at a loss. "But it doesn't look nice. People are talking about it!"

"People are talking?" Elaine turned on her. "Who is talking? Please be clear!"

"Why, the servants among others. . . ."

"So I'm to be beholden to servants for what I do?" Elaine burst out laughing. "What next? . . . Well, my dear, if it gives them any pleasure, let them talk! I shouldn't lose any sleep over it if I were you! I'm not, I assure you!" And she swept out of the room, leaving the discomfited lady pondering on "the sort of creatures decent men marry." And she murmured, "Poor Henry!" —adding under her breath, "The poor boy will need me!" She was more determined than ever to give no offence to the mistress of Ravenford, such as might force her to leave poor Henry unprotected.

It is hard, however, in this life to keep to any resolution which in an extreme situation might prove a violation of one's own fundamental character. And, indeed, scarcely a week passed before the good Emily was in hot water again. She was having dinner with Henry and Elaine, when she casually said:

"Molly was just showing in the pantry the dress you've given her."

"I hope she was pleased," said Elaine.

"Pleased? Why, everyone in the servants' quarters is all agog. They all wondered how you could give away such a lovely dress to a mere servant!"

"Why shouldn't the poor things occasionally enjoy the same things that we do? What do you say, Henry?" Elaine asked, turning to her husband.

"I quite agree, my dear," he replied, smiling whimsically. "The Christian idea appeals to me. The other day in London I saw a beggar to whom I felt strongly inclined to give one of my suits, when it occurred to me that he couldn't possibly use it. It wouldn't have been good for his particular trade. He'd miss the ventilation! So I contented myself with giving him a half crown."

"That was very sensible of you," said Aunt Emily gravely, ignoring the lightness of his speech. "I'm the last in the world to deny charity to the poor. But it seems the lower classes are happier kept in their places. For a poor girl like Molly to strut about in all that finery sets a bad example to her companions and neighbours. I'm sure it makes for envy and bad blood!"

"What exactly do you mean?" asked Elaine, in a tone which the lady thus addressed thought rather ominous.

"I mean," proceeded Aunt Emily, very much against her will, "that it's unfair to awaken feelings in persons of the lower station. Molly's a nice deserving girl, to be sure. But do you think it makes the other girl—Jane, I mean— any happier to see Molly rigged out in that fashion?" The speaker was treading on dangerous ground, and she knew it; there was no help for it now. Her indignation and irritation had gotten the best of her, and she saw no way of retreat. And she was, really, terribly vexed with what she considered Elaine's profligacy. She regarded the dress which had been given away—it was purchased from one of the most fashionable of Parisian couturiers—quite good enough for longer wear, and she had thought of Henry's purse which paid the bills. She did not like seeing the modest Thorley fortune dissipated. No, not she! The thought rankled, and it made her reckless. A sudden fury possessed her. What cared she what she said?

Aunt Emily scarcely looked up from her plate while she spoke; it was only towards the end that she looked up, and rather challengingly. There was repressed thunder in the air. A tense silence followed, momentarily relieved by the approaching footsteps of Jane bringing in the roast.

"Jane!" called the mistress, when the girl had set down the roast and vegetables on the serving-board.

"Yes, ma'am?" Jane, a pretty, red-cheeked country maid, stood at respectful attention.

"Miss Thorley thinks you ought to have a dress as pretty as the one I've given Molly. She doesn't think it right that Molly should have something that you haven't? . . ."

"Me . . . ma'am? . . ." The girl stood open-mouthed, very much embarrassed. A deep flush crept over her cheeks.

"Jane," went on her mistress, "after dinner, I want you to go up to my room, and in the wardrobe there you will find the black lace dress . . . you know the one I mean. . . ."

"You mean the one with the flounces of lace, ma'am?"

"Yes, the one I wore last Sunday!—my best one. . . ."

"Yes . . . ma'am. . . ."

"I make you a present of it, Jane. . . ."

"A present . . . me . . . ?" The girl stammered. Her

flushed cheeks suddenly grew pale. She stood there, transfixed, uncomprehending. The girl caught the unfriendly
stare of Aunt Emily, and was further confused thereby.
There was silence.

"Can't you understand?" flared up the girl's mistress.
"I give you that lovely black dress! Go and take it! Now!
And don't stand there gawking!"

The poor girl, not knowing what to do, bestirred herself. "Thank you, ma'am . . ." she murmured in timor-
ous, almost lachrymose accents, and disappeared from the
room.

There was a dead silence. An explosion was imminent.
And it came. Aunt Emily, who had never before in her
life shown a temper, now magnificently exploded.

"I can't stand it! I can't stand it!" she cried, flinging
down her napkin and, rising to her feet, swept out of the
room.

"Elaine!" Henry whispered reproachfully, giving his
wife a look of appeal, and, leaving his food uneaten, ran
after his aunt.

He pleaded with her to stay, but she would not listen,
and went on packing her bags. She would not stay in
that house. Not so long as "that creature" was there. No,
not for anything.

He saw his aunt off, and, sad of heart, returning to the
Manor, meditating upon the singular fact that of the two
women who loved him—were they not his Mary and his
Martha?—neither, in the personal quarrel, which had en-
sued, had stopped to consider him or his welfare. It had
been each for himself. And the fact irritated and rankled.

He went to his room, and studied the portrait of his
mother intently and long.

CHAPTER NINETEEN

Irony

TIME is a very strange thing. So much can happen in an instant, so little in a stretch of years. Time's isolated high summits, looked back upon, appear to run into one another, telescoping as isolated hills may at a distance appear to telescope to form a non-existent range. Thus looked at, miles may telescope into furlongs, and years into a series of moments closely grouped.

In the lives of human beings time and space are closely inter-related. Dull times are associated with dull places, the monotony of plains forces monotony upon the human beings who inhabit it, vast flat spaces inflict their mood on the soul of man, which sees time as flat, endless and tedious. And as the sight of a summit breaks the monotony of space, so an intense living moment breaks the monotony of time.

How hard, then, for human beings who, for six months, passed from summit to summit of rapture, from one enchanting spot to another, to settle in a valley, shut in by downs and sea! You've moved about so long, then have ceased to move about, and time suddenly stops still, and space moves only when you move, when you are on the train or aboard ship.

To such a pass have Elaine and Henry come.

The trial marriage, lived intensely, in constant motion, had been a complete success; the legal marriage, lived in stationary quiet, in a world of outer monotony, had become an effort at readjustment in a world in which the moving beckoning flame had become extinguished.

They loved one another as much as before, yet loving was not enough. Why not? The question vexed Henry almost to madness. They had been a world in themselves —so he had thought—immune, in the love they bore one another, from the outer world pressing upon them; and he and she had based their legal tie on this, the rapturous existence they had led for six months immune from the persecutions of the outer world. He had had every reason to believe this to be due to their living in one another, to their keeping the outer world out; but if this was not so, then those six months of bliss had been an illusion and the bottom dropped out of life for him. And, oh, what irony of ironies that the rapturous trial marriage should have led them both to a wretched legal marriage based on falsehood! He did not want to believe this; it seemed incredible to him. Then the vile thought recurred: he had cursed God, and, perhaps, this was God's way of replying with a jest, a grim jest. The Catholic order was reversed, and He had provided heaven before purgatory. For, after those six idyllic months, a purgatory Henry's life had become: a purgatory—not however without idyllic moments to remind him of what he had had and lost. He had cursed God, and he was now the accursed of God. The thought pursued, he could not banish it from his mind.

The first year at Ravenford passed fairly happily. This was in no small degree due to Elaine's condition. Pregnancy and care of the infant after birth—there was the pleasure of its being a boy—caused her to overlook the environment which her romantic spirit deprecated and loathed. At this period, the hysterical attacks which began on the day of Jenkins's death were few and far between. She was not interested in household affairs, and Aunt Emily's duties had been taken over by a youngish good-looking Frenchwoman, who later was to undertake the additional duty of imparting French to Richard. Elaine chose Mlle. Panchaud herself; she liked good-looking sprightly people about her. The servants and neighbours were chagrined at the introduction of "furriners" into the honoured household, and they ominously shook their heads. They felt sure it would lead to no good. In this part of the world all men owned to being stalwart "Britishers," and were proud of it. Moreover, Elaine insisted on Mlle. Panchaud sitting at the table with her and Henry, making her to all intents and purposes an intimate member of the household. This was thought to be a breach of social etiquette: it was not meet for servants to sit at the table of their masters. All were agreed that men and women of a higher station in life should maintain that place and not allow themselves to be contaminated by the presence of those of a lower order. "What next?" everyone murmured.

Beside—besides—the bolder ones protested—the French lady was a "pretty piece," and she dressed—well, well—there was certainly a lot of flounces and frills about her—and she had satins and silks—and French ladies, generally speaking, especially when they were pretty, were not to be trusted in a decent British household—and the mistress was running chances, putting temptation in the way of a man! It was tempting Providence itself.

Oblivious of rumours and criticism, Henry approved of his wife's ways and decisions. If these things pleased Elaine and added to her happiness, why cavil?

Far graver matters worried him. Elaine had not gotten over her feeling about Ravenford, and was becoming increasingly restless. Nine months after Richard's birth, he became concerned about her health, and whisked her off to Italy, hoping that the scene of their original happiness would revive her spirits and their previous joys.

Everything happened as he wished. They recaptured their former perfect if limited world. They lived for the day, in and for each other. And every day was the same, perfect if limited. They ate Italian food, and drank Chianti, and touching feet and knees under the table and exchanging glances above played at being lovers, which they were, and, holding hands, they skipped down the nocturnal deserted streets, until reaching their door he would lift her with a fierce tenderness in his arms and bear her, as if she were no more than a feather, up two flights of stairs. Then they loved, as if loving were all, all . . . as if life were made for loving, and for nothing else.

Why should one worry and fret about what was past? Yet Henry, for all his happiness, did worry and fret. For in instants of meditation he could not reconcile himself with the circumstance that only in a perfect setting could their limited perfection exist, and that Elaine and he were not sufficient unto themselves in less perfect settings. It vexed him to think that his power over Elaine waned at Ravenford, and that in caressing Elaine his fingers lost some of their healing virtue in climes other than this. To be sure, he made the most of his happiness here, but the accursed thought persisted: the past, through memory, insidiously projected itself into the present; and the future, future sorrow—certain, because they could not always remain in the perfect setting—reached out with prescient claws and, likewise, scratched into the shell of present happiness.

So even here, in surroundings they both loved so well, he found himself looking as it were through the tiny window of his perfect shell upon a world hostile and portentous, whose fitful lightnings would sometimes light up the interior of the shell and reveal its fragile nature and wavering instability. It gave rise to brooding when he was alone. A nostalgia, for heaven knows what, would seize him. It was no common home-sickness, no mere desire to be back in Ravenford where he was born and which was his home, but a fearful longing, a terrible gnawing at the heart, for something elusive and not within reach. It was homesickness for a home which was not here on earth; it was a yearning for heavenly perfection, enduring and changeless, which might be on earth had men chosen that it should be so. Here was potential paradise, all but for immortality; yet men chose to make hell of it.

And he thought: were not homesickness and wanderlust —one and the same thing, in the sense he meant it—but symptoms of the incurable malady contracted by man when he first put his foot on this side of Eden? Life was an eternal wandering to find the original heaven-granted shelter, where happiness was an eternal reality, not an illusion whose false beacons lured men on to quests unattainable.

He had thought his Eden was in the heart of Elaine, and that her Eden was in his. . . . The precariousness of happiness, dependent on the fitting environment, the perfect setting, once made clear to him, made him wretched. His happiness did not appear to belong to him, it was the setting's—he merely enjoyed it by virtue of his presence, and Elaine's presence, within the perfect frame. The thought obsessed him, was the inevitable fly in the precious ointment of his joy.

What of Elaine?

She was experiencing her own emotions scarcely less intense than Henry's. Her emotions were pure, as a woman's often are, unmarred by admixture with extraneous reasoned thought. She loved or she loathed; between these two points there was little gradation. She was all light or all darkness, no intermediary penumbral shadows intruded on her nature. She loved Henry the lover, not the husband; she loathed Ravenford for what it was: a fortress of stalwart, respectable life, made for stalwart, respectable persons, good enough in their way but not her kind. It was not her place. And if Henry was what she had at first taken him to be, it was not his place either. It was made for Aunt Emily, and Aunt Emily's kind.

Ravenford exercised a strange effect on her. She admitted that the house was beautiful; yet she also felt that the whole place exhaled an aroma of dead men and dead women hostile to her, alive only in their hostility. It was as if there were hidden evil here lurking in the corners; and at times, more particularly in the twilight, she was acutely conscious of spirits hovering in the shadows: in vulnerable moments, ready to spring at her and cause her inwardly to cower and to shrink. And it always made her feel as if she were on the verge of dire calamity. Unwillingly, scarcely aware of what she was doing, she would turn upon Henry, and, always to his astonishment, abuse him roundly for bringing her here. At such times, she would appear to be beside herself, and she would use language not to be expected of a gentlewoman, much to the distress of her husband, who used all the persuasion of his love in the vain effort to appease her. It was true that later, issuing from her mood as from a trance, she would act as if nothing had happened, or, more rarely, appear repentant, accusing herself of being "a bad, wicked girl" for acting so wilfully and ungratefully toward so devoted a husband and lover; moreover, one who regardless of provocation, never went out of his way to reproach or upbraid her. Only why in the name of Jehoshaphat didn't he take her away from here? Intelligent man and devoted lover that he was, why did he do nothing to remove the cause of her discontent? What if it did mean abandoning Ravenford? Of course, she knew it was hard for him. Men are prone to cling to the haunts of their forefathers; here was a manor house handed down from father to son, through many generations. Yet what was a manor house, however old, however precious, against the most precious of all precious things—Love itself? With the birth of Richard, she somewhat modified her attitude: she must live here for Richard's sake. Richard must not lose his inheritance because of a woman's whim. If she gradually reconciled herself to the idea of preserving the Manor for the Thorleys to come, she did not abate an iota in her loathing of the place; and if anything, loathed it the more. It was during a particularly intense outburst of loathing that Henry decided to take her to Italy for a holiday—or "new honeymoon," as he put it. It happened towards twilight. They were sitting in her spacious bed-chamber, by the broad bow window, whose casements had been flung open, and they were looking out to the sea. The tang of autumn was in the air, and now and then a fitful gust circled among the tree-tops, causing flurries of leaves to sweep through the air and fall to the ground. Elaine felt unusually sad, and Henry vainly tried to cheer her.

"Take me away from here! Take me away!" she cried, at last, in answer to his persistent entreaty.

"Why do you so hate this place?" he asked her, not for the first time.

"I can't tell you. But I just l-loathe it—I l-loathe it!"

"But there must be a reason," he expostulated.

"If you must have a reason," she answered after much urging, "it's this! Someone was murdered here!"

The answer astonished him; for she had said the same thing on the day of her arrival.

"But, my dear, no one was murdered here, I assure you! The records of the Thorley house are an open book. I've opened all its pages to you. You know as much about Ravenford as I do!"

"More than I want to know!" she snapped. "But you yourself have told me that someone was murdered here!"

"I? . . ." He sprang from his chair and faced her. "What do you mean?"

"You know as well as I do!"

Now he knew what was coming. "You mean——?"

"Yes. You know what I mean. Let the stupid take things literally. You and I know better. . . . Murder with a knife is kinder than subjecting a poor woman to incessant anguish!"

"M-my father," he faltered, "my father was kind—to my mother."

"As you are kind to me!"

"But——"

"But he—or this house—killed her just the same! She begged, I'm sure, to be taken from here. How hard, how pitifully, she must have begged!"

"She couldn't have begged! Father loved her, would have done anything for her!"

"Well, what if she didn't! She probably knew it to be useless. They say Russians are fatalists. Anyhow, she must have been one!"

"But I tell you——"

"She was murdered! She was murdered, I tell you!"

He was in despair, and he stared at her in perplexity.

"Why don't you change your room?" he said, at last. "If——"

"Not for the worlds!" she cried. "She's the only thing in the house friendly to me. She knows what it is to be tortured as I am. As for the rest——" She made a helpless gesture of despair.

"The rest?" he pressed her.

"They're everywhere about the house—despotic men and cringing women——"

"What are you saying?" Henry showed exasperation for the first time. "That's nonsense, of course! The Thorleys have been just men to a fault!"

"Just men!" she mocked him. "Just men are always hard men! It's not justice they want, but *their* justice. . . . Go away from me! Leave me!" Her voice rose to a high pitch, expressive of the intensity of her emotion.

He rose to his feet, hesitating; but did not go. Instead, he reached out his hands towards her, hoping they would soothe her, heal her, as they had done so often in times gone past.

She shrank from him. "Don't touch me! Don't touch

me!" came the shrill cry as of one possessed. Then, on his slowly proceeding to the door, she collapsed in the chair, and broke into a paroxysm of grief.

Hesitating, he returned, and, shaken by the scene, he stood looking down at her, wondering what he should do.

"Listen," he said at last, slowly. "What do you say to starting for Italy? At once, I mean. . . . Too late tonight —let's say tomorrow!" And he waited for her reply.

Her paroxysm abated, became a low, almost inaudible moan. After some minutes, this also ceased. He repeated his question:

"Yes, darling, what do you say to Italy? We can start tomorrow. It'll do you good. You need a holiday. We both need one. . . . Well, my dear? . . ."

"I don't need a holiday . . ." she murmured, softly, in contrite tones.

"What's the odds? Let's call it a honeymoon. . . . We haven't had one, you know. . . ." He laughed. "We came here at once after our marriage. . . ."

"I'm a bad, bad girl," she said, seizing his hand and pressing a kiss upon it. "And I don't deserve such a kind husband. Only it's not really a husband I want but a lover . . . the old lover!"

"You shall have him," he said, and, sitting down on the arm of her chair, he smoothed her head.

"I've been dreadfully unhappy," she said. "Ravenford is something to live up to, but what one has to live up to I don't like. It's not a case of improving the place. It can't be improved," she added equivocally, with a smile.

He wondered if she referred to the plan he was cogitating in his mind for making his cottagers happier, and he had gone so far with preliminaries as to plan to begin the actual work on the morrow. The plan included a scheme for making the cottages more comfortable, and provided for the lightening of dull lives with diverse entertainment reminiscent of England of other days. With an inward sigh, unheard by Elaine, he put it all from his mind.

And on the following day they started for Italy, to begin their "new honeymoon."

Elaine felt not a little ashamed at first for having forced her husband's hand. Was he not devoted to her wherever they were? And now she had gone and ruined his long-deferred pet project for making the countryside happy. She remembered with some satisfaction that she had offered to stay. But he had vigorously waved the suggestion aside. Once away from Ravenford, in the midst of their renewed rapture, she forgot her scruples and thought only of the wonder of love, and loved her wonderful lover with even greater zest than during the "trial marriage."

And matters might have gone on well for them if Henry had not delved too deeply into his soul and stirred up insoluble doubts and questions which could not be answered.

Elaine had her lover back, and he seemed as before; yet he was not wholly as before. At times—something—something appeared to trouble him, and she could not tell what it was. In happy moods his face was as a sunny sky to her —and lo—such a cloud, such a shadow, would suddenly pass across it; and his luminous eyes would grow pensive, enigmatic and brooding as the eyes of Night in the Medici tombs, where he loved to linger with her. It was in this marble sanctuary that she tentatively took him to task.

"You sometimes look," she began, "like that figure!"

She pointed to Il Penseroso, so grave and sober in his niche.

"Really?" He smiled upon her.

"Yes, you do!" she repeated with some vigour, and assumed an expression which appeared to demand an explanation from him.

"Well," he admitted, half in earnest, half in jest, "I dare say I sometimes feel like him!"

"Why should you?" she pressed him for an answer. "You are handsome, well, and happy, and you are loved by some one as no one was ever loved before!"

"True," he said. "I must seem a perfect pig to you!"

"I didn't say that at all," she laughed.

"Perhaps, my dear," he mused, surveying the magnificent chapel, "it's something quite abstract. I can scarcely explain. This room represents the end of a great epoch which Michelangelo felt and expressed in these brooding figures. And the end—any end—is always terrible. These figures, after generations of magnificent human endeavour, seem to contemplate the universe, life and all that men have wrought. And only now they seem to ask: What is the meaning of it all? To what end all this created beauty, all this bitter-sweet torment, this agony of creation? Look at the figure of Dawn, whose eyes, as it were trying to penetrate the future, appear to ask, What next? . . . And as I stand here, I seem to feel as though we too are approaching the end of an epoch. We have created much new beauty, we know so much, our bellies are full of knowledge. Men are writing, inventing, discovering,—and yet there's little real joy in the world, little real happiness. It's like a ghastly pantomime, and men no longer believe or love. It is as if the light had gone out of the world and we drifted about like drab automata in the darkening twilight, like dreary derelicts towards an unfamiliar darkness. . . ." He paused, while a perplexed frown formed round his eyes. It was clear that he was deeply troubled.

Elaine laughed. "What a prophet of evil you are! And if this room has that effect on you, the sooner we get out of here the better. I won't let you come here again, do you hear? . . . Come," she said, seizing his hand, "let's go to San Marco, where we will look at the innocent little angels of Fra Angelico dancing about in their brightest colours!"

"Not a bad idea!" he agreed, joining in her laughter. "The world was still young in Fra Angelico's day!"

He felt deeply all he had said to her, but he did not tell her of his personal doubts, of the intimate agony he suffered with regard to her, with regard to his realization that he could keep her happy only in a perfect setting; for he had suffered a great blow to his illusion that he was all-in-all to her anywhere. She would not understand it, he thought.

Then one day, while still in Florence, the blow fell. Henry's solicitors, Grimbly & Grimbly of Lincoln's Inn, wrote him requesting his immediate presence in London. There was a serious reverse in the Thorley fortunes, and a council must be held.

And again, as in many a despairing moment, he remembered: he had once cursed God!

Time is a very strange thing. . . . Time is the father of irony. Irony is of time, in time. . . .

CHAPTER TWENTY

The Waning Dream

LET'S go back at once—this very day!" she had said on
the morning when the news reached them.

The night before they had fittingly celebrated
the anniversary of their first meeting, and they were both
in high mettle when the stack of English mail was brought
to their room on a tray. Henry did not anticipate evil,
and he opened the fatal envelope with the same casualness
as the rest. He read the few lines written with a quill in
the familiar legal script almost uncomprehendingly. Pale,
in silence, he handed the letter to Elaine, who was enjoying her breakfast coffee and rolls in bed.

For some instants she looked downcast. She had counted
on their hiring a carriage that morning for a drive to
Fiesole, and on the way she meant to stop and for the
hundredth time view Giotto's tower, whose graceful lines
and lovely rose tints never failed to give her the greatest
delight. And the weather was simply splendid. The news
spoiled the morning, of course. But she hadn't yet realized
the full import of the letter. His grave face, however,
alarmed her, and she made haste to ask:

"What does it mean?"

"It means," he said earnestly, "that Henry Thorley is
now relatively a poor man. I shall need every penny if
I'm to keep the estate intact."

"Does it mean we can't afford to do any travelling?" she
asked anxiously.

"I'm rather afraid it does. . . ."

It was at this point that she made her suggestion that they should leave at once—that very day.

He gave her a grateful look, and said: "But, my darling, we haven't been away very long, and you don't like Ravenford!"

"Never mind, dear heart. I've had more than my share of happiness, and I shall live on it as a camel on his hump!" She smiled cheerfully. "Only I do want one more glimpse of Giotto's tower before we leave!"

"You shall have it, my dear!" And he flung his arms around her. Sudden joy infused his frame grown cold from the evil tidings. "I love you for saying that! Here-after—for a while at any rate—we must bear Giotto's tower in our heart—yes, and all the rest of the beauty too not within our reach!"

"Yes, we'll do that, won't we?" she handsomely re-sponded. "Promise me that you'll still be my lover in Ravenford—my beautiful lover, and not merely my de-voted husband! Promise me!" she pleaded, with a strange intensity.

"Of course, of course, dearest! Why do you ask?" His astonishment at her question was obvious.

"Why, because there's something about Ravenford—I can't explain it—that makes me act differently. I suppose it's the setting. It calls for a different life. It makes de-mands on me which I can't live up to. One feels one has to act as though one belonged to the place instead of the place belonging to one. . . . And it makes one feel so staid and proper . . . just like an ordinary wife. . . . That's partly why I've loathed it so there!"

"But, my dear, you make me feel guilty. It makes me feel as if I'd been a perfect ogre!"

"No, you haven't been that. . . . I might have stood it better, perhaps, if you had! You've been kindness and devotion itself. But in a place like Ravenford, these things pall on one. After all, one gets devotion from one's mother, from one's aunt—yes, even from one's dog—most of all from one's dog! I want my beautiful lover. . . . I want to skip with him . . . as though there were no Ravenford, no responsibilities which take him from me. . . . I want him to be my Florence, and my Giotto's tower, and my Fra Angelicoes! When I first came to Ravenford, it suddenly came over me that I'd lost all this world, and I thought I'd never have it again. . . . You remember what I then said, and how I acted. . . . And here I've got all that back again, I've got you back again! I don't want to lose all this, I don't want to lose you again! What if we are poor! What if you can't shower upon me expensive gifts! What does it all matter?" She seized his arms in her two hands and looked with intent scrutiny into his eyes, searching there for confirmation of her own mood and a response to it.

"Yes, what does it all matter?" he echoed her pensively. But at the back of his mind was the thought: his affairs having come to such a pass, he would have his hands full and the demands on his time would be greater than ever: it was a rankling thought, because in this hour of misfortune she was dictating conditions.

With her woman's intuition she detected some reservation, and, crestfallen, she released his arms and gazed at him speculatively.

Sensitive to her moods, he tried to retrieve his mistake.

After all, he had no quarrel with her; she had expressed not only her views of life but his also, and where she had a right to expect enthusiasm she received discouragement.

"I didn't mean to be ungracious," he ventured. "Only I couldn't help feeling that there's work for me to do at Ravenford. I don't want us to be beggars, and there's Dicky to think of!"

"I suppose you're right," she said, but her voice did not endorse the statement.

"Darling! Darling!" he pleaded. "I shall find time for being a lover to you and for——"

"And for reestablishing the honour of the Thorley house," she finished for him. "By all means. Only put me last!"

"Don't be cruel, Elaine. I can't stand it today."

"I am sorry," she said contritely. "I didn't intend to be mean. Only don't you see, my dear," she again seized his arms, "I am trying to save something. Perhaps the most precious thing in life. What do I care if Ravenford Manor goes as long as our love remains, and we can still skip in the country lanes as we used to at night in the city streets. Do you remember?"

"Of course, darling! You're quite right. Quite!" Now his voice was full of ardour, in response to which she flung her arms around his neck and wept, while he kissed her eyes and tasted of their salt.

"Let's be happy!" she cried, releasing him, and alertly springing out of bed. "Let's go and feast our eyes on Giotto's tower and find joy again!"

"Right!" he said, warmly, pleased that the misunderstanding had been smoothed out. But something of the salt of her tears remained deep in his consciousness, like a residue of sorrow; for he comprehended the nature of the task yet before him and its inevitable difficulties.

And this was the end to their "second honeymoon." It had lasted exactly three weeks. Their return coincided with the arrival of the first London fog. Elaine's throat tickled; she coughed constantly. "What a vile place after—" But she did not finish her sentence.

"—the Italian sun," Henry finished it for her, and added. "Remember, we must bear the Italian sun in our hearts!"

But she coughed only the more violently.

It was a gloomy man, trying to look cheerful for Elaine's sake, who entered the Golden Cross Hotel, with a choking little woman on his arm.

Next morning Henry faced Mr. John Grimbly, of Grimbly & Grimbly, solicitors for the Thorleys "ever since the flood," as he put it jestingly to Elaine. The head of the firm, he was a man of about fifty, with luxuriant side whiskers and bald head. His face was broad and fairly round, and his wide mouth might have been cut with a knife. There was a twinkle in his round blue eyes. In short, he might have posed for John Bull; but John Grimbly—pronounced Grimly—was not a bad name for him. He greeted his client heartily, in the manner of an old friend, and bade him sit down. Then, by way of preliminary, making a motion toward a tiny cupboard in the wall, he asked:

"A beastly day. Would you like to have a nip, Thorley?"

The familiarity came naturally; he had known Henry's father as a friend, and he had swung Henry on his knee when Henry was but a little boy.

The offer of the drink was declined, but it gave Henry

something to think about. "It must be worse than I thought," he said to himself. It wasn't like John Grimbly to offer a visitor a drink at the office in business hours. A few minutes later the solicitor confirmed his worst suspicions.

"It's just as well," said Grimbly. "Nothing like a clear head to get hard facts straight!" After lighting a cigar and puffing away, he addressed his client in a more legal tone: "It is my unfortunate duty to inform you that the failure of the Australasian Improvement Company, caused by a multitude of circumstances too intricate to go into here, has been a very disastrous failure indeed. If I am to trust reports I have in hand, shareholders will be fortunate if they ultimately receive a return of twenty-five per cent of the original investment. You may or may not know that I was strongly opposed to your father putting his money into the undertaking. But disregarding my counsel, he disposed of his valuable African securities to accommodate his friend, Mr. James Wilson, Senior. It was a rash proceeding, if I may say so, to put all one's eggs in a single financial basket, and I said as much at the time. But your father wouldn't listen. He——"

"Never mind that, Grimbly," Henry cut him short. "I am to understand that I am to have no more income from this particular source. That's what you want to tell me?"

"Yes. It amounts to that. . . . Though I hope the reports of the failure are grossly exaggerated. . . . And I trust that you have sufficient reserve funds to tide you over."

"I haven't very much."

"By the way, I have another thing which I am in duty bound to impart to you, though I cannot counsel you to 'take notice of it. I've been asked by James Wilson, Junior, to convey an offer to you. He would like to purchase all the pasture lands at Ravenford bordering immediately on the sea, and he has offered quite a handsome figure too! But I repeat, I neither expect nor advise a Thorley to entertain the matter." Mr. Grimbly looked at Henry as if he considered the matter closed.

"So Jimmy Wilson wants to buy my lands?" Henry looked dumfounded. "For what purpose, may I ask?"

"Oh, haven't you heard of his hobby? He's been preaching the new-fangled notion of garden cities. And now he has founded a company—the Wilson Development Company—for the purpose of building a garden city by the sea. He has an idea that he can make it pay handsomely."

"A garden city at Ravenford?" Henry gasped.

"Preposterous!" Mr. Grimbly agreed. "You know the sort of thing he'll make of it. A London suburb—with a couple of hotels, tennis courts for tournaments, a few bath houses, and ultimately, perhaps, a promenade, amusements and a brass-band!"

"Horrible!"

The thought of beautiful rustic Ravenford, a natural growth of generations, transformed into a conglomeration of unsightliness, with "arty" houses of a dubious architecture and stunted shrubbery shaped artificially to resemble what not—the thought appalled him, filled him with rage. His feelings were all the more outraged because of his own dream of making Ravenford a spot of so-called Merrie England in reality as well as in name. And now his own dream faded away as dreams do, and the nightmarish reality of James's undertaking—in keeping with his idea of the "march of progress"—was creeping on the world apace, like a dense fog which had come to stay. As in a flash, the ancient village, looked at from the downs, appeared before him, its roofs here thatched there tiled, all mellowed to the tones of the landscape, in which they were lost. And this quiet vision was followed by a vision of another kind— a "garden city" he had seen somewhere, a vision of garish stuccoed walls and bright new tiles loud in a treeless landscape, all shouting as in one voice: "We do not belong here! We do not belong here! We are alien conquerors, and we've come to stay! To stay!"

It was scarcely an instant in which these thoughts came tumbling one upon the other, but this instant was enough: he suddenly felt numb and dumb. It was as if a fog had entered his body and shackled his blood, which seemed to cease flowing; and his tongue could not get beyond the one word, "Horrible!"

An instant, but it seemed endless; and Mr. Grimbly, seeing his client first grow red, then pale, bestirred himself and, presently, stood above the bowed figure with a glass in his hand. "A tiny nip won't do you any harm!" he said, with sympathy, and gave Henry's back a friendly tap.

Automatically, Henry accepted the proffered elixir and, abruptly returning to life, gulped down the drink.

"Horrible!" he groaned again, with some vim. "Curse him and his kind!"

Delighted to see his client return to life, old Grimbly smiled. "Yes, that's what good old little England's coming to! Everything changing, and for the worse. Well, there's the comfort as far as you're concerned. You needn't sell him an inch if you don't want to. And if I know anything about the Thorleys, you won't! . . . Forewarned is forearmed. James Wilson, Senior, has taken in your father, and if the son is careful, James Wilson, Junior shan't take him in! I gave him no hope when he saw me yesterday. He'll be looking you up in a day or two in person, unless I'm mistaken!"

"I suppose he's coming up in the world. He was full of what he was going to do when I saw him last a year or two ago!"

"So you haven't seen Jimmy in a year! You'd scarcely know him then. He's grown quite portly, and if he expands another peg or so his watch-chain will burst!"

"And how's Margie?"

"I haven't seen her for ages. She's very fond of little Jimmy, I hear."

"So they have a son?"

"Haven't you heard? Born a year ago. In December, I think. Yes, it was December! Wasn't that the month your Dicky was born?"

"Yes."

"Well, all I can say is that little Jimmy can't hold a candle to your boy, if that's any comfort to you. He has extraordinary eyes, your Dicky has. Quite extraordinary. So old and so wise. As if he had lived for a thousand years before he came into this world. No, Thorley, you can't forget those eyes, once you have seen them! They look at you as if they tried to remember something——"

Absorbed, Henry listened. He took an inordinate pride in his offspring, and with the zeal characteristic of romantic persons he prayed and willed, during his intimate embraces with Elaine, that their child, if they had a child, might be distinguished in some manner among his fellows. Both he and Elaine thought it would be a terrible thing to have ordinary progeny. He often wondered if anyone noticed those eyes or if he was one of those over-fond parents who exaggerated the peculiar marks or virtues of their children. It comforted him to have his own impression confirmed. John Grimbly was not the man to talk idly.

"Well, I must be getting back to Elaine. She's waiting to hear the worst!" Henry rose abruptly, and smiled like one who did not look forward to a task.

Grimbly also rose. "I have another appointment within a minute or two, or I'd ask you to stop longer," he said apologetically, putting a friendly hand on Henry's shoulder. "We must meet again soon. And do look in when you're in town! If there's anything I can do for you—" He paused awkwardly. "The Thorleys are proud, I know. But there should be no pride between friends. . . . You know what I mean. Your father was my friend. . . . Well, good-bye, Thorley! And don't forget—don't give Jimmy an inch of your land!"

And, with great ceremony, he ushered Henry out.

Like a soul lost, Henry presently found himself walking slowly past the gardens of Lincoln's Inn. His mind was a confused jumble of thoughts, and among them one thought brighter than the rest was trying to break through, even as at that moment the sun was trying to break through the yellow fog. Animate shadows scurried past him, brushed but did not enter his consciousness; and his own thoughts were like these shadows pressing round a luminous dream, smothering the last flickers of a light growing increasingly dim. This thought, this dream, was of a life with another being led at another time and at another place, of eternity of paradisian life snatched from eternity now receding into eternity. Had he ever lived this other life, had he ever known this other being he had called Elaine, had he ever existed as this other Henry, or had it all been a thought, a dream, now vanished like the vaporous evocations of taunting, malignant genii? Life had looked back on life that was past, and life had become a pillar of salt, and of the taste of salt. Come, sun, and dissipate these vaporous shadows! Come, sun, and thaw this life, this congealed pillar of salt, and let it dissolve into tears—magnanimous tears! How futile the fuel, the fire of love, if it was impotent to dissolve the pillar of salt that had once been a woman who looked back on a rapturous past! He was filled with misgiving. Was his love, then, so weak?

He had scarcely the heart to tell her of the full extent of their misfortune. For now it seemed as if she were doomed to stay in the place she loathed forever. And how could she stay there when she loathed it with a prodigious loathing? Was he asking too much of her to sink her loathing in the immensity of a love such as could be theirs if they but willed it so, anywhere and everywhere? Today he felt the slightest thing beyond his strength.

And he walked on slowly, as one fettered by numbed emotions and unwieldy thoughts. He came to the end of the railing, where the garden terminated, and, turning to the left, he saw the main gate loom before him. As he turned, his eyes intent on the gate, there bumped into him a little man, from whose mouth, at the hard impact, there came the most jovial, "Sorry, sir! Sorry!" that one ever hoped to hear; it was almost as if he were glad. But Henry, bent in two, had his hands on his stomach; his wind had been knocked out, and he was unable to speak. On seeing his plight, the little man did not go, but went on repeating in a more grieved tone than before "So sorry, sir! 'T'was my fault. I humbly apologize. Most profoundly, sir! It was this brief case, full of weighty matters," and he looked so reproachfully at the guilty case that Henry who was now recovering from the effects of the collision could not help laughing. Then he looked into the little man's face turned up to his, and there was recognition and astonishment on both sides.

"Why, Thorley!"

"Why, Smallpeice!"

"If this isn't luck! It's nigh on to fifteen years since we've met! Well, well, I'd have known you anywhere! And, really, I've been looking forward to running into you!"

"Well, you certainly have, and mighty hard too!" Henry laughed. "Anyhow, I've often thought of you too!"

CPSIA information can be obtained
at www.ICGtesting.com
Printed in the USA
BVHW041029250819
556740BV00016B/767/P